LOVE AND FOOTBALL

LOVE NEVER FAILS

The FIGHT writer is back, this time with a love story!
Love and Football, now who wouldn't love to read this book?

JOSHUA LEVI BROWN

Order this book online at www.trafford.com
or email orders@trafford.com

Most Trafford titles are also available at major online book retailers.

Printed in the United States of America.

ISBN: 978-1-4907-1075-4 (sc)
ISBN: 978-1-4907-1074-7 (hc)
ISBN: 978-1-4907-1076-1 (e)

Library of Congress Control Number: 2013914253

Trafford rev. 08/16/2013

www.trafford.com

North America & international
toll-free: 1 888 232 4444 (USA & Canada)
fax: 812 355 4082

Contents

This story's characters are fictitious.

Love Rules All

"I Will Always Love You . . ."

Whitney, one of the greatest voices ever known to the human race. She sang loud, pleasant, and beautifully from the four speakers in my bedroom.

I laid on my back, as she laid, peacefully on my ripped, muscular, tatted-up chest.

I love my girl. No lie. No games. Straight up. Real talk, in Real Life Action. I got her back.

I ain't never doing her wrong. Never going to cheat. Never going to hit her or leave her side.

We were the perfect couple!

Match made in heaven! Bam!

High school superstars! She was the prettiest, most-popular cheerleader, and I was the all-star quarterback.

Now, she was resting in my arms. She was so beautiful. I'm just happy man, looking at her sleep like a baby.

"I love you," Ebony mumbled, reading my mind, while she continued to sleep.

"I love you too," I said, smiling, while running my fingers through her long, curly, Indian and black, natural, pretty hair.

Dang! Her body was banging! Her butt looked like a juicy fruit mixed with a basketball!!! Sticking, well, poking out. Round and perfect. Even from underneath our red, silk sheets.

Ebony's body was cold as ice! Rich like gold! Fine as wine! Priceless, like a diamond! Delicious like ice-cream! Sweet as a Georgia peach! She had caramel, smooth-as-silk skin to set off her slim waist and pretty face!

Ebony was top model tall at 5'10". Then, she was funny, loyal, and athletic at the same dang time! Gymnastic moves, video vixen booty, hypnotizing, hazel eyes, and cheerleader energy like WOW!

Ebony was the love of my life. Of course, I'm a brown-skinned, hard-core, pretty boy with a gangstafied attitude. Lol.

Pow! Pow! Boom! Boom! Boom!

"God!"

Gunshots erupted from every direction. Bullets ripped through the windows and walls in my bedroom.

Instantly, I grabbed my queen, and shielded her body. I laid on top of her, covering her body completely.

Glass shattered everywhere! My heart beat faster than a drunk driver in a race car!

Boom!

Someone kicked the door open . . .

Thump . . .

I rolled our bodies off my king-sized water bed and rolled us underneath the bed.

"Who shooting, baby? What's da-"

"Shhhhush baby. Quiet," I whispered to my trembling, terrified queen. I held her body tight and close to my heart, like a pacemaker.

The room was solid black . . .

"You will die! You and your pretty, innocent, cheer-leading girlfriend! You may be a NFL star quarterback, but you still have dues to pay. You violated the Blood gang. No need to hide under the bed."

Click . . .

The lights came on. I peeked from under the bed. Three killers. They had on red shoes, black clothes, red ski masks, and red, evil-glowing eyes!

Sniffling. Crying. Trembling. Body vibration.

My girl was shaking with fear. The fear of dying an early, young death. Who wants to die? We can't die. God. Not like this!

A week before the Super bowl. Atlanta is picked to win, by ten. I'm the rookie of the year! Plus, the first, black, starting quarterback ever, picked to win the Super Bowl, by Vegas, in history!

Now, my high school sweetheart was about to be murdered with me, in my arms. Because of my mistake . . .

Boom!

"Cim! Cim!"

"Huh? Hu . . . Huh?" I stuttered, drooled and jerked.

"Wake up, baby! You had a nightmare! You are sweating like a Friday night slut! I know you got the biggest game on Earth coming up, Sunday. The Super bowl is gigantic! Everybody knows that, baby. But stop sweating. Relax. You made it this far, you will win. Believe me, baby. God is with you," Ebony told me.

She was so confident, positive and sure. She was always my motivation. Ebony believed God gave us the natural ability to accomplish anything. Period.

"Ouch. What da?" I quickly snatched the silk sheet off me and looked at my right leg. Dang, Mary Jane, Cain and Zayne!

A red, fire ant bit the living hot sauce pain out of me!

Hold up . . . A red ant?

Dreaming of red ski masks . . . red shoe . . . where they do that at? Was this a sign? My team wear red and black. That gangstafied, powerful, Atlanta color.

"Forget—it!! I'm ready! Give daddy a kiss," I told my sexy, sweet love.

Then, I climbed on top of my future wife for life, and we passionately tongue kissed like erupting volcanoes; sexy hot!

We Ready

"Go! Go! Go! Deep! Go deep!" Deon yelled to my star wide receiver, Sergio.

"Bam! Touchdown!" I shouted.

"Yeah, playah! Boop! Boop! I told you, I got that goodle, oodle, noodle, fye game, baby!" Deon joked and bragged.

He was our rookie wide receiver. Very talented and quick as the speed of light. He ran 4-2, just like me. We also used Deon to return kicks on the special teams.

Boy, he was so excited to throw a touchdown to Sergio in practice!

He was sticking out his tongue, doing the Moonwalk.

"Wooh! Oops!"

He fell! The entire team laughed.

"You silly. Get up, De," his twin sister, Shawn, said, as she grabbed his left and right hand to pull him up.

Shawn was one of our forty beautiful cheerleaders. Light-skinned and innocent cute.

"Hey! Huddle up. Motivation. Dedication. Preparation. Determination. This is our game, our shine, our show, our glow. Our game to win. We must not slack. Go hard. No slipping. No turnovers. No mistakes. No doubts. We cannot, and will not, underestimate the underdogs. This is the biggest game on Earth. We live our whole lives to play and win. This game, this is it. One, two, three . . ."

"We ready!" We all shouted simultaneously when Coach Joshua Brown finished up his pep speech.

Coach Brown was one of the coolest in the NFL, at 37. He could motivate a pig to score a touchdown! Touchdown Porky the Pig! Lol. Coach Brown made you feel like you could do anything!

The team separated. Practice lasted five, long hours.

"Look, dawg. I want this game. I was born and raised in Atlanta. Forever, I love Atlanta. My dreams as a kid were to bring a championship to my city. We need that man, bad!" Sergio told me as we walked out of Pantersville practice field in Decatur, GA.

Sergio was my best friend. He was the top NFL wide receiver, four years in a row. He had fourteen-hundred receiving yards this year.

Super Sergio could catch a bullet with one finger if I threw it!

That boy could catch anything! Plus, he could jump sky high!

I was fresh in the NFL. I took his advice, because he was an experienced vet, and I was an energetic, young rookie.

"What up, nicca?" Micki, a.k.a. Red Bone Shawty, asked me.

I was standing in front of my H-2 Hummer, red and black, of course.

Micki was twenty-one, young, and pretty. She was Coach Brown's feisty, hot girlfriend. You know they met because she my sister. She had that real, red bone attitude, with a little Candler Rd, killa personality. Cause she was humping the best coach in football! You couldn't tell this red chick nothing!

"What it do?" I asked Micki. She swore she ran this team too. Coach Brown was coach of the year, and got a fat eight-million dollar contract. He also had three-hundred million in the bank, from when he played professional football himself. Hot damn and ham if Red Bone Shawty ain't blowing every penny!

"Look! Everybody and their momma asking for the hook-up! Give me free Super Bowl tickets. Your brother is the quarterback. Blah, blah, blah. My step, great-grand cousin and even my god-cousin want free tickets!" Micki said laughing, but shaking her head.

"Lol. Guuurl, god cousin? Where they do that at? That's a new one," Erica said, smiling. Sexy-chocolate, candy body, cutie. She was my powerful running-back, Levi Bailey's wife. Levi just got a one-hundred and twenty million dollar contract.

Ka-pow!

He was a beast! He once carried five players ten yards on his back, and scored the winning touchdown against Green Bay, to get us to the Super Bowl!

"That's crazy. Some chick named Ice Bread, a male stripper named Juicy Fruit Johnny and another one named Butt Licking Bobby asked me for free tickets, say they went to school with me, girl. Hah, Hah," Ebony, my queen, laughed.

"Guurl. No, they done lost their mind, and their foreheads. Forget—that! I don't care who don't go to the Super Bowl. I'm going! V.I.P. baby. That's right! Micki a.ka Red Bone Shawty, we'll be up through there!" Micki laughed, snapping her fingers.

"True. True. The after party is what's really poppin', anyway!" my baby sister, Pretty Kishauna added, with her Cedar Grove High School cheerleading outfit on. She was the only girl at the school with a Benz.

"You're right! We win! I'ma tear the city up! Paint the city red, baby! A blunt of loud in one hand, and a bottle in the other, that's word to my mother!" Micki added.

"I just want to win. Levi ain't even talking to me right now. He ain't said one word in two weeks! He want to win!" Erica said, crunk.

"Well, I apologize, yall. Everybody can't get a ticket. I did what I could do. I just got to win. We are undefeated. So, I want to stay undefeated. Give me a kiss," I told Ebony.

Then, we got into my big boy truck. I drove off, in deep thought. So much intensity. So much hype. So much pressure. All eyes on me. The starter of the biggest game in the world, the Super Bowl.

Beyoncé is performing at half-time. My whole family and city is cheering. The whole world is watching. The 2012 Super Bowl was the most watched program in American TV history. With an audience of over one-hundred and fifteen million viewers. We will top that! So we MUST bring home the Lombardi trophy! I got to win this! I got to, baby! I got to do this for my dad, who got killed last year. He always believed I would do this, even when I had my doubts. I love you, dad. For Ebony, my high school love . . . in Columbia High school, she was the beautiful, brown cheerleader, while I played ball.

In college, at Georgia Tech, we won the national championship. Ebony was a cheerleader. Before each play, right before I got the ball, I would glance over, to see my baby cheering every time.

I love my baby. I love this game.

"Cim?"

"Huh?"

"I'm pregnant . . ."

"What?!"

Screeeeeeach.

I slammed on the brakes.

Bam!

So shocked, I crashed . . . slap, smack into the back of a grey Honda.

I squeezed my baby's hand.

"Are you ok?" I asked her.

Her eyes were as big as a football. Her right hand was covering her mouth. She was a little shook up, like dice.

"Ye, yea . . ." she replied.

Tap. Tap. Tap.

I rolled down my window. It was a mad, Mexican midget. She was adorable, but visibly upset.

"Sir, do you have insurance?" she asked, with a nasty, three-foot tall attitude.

I laughed.

"Insurance? Take this and fix your bumper, baby," I said in a cheerful voice.

When she saw the four-thousand dollars I gave her, she ran faster than a kangaroo on crack!

"Cim, baby. Can you please calm down?"

"Ummm. Yeah, but why you didn't wait till after the Super Bowl to tell me?"

"I know. I thought about that. But, now you should have more motivation to win the game. You have to win this for your wife, your family, your fans, your haters, and now, your unborn child."

When those words came out of her mouth, unborn child . . . , I instantly felt a glow. My first born. Cool . . .

"Hello?" I said into my ear phone.

"Someone broke into grandma house!" my little sister, Kishana screamed.

Oh God.

"Ummm. I'ma take care of it. Is grandma ok?" I asked.

"No! She is very mad! I'm pissed! Can you come now?"

"I'll be there, Kishana."

What now? My line clicked again.

"Hello?" I asked.

"Hello Cimeon. This is Michael Lackey, the owner of the team. I have a little bad news. The storm from the tornado caused the roof in the dome to collapse. We may have it repaired before Sunday. So let's hope so. The main thing though, let's just win!"

"Sure," I said, shocked.

How much pressure can one man take?!

Just win. Just win. Easier said than done. I sat at the next light, pondering about all the extra pressure that just exploded in my lap, a week before the game of my life. What could happen next?

Get hit by a drunk, race car driver? Get pimp-slapped by a skinny elephant? My star running back, Levi, break his arm? I got shot? I mean . . .

Bam!!!

"Ouch! Baby, what you do that for?"

"Hah, hah. You got to wake up and smell the coffee!" Ebony said laughing. She scared the living toe nails out of me; yelling in my ear and punching my right leg.

"Boo, I'm woke. Just focused on my destiny, dreams and my goal."

"Cimeon baby, be easy. Stay calm. God is with you. You can't lose, because you are a winner. I love you. Look at me . . . I loved you before the fame; before the game. I been here. Before you had any fans. I was your number one fan. Before you heard any cheers, I was cheering for you; holding you, loving you. You're the only man I ever slept with. Now Cim, I want you to put this city on your back. No matter what obstacles come your way. You're a soldier, built to last. You shine under pressure, baby. You always have. You always will. I love you. You will win," she said, staring into my eyes, squeezing and sliding her red, manicured nails slowly up and down my right arm.

I took a deep breath . . .

"Awwe Ebony, you always know what to say. You're the best, really. The very best, everything. The best motivator and best person. The best person I ever met. I love you. No doubt. It's just so much on the line at one time. Like a zillion things going wrong all at once."

"Shiiiish. Our love will always win, in the end," she spoke, like my angel, while gently placing her pretty index finger over my lips.

"Muwah," her soft lips kissed mine.

"Love will always win in the end . . ." I repeated her words in my mind, out loud; so short and simple, yet powerful and true. I have love. Love for my family, love for my lady. Love for my God. Love for the game. Love for myself. Love for my fans. Love for the world.

Cheating, Beating

"Shut up! I know what I saw, man! Now, who you want? Me or her?" Micki yelled at Coach Brown.

"Micki, listen. I can't leave my wife. I will be a prune face! Micki, she would suck me dry!"

"Coach Brown don't get beat down. Listen-"

"No Micki, you listen. You little red, candy yam. Kids are involved!"

"Stupid! Cut your butt is involved if you don't choose me! I'ma burn this three-million dollar mansion down to the ground! T.L.C. style, baby. You think I care about your measly eight-million dollar contract?! Ank! Wrong answer, buddy roe. I got NFL ballers with fat, one-hundred million dollar contracts begging to taste this strawberry short cake!" Micki yelled, smacking Coach Brown's face, looking like a foxy, female wrestler.

Bemp!

Coach Brown snapped, but in a cool way. He just punched the wall.

"Walls don't punch back, punk," Micki barked, like a cute, female boxer. Then she walked away.

Instantly, Coach Brown grabbed her petite arms, yanking her backwards, causing the foxy girl to stumble.

Wrong answer.

Like the Candler Rd. killa she was, she pulled out her gun and shoved it into his jaw. The day before the Super Bowl, Atlanta would be coach less.

Pow!

She pulled the trigger.

Micki, a.k.a. Red Bone Shawty, had struck again. So what? Ain't nobody on earth getting over on Micki.

"Ahh! Ahh! Dang! You crazy pink trick!" Coach Brown took off running, holding his jaw.

Bimp!

He flew through the bathroom door, and slapped his bloody face to the mirror.

A hole was straight through his jaws! Well, at least it was only a pellet gun!

Bam!

Red Bone Shawty kicked the bathroom door open with her three-hundred and fifty dollar, black, UGG Raya boots.

"Next time, it will be a real gun," Micki yelled, and stormed out in her tight, short, red, lace skirt.

Coach Brown was still staring in the mirror. Stunned that his pretty, little mistress was losing it!

Red Bone Shawty growled like a light-skinned ware wolf, with micro braids! Boop!

Then, the run-way model walked out of the three-thousand-dollar-a-night, down town hotel, after she stuck her gun back into her Gucci purse.

Red Bone Shawty hopped into her delicious, candy apple, red, new sparkling Benz. Yea, the one Coach Brown bought her last Valentine's Day.

Snap!

She turned on the new Kelly Rowland and Wayne. Then called her big brother.

"Cim?"

"Yeah?"

"I need a million dollars."

He sighed deeply . . . "Oh, Micki."

"And some gasoline. Hah, hah," she mumbled to herself, the second Cimeon hung up.

Money and Da Power

Michael Lackey, the multi-billion dollar owner, paced the elegant, most-expensive, type of floor on Earth. Like a royal palace, the Pietra Firma's LuxTouch tile had diamonds and black marbles in a sumptuous, flower-petal pattern. Then, hot money heaven, every ten square feet of Lux Touch tiles cost one-million dollars!

"Sexy Shawn, you are worth more than a zillion of my dollars. You, my precious, gracious sweetheart are the blood in my rich veins. I adorn you, darling dear. Anything your eyes can grasp, you can have. A skinny elephant, a tall pig, an eighteen-room castle, a flying fish, anything. Sexy Shawn can have it."

Shawn blushed like a shy kid. She loved the nickname, Sexy Shawn. Growing up on the west side of Atlanta, dealing with so much neglect and pain, her brother finally hooked her up for life when he introduced her to the wealthy owner of the Atlanta Tigers Football team.

Mike was one of the wealthiest men on earth. Shawn sat with her legs crossed.

"Wow," she sighed, reading Real Life Action, on her twenty-thousand dollar Mervis Diamond Importers' iPad, of course; no green gummy bear joke. This was the most expensive iPad on Earth. Can you say, Jackpot! Baby girl from the hood just hit the lottery, baby!

She sipped on her sparkling forty-thousand dollar Dom Perignon White Gold Jeroboam champagne.

"Hello?"

"Mr. Lackey, this is Joshua Bell, with the ZMB repair service."

"Stop. When can you repair my dome?"

"Well sir, we might not be able to-"

"Wrong answer. You will be able to! This is the first time in NFL history, a team will host the Super Bowl, in the same city the team plays in. I don't care if you have to borrow the Incredible Hulk and bring the Egyptians that created the pyramids back to life. Fix my Georgia Thunder Dome before this Sunday."

"But sir, that's forty-eight hours away."

"And you will be forty-eight hours away from not having a job if you don't FIX MY DOME!

Click.

"Now, back to you, my marvelous, delicious sweetheart," the fifty-five year old, handsome, blue-eyed, blond-haired, billionaire said to Shawn.

Not only did Michael Lackey own the Tigers, he was the CEO of Slap Jack Record Label, Peter Pot Trucking Company, and had ownership shares in ten professional teams. He owned Silly Wet Willy Franchise Restaurants, BBD TV Station, and Riley Clothing Line.

Shawn texted her twin brother, Deon.

This white man got that bread!!! You was right, bro! Kah Pow!

LOL. I told yah. BOOP! Deon replied.

"Ahh! God!" Shawn yelled from deadly, off guard, paralyzing panic and fear.

"Yes, I know you are surprised," he said, flat as a pancake under a tire.

"I can't believe you!" Shawn yelled again, holding her heart, with her mouth wide open.

"It's just a measly 3.17 million, H. Stern Venus Diamond necklace. The clasp, right there is exquisite. That fourteen point diamond star is truly a piece that is beautiful on every angle, just like you, my adorable angel. Sexy Shawn. But here, I'm going to handle some business. Take the Porsche, the Bentley, or even platinum Limousine."

Bam!

Then, he dropped a suit case full of hundred dollar bills in front of her pretty, pink, pedicured, perfect toes.

"Hold up, what's this for?"

"Awwe. Play, play money. I'm game, honey. Have fun," the billion-dollar man said, and walked out like a king in his castle.

Shawn was stuck like Chuck!

Boop!

Dive In

"197, 198, 199 . . . 200! Push-ups in a row. Five-thousand all together," I said, getting off the floor, from my nightly exercise.

"Baby?"

"Huh?" I answered, feeling like a lion on steroids!

Roar!! Hold up. I'm not on steroids, though. One-hundred percent natural, baby! Wooh!

"Cim, are you jogging today?" Ebony asked, staring at my ripped-up chest, then kissing her name on my shoulder.

My chest always made her melt like butter, and get weak, like paper.

The sweat made my muscles gleam and look like a sweaty boxer, and a sex symbol all in one.

"Yea baby, I'm about to jog inside of you," I said pulling her closer to me, as she gently caressed my chest with her fingers.

She was softly kissing my neck and licking my ears. I picked her up, and carried her to the wall.

Smack.

I slapped her juicy booty, as I palmed it with my powerful hands.

Like two fighters in love, we battled and wrestled with our tongues, taste for taste. Lick for lick. Kiss for kiss. Our love was deep. Entertainingly different, spontaneous, sticky, passionate, hard, fast, slow, good, great, nice, hot, cold; never the same.

I squeezed a strawberry on her breast, then placed it in my mouth, like a pacifier.

She moaned and her eyes rolled to the back of her head while she was slanging her head against the wall. Clawing and scratching my back. Biting and kissing my neck.

"Daddy!"

"Give it to daddy," I said, with force, as I went deep into her juicy, tight, perfect-fit love.

She met me with every stroke.

The bed of a marriage is honorable, pure and perfect in every way! Hebrews 13:4.

No one knew we had gotten secretly married yesterday. We planned to have a luxurious, lovely, romantic, large wedding a week after we win the Super Bowl, in which I was the quarterback in, and she cheered in.

That's love.

This is love.

Strong love.

Now, we made it to the floor. Our bodies were tight and tied together, like a shoe. Her legs were wrapped around my body.

'I Adorn You' was on. Then 'Dive In' came on.

I dove deep inside my wife's sweet, delicious, sweating, hot, soft, loving body. Her toes was curling, her body temperature was hot, and my tongue was wet . . .

"Oh baby. Yes. Yes. Cim! Cim! Cim! Ciiiiiiim!!" my love screamed as I picked her up and sat her fine behind on the thirty-thousand dollar mahogany dresser.

She spread her legs and I dropped to my knees to kiss and please . . .

Practice Makes Perfect

"Down! . . . Blue 42! . . . Hut!"

Owens, my center, snapped me the ball. I did my thang. I dazzled and danced! My 4-3 defense was biting like them killa fish with razor sharp teeth!

The best two defensive ends in the game zipped straight for my body! Bam!

No sir, can't touch this! I refuse to get hit or sacked! Even in practice, baby! Ben and Render, both slipped and ate a grass sandwich, when they missed! I Booped them, baby!

Now, I was loose as a goose. The play I called was a slant for my Super Pro Bowl wide receiver and my favorite target, Super Sergio, who was also my best friend.

Shoot!

By this time, he had shook the corner backs and he was wide open like gorilla couchie!

BAM!

Sergio caught the ball at mid field, then dashed to the 40, 30, 20, 10, 5 . . . Touch Down! Nope!

Bang!

Out of nowhere, Dwight, a.k.a. D.J., power hit the day light sunshine out of him! Numbing Nasty! At an angle! One yard away from the end zone!

D.J. was our speedy corner back that led the league in interceptions. He was also the number one tackling corner back, this season. In other words, D.J. is a Beast!!! Godzilla the Killa!

"Gee willy cards, Batman, that hit looked paralyzing and as thundering as a jet crashing into McDonalds!!!!"

The ball fumbled out of Sergio's hand and disappeared faster than the first happy meal ever created. The one that came out for a dollar in 1979! Boop!

Zipping Zack, our safety, scooped up the loose ball and zoomed towards the opposite end zone. He was running like a runaway slave!

Touchdown!!!!

"Good! Go! Excellent defense. Darn good defense, guys. Now Cim, you know New England live and die by blitzing the quarterback. They have a huge, fast defense. They coming, baby. Full speed! D.J., Zack, that's the defense you must play Sunday. All the way turned up! Wesley is an awesome quarterback, with multiple offensive weapons. Good dee, guys!" Coach Brown said, complementing his Pro Bowl defense, patting Dwight on the back.

"Bull crap! Sergio, you were slow as a turtle on crack, with a broken leg! You shoulda scored the touchdown! You do that slick, slow crap on Sunday, and we will lose! You must don't know how fast Omar is? He likes me too, but that's another story. If you even blink wrong, BAM! He will get you! Now look, no fumbles. Run out of bonds. Look back, dive, dodge or fall. Just don't lose that ball! Levi is always a good option, Cimeon." Micki redboneshawty said, pointing her finger at Sergio.

"They don't have a good run defense. I want yall to try trick plays. Flea Flickers, Double Pass and all. We gotta win or I'm slappin' all yall in the mouth with my personal, pink and gold ATL football!" Micki, a.k.a. Redbone Shawty, said.

Yea, my sister was not the average cheerleader. Micki was the the boss! Plus. She was the secret girlfriend of the baddest coach on the planet! Coach Joshua Levi Brown, NFL coach of the year! Plus, the sister of the rookie of the year, me. So she always tried to run the team.

"Hold up, Shawty, are you the coach? Like, since when did females start coaching in the NFL? This ain't softball. This is football!" our linebacker, Terry, said.

The whole team laughed.

Terry was always going toe to toe with my sis. I think he had a tiny two-hundred and ninety pound crush on her! LOL.

Oh, my sister knew she had the power of the P. She just looked at him, smacking her red bubble gum, and chewing on a corn dog with ketchup on the tip. She wiped her lip, other hand on her hip. Then stepped her 5'3", foxy, slim figure dead in the 6'5" giant's face.

"Look, beer belly billy. This is Redbone Shawty's team. I call the shots. I don't like it, yall don't hike it!" Micki snapped, then cat walked away in her mini skirt and knee high Jimmy Choo boots. She rolled those pretty, sassy, brown eyes.

"Whateva. We will win. I bet my kids on that!" Terry roared.

"Hah, hah, Micki, you crazy," her brown-sugar, beautiful, virgin, cheerleading best-friend, Shylin said.

Shylin was thick in all the right places, with long, good hair. She was Indian and Black, with a touch of Cuban. It made this untouched cutie stand out like, Bang!

Micki was a sexy, red, athletic cutie, with an attitude. Beautiful, but bad to the bone! She never took any crap! Why would she?! I'm her big brother!

Micki looked like Mariah, Lisa Raye and Megan Good, mixed together with Left Eye's attitude! Lil' sister was bad!

Red Bone Shawty pulled off in her candy, apple red Benz, her red skin and sipped on some gin, with an evil grin!

"Look, disregard her. Excellent 4-3 defense. Great execution, D.J. Good on field awareness, Zippy Zack, we will need every inch and muscle of defense known to football; known to mankind. They have a gigantic offensive line. Lining up in that fast, Shotgun Formation, they pass the ball seventy percent of the time. Most of their rushing yards come from their quarterback, Wesley. So Wesley, you help spy on Wesley. This will not be the disappointing repeat of 2013!" the defensive coordinator, Manilito A. Dunlap barked.

He was short, but mean. He had the biggest mouth on the east side of the Mississippi River! He was pumped up like a wrestler!

This coach would actually work out with the team! Boop!

My mind was in a zone. I could feel the adrenaline pumping fast in my body! My heart was beating fast as a cheetah, increasing my energy and ability to move quicker and stronger. I was hyped and psyched! I could eat a bike! Man, the whole world will be watching. I reminisced on all the Super Bowl parties we had in Saint Louis and Atlanta. It was so hype. So much energy. Now, I'm the main event. All the pressure is on me.

All eyes are on me. My mom will be watching. My wifey for lifey will be on that side line, watching, cheering, and holding my unborn child. She never saw me lose a big game. Now this was the biggest game of my twenty-one year old life.

Then . . . this is hard . . . My dad's face flashed through my head. I miss him. Why did he have to die so soon? I know he would love to see his son play the biggest game on Earth. He was one-hundred percent Jamaican; my older, handsome twin. Sadly, I never met him. Never seen him. But, I know, I'm a part of him. Everyone said, I'm his soul. And in his death, I will win this for him!

"Hey! Next play!" Mr. Pettis, our offensive coordinator shouted.

"Down! Green 38! Hut!" my other center, Elijah, yelled, snapping me the ball.

I had to quickly call the audible and change the play. The defense switched from 4-3 to a 3-4 corner Blitz! I was four yards behind Elijah in the Pistol Formation. D.J. and Terry flew at me. Boom!

"Man," I mumbled on my back, from the sack!

Terry hit me down low and D.J. flew, diving over Big Butch, smacking my helmet off! BANG!!!

"Ten yards lost! Come on!" Pettis yelled in my ear piece.

Dog, I had to get helped up by Big Butch. Then, I had to adjust my pads!

I signaled for my offensive to huddle and called the play.

"69," I told them, as I winked at my wife.

Clunk! Clunk! Clunk!

We ran to the line. West Coast offense, baby!

"Down . . . Hut!"

I got the ball, and read the 4-3 cover 2 man defense quickly, cause these big boys are fast as light and strong as polar bears. I was sore as a five-year old with a fresh, raw wound after falling hard, off of his bike!

Bloop! Bang!

Cameron knocked the Boom, Bang, Bam out of Terry! My offensive tackle hit hard! Super mean like Godzilla in the Ghetto! Perfect Beast Mode in man-on-man blocking!

That's all I needed as I zooshed and mushed Andrew with my right hand. He tried to dive at my legs, but I mushed his big head! Like wet bread! Then, I ran like ants in my bed!

Boom!

I zipped a 20 yard pass to Deon, who was wide open.

"Ahh! Ahh!"

D.J. tipped the ball in the air. Deon caught it!

Nope! Interception!

D.J. took the ball out of Deon's hand, and flew down the sideline, with his dashing, grey hound speed.

Kah Pow!

Wrong answer!

I hammered D.J., throwing my helmet into his side.

Bemp!

The ball popped out, and hit the ground. Boom! Boom! Bacon! Butterballs!

Big three-hundred pound Butch picked up the ball, and slow, wobble ran the touchdown!

"Boom! Big Butch! Baaby, baaaaaby!!!!" I yelled as we all laughed at the big boy.

Hah. Ha. Butch was tired as a jogging elephant, with a Toyota on its back!

I ran to the end zone to join the hilarious celebration.

"Big baby! Boy you look like a Marta bus with four flat tires, rolling down a hill, with no brakes!"

"Hah. Hah. You crazy, Cim. I can't breathe. Get me a stretcher! Carry me to the house!" Big Butch muffled, as he laid in the end zone, on his big belly!

"Mwah. Good play, baby," my beautiful boo said, rubbing my back, then kissing my lips.

"Yeah, thanks, boo. Hah, hah. I'm exhausted."

"Awwe, poor, powerful baby. I'ma hafta ease your pain," my angel told me, sounding so warm, healing and polite.

Ebony was even my practice cheerleader! Real ride or die chick, baby! She never missed a practice! Even when she had the flu! That's my boo! Shoe-be-do!

"We will REVERSE the curse! An Atlanta team will finally win the big one! I see it! You can be it! There will be no relaxing. No sleeping! No stopping! No giving up! We get a big lead. Crush them!!!!!" Coach Brown roared.

"Come on, together."

"1,2,3,. CRUSH THEM!!!!" we all shouted, simultaneously.

Ebony squeezed my sweaty hands as we walked to my Hummer truck. Man! That red and black looked good!

Mwah. She kissed my lips like Chap stick. Never, can you get too much love and kisses!

"I'm so amped up. I got to win this one for my city."

She just looked at me with those beautiful, loving, brown eyes.

"Awwe. I understand, baby. I'm here for you. You are a natural born winner. You are a fighter. Plus, you have everything it takes to be the championship quarterback. You have the vision, the quick release, the size, the mobility, the intelligence, competitiveness, arm strength, the heart, oh, and good looks!" my boo said, laughing and leaning on my shoulder.

I had to crack a smile. Boop!

My baby always had the right words to say. She calmed me down, like a hot, pregnant woman, getting a body massage, or a hot bubble bath after a game.

"Aweee. Cool. Soooo cool," is all I could say, smiling, feeling myself!

"Cim. It feels so good to cheer for my husband. Your entire life, even when you was catching those little cotton footballs, at five years old! Hah, hah, hee, hee. Wooh, lawd. Can you say, grown up! And football upgrade!"

Bingo! She made me laugh again, while I drove.

"Yeah, I know, right? Long way from football on the playground, and in the middle of the street, to the Super Bowl starting quarterback!"

"Hah. Cim. Boo, don't forget those high school titles at Columbia! We were undefeated and smashed! Lovejoy for the state championship!" Ebony reminded me.

"Hah, hah. I know. Deon and Earl. They were race-car fast! Then in college . . . Wooh!!" I yelled., reminiscing on those Georgia Tech days.

"Yeah, it was sad how Earl got popped and dropped."

"Yea, set up by his best friend, James. I shoulda killed him that night," I blacked out, thinking about the night the ten DeKalb County cops kicked Earl's baby mama door down.

James was laughing at my running back/best friend. Africa was cussing! Yae was screaming! Micki and Kiki were fighting the police. I snapped. I jumped off the couch, and hit that nut with a Pluto Power Punch!

Kah Bam! One punch! Knocked out four teeth! Ching! Ching!

Scccreeech!!!

I slammed on the brakes . . . my truck slid to an uncomfortable, immediate stop!

Rip. Rip. Tear. Tear. Snap. Pop.

My buttons popped off my four-hundred dollar black and red JLB shirt.

"Give it to me daddy! Right here! Right now!" Ebony yelled, shocking me with undeniable love.

I mean, whoa . . . at the red light, in the bright afternoon, on the super busy Tara Blvd.

She was spontaneous, so unpredictable, so seducing, so exotic, so hot and arousing! She slung the truck into park. Yank! She snatched my buttons off my shirt, and ripped my shirt open, desperately rubbing my chest and kissing on my neck, sticking her tongue inside my ear. Umph!

She grabbed in between my legs and jumped into my lap. Sexy wet surprise! No panties under her black mini skirt!

I could no longer resist! I surrendered! Threw in my sex towel!

R. Kelly was bumping romantically with a sexy, dancing rhythm as our bodies turned the bright, busy highway into a motel at midnight!

"It's the remix to ignition, hot and fresh out the kitchen, mama rollin' that body, got every man in here wishin" . . . .

Beep! Beep! Beep!

Ten horns blew loud! The lights flashed red . . .

A few sexy screaming seconds . . .

The light flashed green . . .

Her body flashed hot . . .

My heart flashed fast . . .

Click.

I let the seat back.

Tap . . . Tap! Crack!

"No! He didn't just crack my dang five-thousand dollar windshield!"

Wham! Clatter . . . the glass hit the pavement. I swung open the door, smacking the dookey day lights out of the dark-skinned, three-hundred pound chump!

Yank! Yank!

I grabbed them long dreds in his head, and directed his body like a bike!

Wham! Kah Bam!

I rammed his back into his own car! Then, picked him up in the air. Looked around from side to side like a powerful wrestler in the main event, baby! Everyone in their cars, back to back, had their mouths stretched open like the Waffle House!

I got muscles and can bench press four-hundred with ease. As this huge glob of a man, lay across my shoulder like a horse . . .

Wham!!

"Woooh!" I yelled in my Nature Boy voice.

"Wow . . ." I heard from at least ten nosey bystanders.

Snap! Flash! Snap!

Cameras were flashing.

"Cim! Big Cim! There he is!!"

"Oh, junk! Pose with him, boy! That's the rookie of the year! Go Tay! Go over there!" a guy said, pushing his three-year old son over towards me, then snap! Taking a picture with an old, 1949 Polaroid camera!

The little curly-head boy was looking too lost. Hey! He did have on my jersey! Number 10! A dime, baby!

"Stop! Stop! Stop taking pictures of my man. Baby come on. You out here posing in a dang street fight when you are the starting quarterback, in the Super Bowl this Sunday!"

Slap!

Woah. Ebony slapped the camera up into the man's nose.

"I told you, stop taking pictures of my man!" she roared, like a fine, female werewolf.

Ebony grabbed my hand and led me back to the truck. Fans were now out of their cars, taking pictures of me and the jolly, juicy giant. He was knocked out! Sleep like a homeless drunk, on his trunk! Dang! This is not a good look. My girl was right.

"Hey, who won the tennis match, mama!" big man yelled, waking up from my knock-out power slam!

ZOOM! A nine-hundred thousand dollar, pink and black, expensive motorcycle with platinum gas pedals and a platinum steering wheel pulled up beside me.

"Bro! Cim!"

"Yeah?"

"I bet I can beat you to grandma's house! BOOP!" my cute, but funny little sister, Kishana said.

Then she sped off!!! Blazing rubber on her new, jet black tires! So that's what she did with her birthday money today! BOOP! Alright. I gave my little sister one-million dollars for her birthday. I made myself a promise. With my one-hundred and twenty million dollar, record-breaking contract, I was blessing every one of my close family members with a million dollars! Even the babies! Heck, I got a two-hundred million dollar shoe contract, and a one-hundred million dollar, apple, gummy cereal contract!

Yes ma'am and yes sir! I pose on the front of the Apple Gummy Bear Cereal box! So the least I could do was break bread with my loved ones. When God gives abundantly to you, you should have the heart to give to those in need.

Man. Whateva. I let the system play my Columbia High, Decatur, GA homies, B.O.B., T.I., and Juicy J. The hot, old track, "I'm in my zone, I'm feeling it. Stop blowing my buzz, quit killing it. So buy another round, they tried to shut us down, bout an hour ago, but we still in dis bi . . . ."

I held my baby's hand.

"Awwwe. Thank you, daddy," Ebony whispered, when I moved my right hand to rub her pretty, pregnant stomach.

-I pulled up at grandma's house, like a real, rich baller!

"Bro! Bro! God! Get out! Get out! Hurry! Grandma! I think she dead!!! Kishana yelled, while pulling on my shirt and crying like crazy.

She ran out of the house, full speed, in her pink, Polo socks! She was all the way inside my cracked, rolled-down window!

Dash!!

I sprinted into granny's house, and wham! Shoved the wooden door open! I have to check on granny! That's my heart and soul! I love grandma!

Stumble, trip, slip, boom!

"Grandma!" I yelled, sliding into the bedroom. I froze like a dinosaur on ice!

I could not muster the sight. The power I once had, leaked out of me, like a balloon! No matter how tough you are, no one can handle the death of a loved one.

Grandma was lying on her wooden floor. Blood was running out of her nose like thick, red snot. Her body jerked twice. Blood squirted out of her mouth. I couldn't believe my eyes. She is the strongest woman I've ever known in my life. The sweetest woman alive!

"Grandma!"

I was crying, man. I couldn't help it. I love grandma. I can't see her like this.

"God help her," I mumbled, low in sound, but loud in my soul. She is so beautiful. I was on top of her, rubbing her long, silky, beautiful, gray hair. It seemed to gleam. Tears flowed from a 100% real man. I love this lady with every inch of my mind, body, and soul.

Flip.

I sat on the floor and put her head in my hands, praying.

"God. Did anyone call an ambulance?" Ebony stuttered in tears. She was in a nervous, head-scratching fit; shaking in fear. EB was walking fast; going nowhere; in circles!

She loved grandma too. I'm lying. She super loved grandma. Adored her in the greatest way known to the human race!

Do you know how it feels to loose someone you love? Imagine it . . . . It hurts . . . Stings . . . Bites . . . Imagine the heartache . . .

Nothing mattered at the moment. Not football, winning, losing, love, sex, money . . . nothing.

Life is more important. We take so much for granted on this planet. Then, I made all these plans for grandma, like tomorrow is promised. You never know. Accidents are never planned. Death is never planned. Life is unpredictable. I realized it, when death hit me.

Boom!

"What? Grandma!" Micki shouted, storming into the bedroom, like a serial killer from the jungle, running, kicking the white rabbit in the air, like a football! Arf!

"Mah!" Micki cried. It was too late.

Grandma was gone . . .

Game Time

The Georgia Thunder Dome was loud as a rocket, with deafening, exuberant noise and cheering. The fans were on their feet, roaring! The blue and silver confetti blasted out of the cannon, as the announcer introduced the AFC champions.

The huge screen showed all the winning plays that got the defending champions back to the Super Bowl.

The Bullets shouted and pumped their fists, as the entire team ran onto the field.

"Ready!" I told myself, as we anticipated the Super Bowl, home team introduction! We were all dancing in place; rocking, shaking!

"And now, your awesome, never ever quitting, National Football Conference Champions . . . . THE ATLANTA TIGERS!!!!"

Our forty, foxy cheerleaders ran in front of us. I saw my Ebony in front of me. Her legs were spectacular! Her skin tone and panty hose that the NFL required them to wear looked amazing! Her shape was hollering fine! RAW! In her all red mini skirt! Boop!

I ran on the field with my teammates and coaching staff. I looked at the huge TV screen above the field. All of our wining plays flashed. No lie, I was in my zone, and feeling it! I stood side by side, in my red and black, with my teammates. God, I hate he died. Cancer is hard.

I watched the late, great Oakland Rangers, NFL running back do his thang on the big screen.

Then Cedra gave the award to the New York Lion's running back,

Harper.

"Go, girl!" Levi shouted, when he saw his sixteen year old, Decatur born, R&B sensation sing. Bre'shauna was awesome! Her CD went platinum! The song with her and T.I., called 'Super-Hot' was the bomb!

Sadness quickly overtook my thoughts, the second I realized this was a dedication to the elementary school students that were brutally murdered in Portland.

Why kill innocent children? What a cruel, insane, evil, devilish, horrible act.

"God bless the families of those innocent children" . . . I quietly prayed while Bre'shauna continued to sing.

Bre'shauna sang like a young Whitney! Straight from Illinois, baby!

I was really feeling myself now. I glanced over at my wifey.

"Mwah." I blew her the kiss of victory!

Double mwah. She blew two kisses back.

Let's get ready to rumble! She never saw me lose, and I didn't plan on losing today! I always won the big games!

Ebony did her stretches, standing between Erica and Shawn. She bent over, and touched her toes, yep, without bending her knees, baby! Too sexy!

Bam! Wow. I always thought that was sexy. Shawn dropped and hit a perfect split!

"OOOH!" Now I was slap a snaggled-tooth, bull frog shocked!

My sister, Micki! She was sitting at a golden piano, playing Alicia Keys! Then, she sang the National Anthem!

I be juicy junk darned! I knew she could sing, cause she always rocked the choir! Micki used to have the entire church dancing, clapping, and falling out!

Now, lil sis, a.k.a. Red Bone Shawty, was singing at the biggest event on Earth! With more TV viewers watching ever in history! I know I'ma win this one, baby! Wooh! However, I wondered . . . . how many people even know the 'Star Spangled Banner' was first a poem, written in 1814 by Frances Scott Key? It was originally called the 'Defense of Fort McHenry.' Bang, baby!

The poem was later added to a tune, chopped and remixed. The title was called 'The Anacreontic Song.' The great John Stafford Smith changed the title to the 'Star Spangled Banner.' Hot Football dog!

And of course, my sister didn't know the history. She didn't give a flying peanut butt either! This was Micki's moment. She was in "Red Bone Shawty" zone. Boy, she sang it!

"Nooooo!" LOL.

I was caught off guard! Lil sis was doing a brand new National Anthem, Micki-remix of her own!

She leaped on top of the golden piano, pulled a red, rubber football out of her back pocked, and started dancing like Beyoncé, mixed with Michael Jackson!

"No. She. Didn't!" Deon laughed.

"Yes. She. Did!" Micki did the Moonwalk on top of the piano!

The Congress would be happy as a kid on Christmas! Lol. Because Micki a.k.a redbone shawty put on the greatest show ever seen! Bam! They proclaimed the 'Star Spangled Banner' the U.S. National Anthem in 1931. They probably would be crunk and live right now! LOL

Dancing, rocking, shocked and happy. Like everyone inside the dome, and watching on TV was right now!

Both football teams were dancing! Her D.J., D.J. Earl the Pearl, sped the beat up, while she danced.

"Boom!" Micki yelled, in her skin-tight, sexy, red, leather outfit. She hit a split! Whoop! Jumped off the piano, then continued to sing, but in the normal tone.

"Oh say, can you see. By the Dawn's early light . . .

What so proudly we hailed, at the twilight's last gleaming.

Whose broad stripes-"

What the . . .

I jerked from the sudden, off-guard fear, like everyone else in the world!

That thundering, thumping noise! Shoe be do! Got me! LOL.

I dozed off, baby! Caught in the hyped-up, dance zone. I forgot about the zipping, booming, five Navy F-18, Fighter Aircrafts. They always zoomed across the Super Bowl game, before kick-off.

The Georgia Thunder Dome was brand new and repaired. The red roof could open and close. So everyone saw the red jets flying over. Five seconds, they were gone! Flying back to Virginia Beach, home of my fried chicken, finger-licking family-Saniya, Jada, Sook, Jasmine and Jameka, baby!

"Cim! Wake-up!" Deon said, bumping my elbow.

"Oh yea, yeah. I was gone." I missed the introduction to the Hall of Famers and legendary coaches that were present for the coin toss.

"Oh! The coin toss is one of the most heavy, bet on events in sports! Dog! If my crazy, Jamaican daddy was alive, he would be somewhere drunk and crunk in Edgewood, making bets. Throwing so much money, drinking so many Budweiser's, he would forget who was winning! Then forget how much money he had! Laughing hella hard! R.I.P. Earl Brown. I love you dad. I'ma win this ring for you!

"OK. Head or tail?" Bonner, the Dominican referee asked.

"Head." I reflexed, staring directly into the eyes of my opponent, Wonder Boy Wesley-New England's, last year, Super Bowl MVP.

I wanted what he had. The world championship ring! That Vince Lombardi trophy. I could care less about the one-million dollars that each player on the winning team, receives. I was donating that to breast cancer. My thought was for my city, my deceased father, my pregnant wife, and for all my fans around the world. Also, the ATL haters! Who said Atlanta will never win the big one?!

Wrong!!

"Head win! Give or receive?"

"Receive!" I yelled, already feeling victory! It's already going my way!

Me and Sergio sprinted to our sidelines, since we won the coin toss. I waited for the Bullets to kick off the ball to my boys!

The air . . . you could feel it in the air. The atmosphere was exciting and awesome, with world-wide anticipation. People were drunk in bars. People were having Super Bowl, house parties. Every city in the world had their eyes on this! Even prisons and jails had their noodle soups and Greendot bets on this!

"A pack of Newports, and two packs of Burglars on Atlanta!" Some hyped-up prisoner with a life sentence was probably shouting!

Some females were not even football fans! Couldn't even tell you what a field goal was! Boop! But, big booty in boy short shorts, you best believe, those ladies were the life of the Super Bowl parties! Some girls just cheered for the team that wore their favorite color! I hope it was red and black!

Deon was deep in the end zone, anticipating the kick. That ball soared so high in the air, nearly touching the sky-high Thunder Dome.

Flip, flip. The ball skipped and flipped into the end zone. The blocker on special teams, BOOM!!! Knocked the dazzling daylights out of the New England defender!

Deon picked the ball up, with no hesitation! Nooo! BOOM!! He knocked the grass off the bottom of Deon Shoes!

Wrong answer! Deon danced, dodged, and ducked the two diving tacklers! They smashed into one of our blockers, like a truck!

"That's it! That's it! GO! GO! GO! GO! Oh, no! Oh, no! Yeah! Yeah, baby! He gone! He gone!!!!" I jumped and shouted from the sideline!

"TOUCH DOOOOWWN, ATLANTA!!!!"

The announcer shouted, world-wide, with all of the players and fans watching everywhere!

"Awww. Go, go, Tigers!" Ebony and the other beautiful cheerleaders shouted. Leaping, dancing, and cheering, while shaking their red and black shiny pom poms.

"Yeah! Yeah! Yeah! Deon! That's what I'm talkin' bout boy! Draw the first blood, baby. Go for the kill!" I told Deon, when he came back to the sideline to thousands of loud, rowdy, cheering fans and teammates patting him on his back. As a quarterback, when the defense or special teams scores, it makes my job easier!

"Girl, that's my brother!" Shawn shouted in Micki's ear.

"Ha, ha, I know. I know. He went in, girl!" Micki added.

"Ha, hee-he. I'm on Twitter, yall. They gone wild!" Cheetara, told the girls.

"Huh, what you say, Cheetara? I can't hear you. It's too loud in here, girl." Micki told her chocolate, brown, cheerleading friend.

"I know, girl. They going crazy! Deon brought the house down in this mother sucker!" Sassy yelled, while leaping up and cheering her heart out, with the rest of the badest females on the planet!

Atlanta cheerleaders were so hot! They have an interview on Tyra's TV show tomorrow.

"Girl, I just got a text from Jordan and Vick, at the same dang time!" Red Bone Shawty cheered and bragged in shock.

"No! Trick! You lying!" Erica joked.

"Trick you! I'm for real!" Micki said showing the messages.

"Gurl, you gone make Coach Brown beat you down!" Erica added, as they both kicked their legs in the air and cheered.

"Shid, it will be a cold day in hell, and a hot day in heaven before that happens! Ain't nobody hittin' Red Bone Shawty!" Micki said, with an evil laugh.

"And Erica, who texted you, cause I seen yo iPhone flash?" Cheetara said.

Woof! All forty girls leaped in the air with both hands over their heads.

"Ummm. Timberlake, girl."

"Whaat! The singer!" Cheetara asked.

"Hah, hah, no. Dustin Timberlake, the plumber," Erica said, quickly deleting the message.

"Yes it was! I'ma tell Levi!" Janice, a.k.a. Philly's Yellow Bone, joked, while laughing and hitting Erica on her smooth, left arm.

Ebony continued to cheer her heart out. She could feel the victory in her heart. She stared down at her man. The man she had loved the majority of her life. How many females can actually say their man has never treated them wrong? Ebony could. Cimeon was the perfect man. Not Mr. Right or Mr. Wrong. He was her Mr. Perfect! No one knew she was pregnant but her man. They had their own special secret.

"Nooo!" the girls shouted!

"Defense!!!" they cheered. Ebony woke up from her Love Dream World and chanted for her A-town tigers to make a defensive stop.

New England's speedy receiver, Dailon returned the kick-off, all the way to mid field! Boy! He almost had a wide-open shot for the end zone as he tip-toed with rocket speed down the side lines.

Kah-Boom!

Butch put the hardest hit ever on Dailon, hitting him head-on, from the side, immediately knocking his helmet out of bounds!

Wiff!

I caught his blue helmet in my hand, and shook my head. "Dang, he hit hard!" I said. That hit made me curl!

Wooh! Like a truck crushing a turtle!

Keep Pushing

I sat on the bench. Forget that! I stood up. Then I sat back down. Then, I rocked back and forth.

"Water?" the corny, goofy, shot-out water boy asked. I just looked at the clown. White male. Maybe twenty at the most. Looked high as a kite and crazy as a demon, but silly as a two-year old, with the brains of a lizard licker!

"Come on, defense! Make the play!" Sergio yelled in my ear, while standing up, trying to coach the team in his heart.

New England's Wonder Boy quarterback, Wesley, had the ball. Their offense was in shot gun formation.

Bam!

He zipped a quick 5 yard pass to Zachariah! D.J. tackled him.

"No!"

Zach shook D.J. off his legs, and continued to run 5, 10, 15, more yards.

Bang!!! Terry knocked him into the turf! His face was inside the ground! Terry was still on top of Zack, bragging and taunting him from the paralyzing, power hit.

The refs ran to the spot of the tackle. Zack didn't move a tiny inch. He laid there on the 25 yard line. His mom's eyes were wide open, like McDonald's on Friday evening!

"Yeeah!" the crowd chanted. When he stood up and waved. Then Zack gave them the thumbs-up, indicating everything was ok. Getting hit by a Mac truck don't feel too good!

"Come on, defense! ATL defense!" Ebony and the cheerleaders yelled. She could feel her 5 week old baby cheering inside her mind and heart!

"TIGERS! TIGERS! DEFENSE!!! Atlanta cheerleaders shouted from the top of their sexy lungs. All the girls had been Beauty of the Week! Micki a.k.a redbone shawty, won the prettiest girl of the year award! Two years in a row, on ten different magazines! Plus, Ebony won Ms.America last year! In other words, Atlanta has the baddest cheerleaders on the planet!

I watched Coach Dunlap call the defensive play. "Red Dog!" he called, the code for blitzing the quarterback.

This was a dangerous call because Wesley was too fast. Someone would be open.

"Hut!"

Wonder Boy Wesley got the snap. Two Tiger linebackers came at him, full speed! Bam!

Before you could blink!

"Ahhh! Ouch!!" Ebony said in her cheer!

The second Wesley got the ball, Terry nailed him to the ground!

"OOHHH! Get it! Get the ball!" Coach Brown yelled.

Wesley got hit so hard, he fumbled the ball. D.J. tried to pick it up off the ground.

Dang!

He couldn't control it. He was too anxious.

Bam! An offensive tackle hit D.J., knocking him to the ground.

"Yeah!"

Terry dived his huge body on top of the loose ball!

Boom! Jump! Jump! Dive!

Ten humongous, school bus-looking players all dove on top of Terry's stiff body, trying to tussle, muscle and fight, or knock the ball out of Terry's possession.

America was on their feet.

Bank!

Money was thrown on gambling tables! Females ran to the living rooms in the houses that held Super Bowl parties! We were on our feet, with the thousands present inside of the Thunder Dome in Georgia, hungrily waiting on the call.

The refs slowly moved the big pile off of Terry's body. We waited to see if the ball came out of Terry's hands. I was ready to play. I ain't even had a chance to do my thang!

Wink. Wink.

I winked at my wifey.

"Yeeeeeahhh!" my Tigers roared! My cheerleaders cheered! The Georgia Dome thundered! Fans shouted!

"Tigers' ball!" the announcer yelled.

Great! I anxiously ran to the field with my hungry, hot defense. I was ready! Not nervous at all! I loved the pressure! I loved the attention! We ran to the line of scrimmage. I bent down. I glanced left and right at the 4-3 defense. I spotted the blitz! Disregard the play that Coach Pettis originally called. I spotted a weakness and I changed the play.

"Red 911!" I shouted the new play. That was also my wife's birthday year!

Huh?

I got the ball at mid field. All eyes on Cimeon, baby. First snap for me in Super Bowl history. I had no chance to glance at my wife or family. No time to think about the past or the future.

I dazzled. Boom. Ugh!

I backed up too far! Dog git! I stiff-armed two powerful line backers, back to back. Boom! Boom! I shoved them into the turf like pancakes when they ran at my legs. I was 15 yards behind my original line of scrimmage. Man!

If they hit me here, that's a huge 15 yard loss! Dang!

Why was nobody open?! I continued to scramble like eggs, and boil like white grits!

"Husband! Husband! Run! Run!" Ebony yelled and jumped.

Kah Bizzle, Dizzle, Bam!!!!

"Ouch . . ." blood poured down my face. My lip was bleeding like a wounded soldier. The strong safety smacked me, unbelievably, numbingly hard! Did dude try to kill me?! I couldn't feel my body parts! The back of my head dropped on the ground like cracked eggs.

Hey, this ain't right.

I couldn't move. I never been hit this hard. My head. My head beat with marching band, rock concert, pounding pain. Only my eyes could move. It was right in my ears! I could hear the loud silence . . .

The entire Dome was on their feet. I felt bad. The stretcher came to the field. The team doctor, Coach Brown, and Coach Pettis stood over me. My teammates had fear all over their faces. Sergio stood over me and gave me a very scary stare. He knew they would lose without me. Naw! They would get murdered without me!

Ebony, Shawn, Mickey, Kishana, Erica, Janice, Akilah, Ashley, Shylin, Kenesha, Cheetara, and all the rest of the worried, beautiful cheerleaders came together for a prayer.

"Lord, this can't happen to my brother! In the name of Jesus! This WON'T happen to my brother! Not here. Not now. Not like this. Lord, God of Gods, King of Kings. You said in your word, Psalm 25:3, no one that puts hope in You will NEVER be put to shame. You can heal Cimeon with just one word. Your word. Psalm 107:20. You sent Your word and healed them. We believe, touch and agree, that You will heal Cimeon Levi Riley. Now Lord! Amen." Micki prayed, anointed and bold, in tears.

The forty cheerleaders held hands and simultaneously said, "Amen."

Ebony was pregnant, pitiful and paralyzed. She squeezed Micki's hand in tears. This was the first time she had ever seen her man hurt.

"No, Ebony! What are you doing"! Micki yelled.

Too late! She was not hearing nothing but love! She dashed onto the Super Bowl football field in her black dance shoes!

Flash. Flash. Snap. Cameras flashed all over the hurt Rookie of the Year and his scared, loving, cheerleading wife! She ran in tears, love and beauty. This was another Huge Love Story, and Sad Super Bowl History!

"Baby! Baby! Cim!"

"Ma'am. You can't come onto the field," the stick, skinny, old referee told her.

Thump!

Ebony pushed through the crowd and held her husband's hands as he laid on the stretcher, motionless.

That earth quacking, devastating sack was a 25 yard loss! In other words, Atlanta was in big trouble!

Only the Strong Survive

I stared straight up in the air, at the seventy-five thousand plus, quiet fans. I wasn't even able to wave or give them the thumbs up.

"I'm with you. I love you," my wifey said.

"Ebony, get over here! If you don't get back to cheering, you are fired! You are not medical personnel, or a team doctor! That is not your job! Your job is to cheer!" the serious, forty-year old, cheerleading captain told Ebony.

No she didn't!

Ebony got right up in her face. "Listen, that's my man. You can take this job and shove it so far up your butt, that you will fart cheers for a year, and blow pom-poms out of your nose like boogers! My man's life and health are more important than any dang cheer!" Ebony said. Right in her face. She was so close, their noses were touching!

"Water! You need water, Mr. Cim?" the goofy water boy asked Cimeon as he rolled away on the cart. The water boy was running behind them, trying to give Cimeon some water.

Whap!

Ebony kicked the water out of the water boy's hands.

Splash!

Water spilled all over the goof ball's face!

"Do my man look thirsty fool?"

Bam!

Micki punched the water boy with a right hand, powerful, pom-pom blow!

"Whoa! Water boy Bell got knocked the heck out! OK girls, calm down. Ebony, Miss Lane, Micki, come here," the owner, Michael Lackey said. Then, he waved for them to continue driving his Pro Bowl quarterback to receive medical attention.

"Ok, what's the problem, ladies?"

"First of all-"

"This dumb b-"

"That fat head fool-"

"Hold on. We can all sing the same song at one time, but we can't yell different statements at one time. Ebony, you explain first."

"Well, that's my man, I love him to death. I'm not leaving his side-"

"Then, don't." Mr. Lackey said, with speedy power. He then waved for her to follow her man/wounded soldier.

"Ok. And Miss Lane, let Ebony see about her husband. Plus, that's my money maker. I have to check on him too! I have two million dollars betted on this game. Mr. Bennit is on my tale! That's the owner of the New England Bullets, in case you didn't know. Carry on. One cheer leader will not be missed. Now, Miss Micki, why did you knock out the water boy, at the 50 yard line?" Mr. Lackey asked the angel-looking, pretty cheerleader, with her long, off-black hair dangling, hands on her slender, sexy hips, brown eyes full of screaming, seducing innocence!

"First of all, Mr. Owner of the Georgia Thunder Dome and the Atlanta Tigers, your water boy is a goof ball! He splashed water in your one-hundred million dollar quarterback's face! While he was paralyzed! In the biggest game of both of yall careers! Cimeon was actually choking, when the dumb water boy dashed the dang water up his nose! So I, BAM! Knocked his butt out!" Micki a.k.a. Redbone Shawty said to the multi-billion dollar man.

Mike just glanced at his forty-thousand, yellow gold, full diamond bezel Rolex watch, then took a deep, serious sigh. Dang. Micki was in big trouble. He began to speak, while she stood stiff and nervous, expecting the worse. Mr. Lackey didn't tolerate nonsense! Hit the road, Jack! And don't come back no more!

"Bam! Ma'am! The water boy is still knocked out! Hah-hah. He ain't woke up yet. Poor Joshua Bell. Well, dang. With that kind of power, we need your one-hundred and twenty pound, five foot three inch figure on the football team! You can be the first NFL female football player in history!" Michael Lackey said, laughing.

"Ha-ha," Micki laughed, unsure of how to take the owner's statement.

"Meaning, carry on! Go cheer, my dear!" he said, waving her toward the side line.

Bam! Bam! Twerk!

The whistle blew.

"False start, offense! Number 55," the line judge yelled. On the Atlanta Tigers, this was a terrible start. Another 5 yard loss. With a forty year-old granddaddy quarterback, taking the snap! Antonio hasn't played a game in six years! Now, this old prune was taking the snap of the most watched TV show in American history! Now, 2nd down and 30.

Backed up to their own 25 yard line, grandpa took the snap; glanced from side to side.

"Blue 22."

The quarterback was now too slow to move.

BOOM!

The defensive end hit him so hard, his helmet cracked! The reffs ran onto the field, again!

"Man down! Player down! Another Atlien bites the dust, baby! Hah-hah!" Wesley cheered form the New England side line.

They rolled the crappy back-up quarterback off the field. He suffered a concussion. So awful, Antonio was gone. Like his sex life! Boop! Coach Brown was in panic mode. Crack head on Mars. Scratching his head. That sack moved, them all the way back to their own ten yard line.

"Ok, 3rd and 40," Coach Brown said, in frustration.

"Hold up! Look!" Offensive Coordinator Mr. Pettis shouted in shock!

"I'm ready." Cimeon told the team.

"Yeeey! Yeah! Cim! Sizzling Cim!" the crowd cheered.

Ebony had the biggest, proudest smile of all.

"That's my man, girl!"

"I know. Look at Cim!" Erica said, eye full of hot joy!

"Hah. Hah. Go get em, bro!" Kishana cheered!

"Good Lawd. Decatur, GA is blowing my inbox up!" Akilah said, checking her thirty-thousand dollar iPhone.

"Ok. Cheer! Cheer!" Miss Lane shouted to the beautiful girls.

Beast Mode

"Time out on the field. Atlanta," the reffs announced.

The down-feeling team ran to their side lines.

"Look, Cim is going back in. It's a long shot. And a big risk to put him right back in the game. Well, its 3rd down and forever! And if he gets hurt, I lose my job. But he is going in!" Coach Brown said, filled with faith!

All the players instantly lit-up like firecrackers! Bang! Bang! Cim back in his thang!

The offense ran back on the field. Super Bowl viewers world-wide were hollering!

"I bet $2,000 they gone make the first down, shawty!" TKO yelled in the Georgia prison, flashing his fourteen digit green dot number, that had $2,000 on it, ready to load on a debit card.

"Cim gonna make it happen! Bet $10,000!" Fab yelled in Las Vegas, at a gambling table.

"No way, Cimeon, Super Man, or the Hulk can make a 45 yard, first down in the Super Bowl. That's impossible! Bet $40,000!" Mr. Pervis yelled in Chicago, at a sports bar.

"Down! . . . Set . . . Hut . . ."

The Super Bowl center, tossed the snap to the rawest rookie in Super Bowl history! Cim took the snap, the offensive line held-up, great pass protection. He scrambled, left to right, looked down the field.

"Dang! Nobody is open!" I whiffed and Dodged the two-hundred and eighty pound, mean line-backer. He was a man eater! Not me! I'm not to be eaten!

"Yeah!" I shouted in my head. I spotted Sergio. My wide receiver was now wide open at the 40 yard line. Just what I needed.

Wham!

Dang! The defensive end nailed me. Wrong! I stumbled 5 more yards backwards, before I hit the ground!

All this for nothing, ok . . .

I desperately threw the ball high, very high into the air. The ball floated, for what seemed like a ten year prison sentence! I was on my back, then I sat up. Wondering. Watching where the ball would land. Sergio went for the catch. He leaped high like a basketball player.

"Dog!" I punched the turf. He missed it.

"Awwwe" the entire dome chanted, disappointed. It was over with. New England would have excellent field position.

"Yeah! Yeah! Yeah! Erica! Micki! Shawn! Look! Look, girl!" Cheetara yelled to the forty, sexy, sad cheerleaders, shaking their entire, slim bodies.

"Who! Booh ya!" Kishauna shouted. All the Super Bowl viewers' mouths were open like toilets, waiting for this sudden, strange decision. The referees ran onto the field. Sergio and Omar were just getting off the artificial grass. Flip! Sergio was frustrated. He tossed the ball at one of the reffs, hitting him on the left knee.

The television commentators were all talking, assuming, speculating, guessing and sighing.

"Apparently, there's a flag on the play," the on field, pretty, chocolate commentator, Ms. J. Pettis said in her microphone. I stood on my feet, after the big three-hundred and twenty-five pound offensive line man helped me up.

"What's the call, Bobby?" I asked Big Bob, from Cobb.

"Oh, nothing. They just trying to decide what spot to give the New England the ball," Big Blocking Bobby said, breathing like a whale on the beach. Breath smelling like kung fu couchie! LOL.

The entire dome was standing, wondering what the call was. The reff ran to the side line, cleared his throat, and spoke.

"Pass Interference. Defense Number 21. First Down, Atlanta!"

"Yeeeeahhhh!!!!" all the Atlanta fans world-wide cheered.

"Big break! GO get em, Cim!" Offensive Coordinator, Pettis, told him. Then, Mr. Pettis texted his wife, Mrs.Pettis a smiley face.

Yes, football is a family, fun-loving sport!

"Mama, what that mean?" Minnie asked Kiana, as they sat in the three-hundred thousand dollar, luxury, owner, club box seats, next to the Mayor of Atlanta, Earl Brown, who was Kiana's husband. Also in the box seats were the governor of Georgia, Lawrence Rutherford, and his lovely wife, and model Kiki.

"Pass Interference, Minnie. That's when the quarterback throws a pass, and while the ball is still in the air, a defensive player pushes, shoves, holds, or otherwise physically prevents an offensive receiver from moving his body or his arms in an attempt to catch the ball," Kiana, the Actress, Author, and Cover Girl explained.

"Mookey, Mook, Mook! Wow. She is a real fingernail! She is a keeper, cuz! You married a girl that knows about football! Wow! I love it! You know not to mess up on that one! Hah, ha. He, hee!" Governor Lawrence joked with Mayor Brown.

"Ha, ha. Yes. Yes. She surprises me. Kiana, give daddy a billion dollar, female football knowledge kiss . . . With your Super Sexy Seducing Stand and your Perfect, Beautiful Commercial, TV Smile!" The handsome mayor of Atlanta, King Earl Brown said.

Mwah!

Kiana eyes was closed and her heart was open, as she leaned in to kiss her husband. Kiana and Earl kissed like Deep, Passionate, Faithful, Thirsty Lovers, in a packed prison visitation room! They were like the Obamas. The perfect role models in GA.

"Ahnn! Ahnn!" baby Ari cried. She was seven months old, holding a platinum baby bottle, with a football on the side of it!

"Billionaires. Yall kill me. We're in scoring position, baby! Wooh!" Michael Lackey yelled, spilling his thirty-thousand dollar champagne, as the billionaires sat in the expensive, Luxury Owners Club box seats.

"Hey! That's what I'm talking about!" I chanted as we ran to Coach Pettis for the next play.

"I love my man! I know we gone win!" Ebony shouted in the midst of their cheers.

"Ok. Two minute drill. We need to blast them before the 2nd quarter. Shoot for the touchdown. The triple stretch is the play. I'm putting in three receivers. Levi, be ready. Yo may have to run the ball if they play man-to-man with the receivers. Let's go! Win!" Offensive Coach, Pettis shouted.

We shot back on the field like rockets. I was geeked out of my mind, in my zone. I looked at the cheerleaders, and waved at my wifey. She blew me a kiss as she waved.

I love that girl. I'm about to do this for you. I settled into my stance, behind my center. Immediately, I noticed the defense was playing man-to-man with my three receivers. I could either run, hit my tight end, or try a running play with Light Em Up Levi.

I looked up at the clock and the score board. Two minutes left in the first quarter. We had a 7 to 0 lead against the defensive Super Bowl champs. I'm a Rookie, first year. Time to shock the world!

"Hut!"

Zip! I took the ball. The heat was on! I scrambled, then, bliff-I decided to give my running back the hand off. Levi protected the ball and Bam! Bam! He ran straight up the middle, smashing through the three-hundred pound defensive linemen! 45, 40, 35, 30

The huge, powerful calves of Light Em Up Levi were steaming and speeding like a flash of light from a rocket! Dawg! Erica musta gave him a little taste of chocolate, cause that boy was gone!

Boom! Omar hit the numbers off Levi's jersey! Ka Boyah! Knocked the big boy out of bounds! Cool. We were in field goal range. Disregard that. I wanted a touch down! I quickly ran to the line of scrimmage for the no huddle offense.

Hut!

I immediately took the snap and threw it in the end zone. I leaned my body back and sideways while the ball was zipping in the end zone, as if my body could make Sergio catch the ball.

Dang!

He missed it! Hold . . . Toss . . . The reffs threw the penalty flag and ran onto the field.

"Off sides. Defense. Number 89. 5 yard penalty. Repeat First Down," the head linesman stated, confirming the cool, cross-eyed line judge. I waved for my offense to do a quick huddle. I checked with Pettis for the play.

"578 Pump F-stop in Two!" we were so close to the end zone; at the 20 yard line.

"Set! Red 91 . . . Hut-hut!"

Bam! I took the snap and made sure Sergio was in position to make the play for the quick out. Sergio ran straight for 7 yards, then he quickly broke to the outside.

Bam! Bam!

My NFL fastest, forty-five mile an hour ball hit Sergio dead in the hands, at the 10 yard line. The lineman crushed me! Like pancake pie! Sergio swiftly avoided two tackles, and Boom! The strong safety rammed my best receiver out of bounds at the 5 yard line.

First and goal now! The red zone defense was tight and extremely difficult to score on. Even though we were so close to the touchdown, it was a lot harder to score because the defense and everyone in the world knew what you would try to do. Score!

Advantage. Us. We had a great, strong, powerful running back. Levi was a mean, physical, tough beast! He would bowl over guys, and fight through three huge defenders at the same dang time! Five feet, ten inch beast! If we got within 5 yards or less to the goal line, best believe you can bet your sex partner on this! Levi is scoring that touchdown!

I got in stance behind my center; thought for a quick second.

"Set.! . . . Hut! Hut!"

I handed the ball to my powerful, bull-legged running back. One. Two. Three tacklers bamboozled Levi! Boom!

He fell one yard short of the goal line. Wham! Cold turkey, Gummy Bear and ham!

"Yeeeaah!!!"

"Touchdown, Tigers!!!!"

The referee extended his arms, straight in the air, above his head, to signal the surprise touchdown!

Boop! I booped everybody. LOL.

The people on TV, and on the field. I faked the hand off to Levi, then I ran to my right; straight into the end zone!

"Yeah! Cim! Cim R," my team shouted.

I stood by my bench and watched the twenty-two players on the hottest football field on Earth!

"Water, si-si-sir?"

I held my arms in front of our goofy water boy's face. My focus was only on the kick!

"Good!" I pumped my fist. Yeah! Then gave Sergio and Coach Brown and the sexy team trainer, Danika a high five!

14 to 0, Tigers. End of the first quarter.

The television played the greatest, most popular and highly anticipated commercials of the year during the commercial break.

While America was watching funny, unique, amazing or sometimes dumb commercials, our awesome offensive coordinator, Coach Pettis, who was a 5'10", brown skin, green eyes, Decatur sports genius, spoke to the entire offense, especially me. I sat down and listened to the strategies.

He spoke with a deep, baritone voice, "OK, listen. We are in great control. But, this is a great come from behind team. Don't think New England is going to quit. We must keep our feet on their throats. Don't play conservative. Go hard. Very hard. By half-time, I want to be up by at least four touchdowns. Let's smack them around like punching bags! Cimeon, I want you to stay focused. Keep your mind and eyes open. Read that defense. I'm trying to win this game. Get us to Disney World!" Coach Pettis demanded!

"OK, Cimeon. Don't forget your arm strength and passing accuracy is a whooping, butt smacking, NFL 107.8, first among any quarterback in history! In other words, even though you are faster than Vick was-running 40 yards in four seconds flat, with more moves than Barry Sanders, Chris Brown, and Michael Jackson put together, you have to throw the ball. Levi is the number one rusher in the NFL, with 2,000 rushing yards. Let him run. You pass. Too much leg work will tire you out in the 4th quarter. We making history today, baby!!!"

BOOOM!

The start of the second quarter started.

"I love you, Ebony."

"Cim!"

"Huh?"

"Win the game, love bird!" Coach Pettis said, laughing.

"Ha, ha. All I do is win." I told my offensive coach.

Muwah . . . I kissed my wife's name that was on the inside of my left muscle; on my throwing arm! She was my lucky charm. Every pass I threw, I threw with my boo! All forty five record-setting touch downs that I threw this year!

"Touchdown, New England!"

"What?! What the-" I fell off the bench, in shock.

"You want some water, sir?"

"Water boy! Shut up!" I said, not meaning to chump him off, but I was orange juice, wet-pants pissed.

Wesley threw a 90 yard touchdown to Jayhlen on the first play! Nuts and butts! Jayhlen was the running back! Wesley tossed the ball to Jayhlen Washington. A 5 yard pass, and the quick halfback ran 90 yards down the dang side line! I was hot! African-in-July-with-two-fur-coats-on-hot! With three red peppers in my mouth and hot sauce in my nose, hot!

"Good!" The referee signaled as they kicked the extra point.

14 to 7, Tigers.

Now, I was hyped and extra turned up (in my Roscoe voice).

I refused to let New England come back. That's on my mama! Kin! I'm about to burn these suckers like hot grits on cheating Dick! That's a cheating husband named Dick! LOL.

To all my kids and Christian readers. I just remembered when my Uncle Dick from Seattle, cheated on my aunty. She waited until he came in the bedroom, and went to sleep. Then . . . "Ahhhh! You fool!" Dick yelled in pain.

She tossed boiling, hot grits all over his weeney wacker! Boop!

Uncle Dick became a sex education teacher at Rainer Beach High School! Never cheated again! Yank! Yank! Boop! Shoe-be-do!!!!

"Go!" Coach Brown yelled for me and the offense to run on the field. I sprinted on the field, like a slave on fire. I got in my stance, behind my center. Glanced at my offense, from left to right. I squinted my eyes at the defense; the corner backs were directly in front of my two receivers.

Hah-Hah. They were playing man-to-man defense. I also noticed New England was trying to confuse me and my offensive linemen. How many people were coming at my head? Four, five, or six people? This was new!

Oh, they were in the zone blitz, created by Dick LeBeam.

So what!

"Down . . . Red 89! Hut! Hut!"

I took the snap, Bam!

Good God on the Kroger store ice cream isle! That devastating hit by the humungous linebacker made me melt like cookies and ice cream!

Dang! Man this time, I was hurt. For real!

Not physically hurt, but dog gone it, my pride was hurt. I was backed up like Juvenile! On my ten yard line!

I was not trying to look bad in the Super Bowl. With all eyes on me. My dead father and grandmother, plus my wife and unborn child. All the people in America cheering for me and betting on me. All the kids wearing my number 10, C. Riley jersey! I can't go out bad.

Dog! Of a hog in fog! Coach Pettis warned me about that 3-4 alignment, zone blitz defense.

"That zone blitz will confuse the mess out of a young, inexperienced quarterback," he told me.

Now I see. These guys are so much bigger and faster in Real Life Action! Imagine getting hit by a two-hundred and eighty pounder, running at you in full speed! Kah Bam!

Ouch!

Back on my feet, I stumbled to the line of scrimmage. It was a running play that Pettis called for Levi. Never be too quick to throw this far back in your own end zone. A turn over back here would lead to a sure New England score.

Bemp! Bemp! Bam! Bang!

The big guys crushed each other, like tractor trailer playing real life bumper cars!

Levi was a punishing, bruising runner though. He trampled over the three-hundred pounders for 5 tough yards. Now, we had to get 15 yards, or the Bullets would get the ball.

We lined up.

Muwah. I kissed my wife's tattoo.

"Hut!"

I ran for it! I knew Coach Brown and Coach Pettis were cussing me out! Jumping and yelling on the side lines like kangaroos in the projects. Calling me all kinds of stupid, hard headed, rookie mother suckers!

So what?! I dipped, ducked, dodged, and dashed. I ran 5 yards, stood still, and faked out two linemen. Then, I ran 2 yards down the side line. Bam! I cut to my right and ran up mid field! Bad luck again! For our water boy, I mean. The strong safety missed me and tackled him, knocking Gatorade all up his nose!

While the goofy water boy was crying, I was flying!

"Yeeah! Tiger! Run! Fly! Run!" the beautiful, sexy, model-shaped, Atlanta cheerleaders shouted at the top of their lungs!

"That's my man, girl!" Ebony yelled. Shaking her pom-poms like black pepper, while jumping and kicking her legs in the air with the rest of the squad!

"Girl, he gone!" Erica yelled.

Gone I was. Nope!

I did not look back. 20, 15, 10, 5, TOUCHDOWN TIGERS!!!

"20 to 7!" TV commentator, Sandra shouted.

"Yeah!!! I shouted, leaping high and then dunking the football on the 10 foot high cross bar like a basketball!

Instantly, I ran to the crowd, and tossed the ball to a pretty little fan. She was in her father's lap, blushing. She had on a pink Atlanta Tigers jersey-with my number 10 on it! I assume her name was Saniya cause it had Saniya on the sleeves. Too cute! She was holding that football like it was a gift from an angel! A football angel, with the prettiest, biggest smile you could ever see!

Man, I loved my fans! The kids always touched my heart. I wonder how my baby will turn out? Cheering for her father? I sure hope so!

"Wooh!" Levi and Sergio yelled, picking me up in the air and carrying me to the sidelines.

"Muwah!" Ebony ran to the bench and kissed me. I smiled, with shy love.

"Baby?"

"Proud of you! Love you! I snook off! Gotta go!" she said, running back to join the cheerleading squad.

My baby was breaking all her cheerleading rules today. We grew up on food stamps in Decatur, GA, on Candler Rd. However, we had made it to the top, baby!

I had a brand new, 2018, red and yellow, platinum rims, black-tinted Chevy Corvette Stingray in the garage, waiting on her. She didn't even know it yet! It was just a surprise to show my baby how much I love her. No matter how many females come at me, she was there first. Before football and after football. She will always be number one in my eyes.

It felt good to be winning. But just like life ain't over till it's over, the game ain't over, till it's over.

Bam!

I sat and watched our defense bark, bat and bite at Wesley, knocking him deep into that artificial turf.

The second quarterback was calm like water.

Half-time. 21 to 7, Atlanta.

Half-time Heat

On stage . . .

"Gold all in my watch . . .
Don't believe me, just watch . . . .
I believe I can fly . . .
I believe I can touch the sky,
And can't touch this!
Ain't nobody messing with my click . . . click . . . click . . ."
"Trick don't kill my vibe!"
Boom!!!

Fire shot in every direction. The dome turned invisible, jet black. Then, the roof of the dome opened up.

A green helicopter covered with real life hundred dollar bills appeared in the sky! Everyone was in shock! Eyes wide, staring in the sky.

"Unbelievable! Never before seen in the history of the Super Bowl! What we are witnessing tonight, is unreal," TV commentator, Sandra, announced with hyper enthusiasm.

Chop! Chop! Chop!

The helicopter lowered down to the stage. The lights were still off. Boom!

"Don't stop, get it, get it!
You know I'm bad, I'm bad!

You know it!

Smooth criminal!"

Kah Bang!

The lights flashed on! The stage was covered in red smoke, like flames.

"Yeeeeeah! Everybody say yeah!!!" Asia screamed on her red microphone, in an all red cat suit. Long hair, body like a Coca Cola bottle, sitting on top of a tiger!

The entire crowd stood up and started cheering for the greatest singer/rapper/actress of all time! Asia Brown.

Money started falling out of the sky.

Boom!

Hundred dollar bills were shot out of the four cannons, in each direction.

"All I see is dollar signs.
Money on my mind. Money, money on my mind!
Watch it fall from the sky
Like the Fourth of July!
Throw it up, throw it up!
That's how we ball out.
Money on my mind.
Money, money on my mind,"

Asia sang. Then, she hit a split! She jumped up, then slid like she was on ice, across the stage. Stop! She ran across the stage, froze, stared at the crunk crowd. Her body was tight as a track star. Skin smooth as silk. Energetic as a cheerleader. Fine as a striper-with the voice of an angel!

The multibillion dollar singer rocked the house down! The fans were standing, cheering, and picking up the hundred dollar bills. Dudes were pumping their fists, watching their televisions in house parties and bars!

From Toronto, Alaska, Chicago, Saint Louis to New York!

Worldwide!

The dudes were possessed by the hot, new actress/comedian/ dancing female rapper, Asia Brown.

Then . . . flash! The lights went off in the dome. Flash! When they came back on, thirty girls in red, miniskirts were beside her, dancing.

Then, oh, snap, Asia was fye! She could dance! Plus, her dancers were good! They paused like a DVD, then hit a 360 spin. Then, all thirty-one of them did the Moon Walk, while 'Beat It' blasted. Throw back M.J.!

"Dang, I'm hungry. I got to cash this check, though," Kishana told her sister, while they zipped into the downtown check cashing store, on the pink cheerleading squad bus.

Kishana was driving the hot pink bus like a race car in Daytona!

"Money on my mind! Money, money on my mind!" Micki yelled, while singing and watching the Half-Time show on the bus, from the 60-inch, pink, flat screen, digital TV on the bus ceiling. Micki was standing in the middle of the bus while her little sister was driving 90mph! Kishana soared into the 24-hour check cashing place!

Bad, bad girl. Kishana stole the bus from the cheerleading captain! Boop! All the cheerleaders got off the bus like rock star rappers!

"Yeaaaah! Oh, let's do it!" Kiki shouted as all forty of the cheerleaders entered the check cashing store.

"Lay it down! Everybody. Anybody move, you die!" Kiki yelled.

"What da? This was not a part of the plan!" Erica said, sliding back out the door.

Ebony's eyes got bigger than the moon! She peeked into the door.

"Hold up! Where yall whoremongers going?! We in this robbery together!" Micki yelled.

Pow! Pow! Pow!

She shot through the bulletproof glass.

Splash! Kick! Bang!

Micki leaped on the counter and kicked straight through the shattered glass.

The Indian lady stuttered in goofy, not-so-good-English.

"Wat-wad ju want?"

"You!"

Pow!

Kishana shot her with her gold glock 40!

"Gold all in my mouth! Gold all on my glock! Don't believe me, just watch!"

Pow!

Kishana rapped and shot the safe open with her gold street sweeper! Was this a dream? Was something missing? Where in the world did these two sisters get their guns? Where did they hide them? How did I get involved in a Half-Time Super Bowl robbery? When I'm a married, pregnant cheerleader, with a husband playing in the Super Bowl? How in the world did I get involved in a robbery that I didn't even plan! Forget this, man! I'm too much in love with my man. I got to support him! Them crazy Candler Rd. sisters just got to kill me!

"I'm gone!"

Pow!

Micki aimed her platinum .44 at Ebony with her back turned!

Pow!

Kishana aimed at her head.

"Nobody leaves!!! And Kiki, the red bone said that! All of us are in this together! Cheerleading robbers! Load this money!" Kishana yelled, pointing her gold gun at the Indian man.

"I'm mad yall came over here and took all the jobs!" Kishana yelled at the crying man.

"Mommie!" a little one year old girl cried.

Zoom! Instantly, both of the cheerleading killas and all the rest of the store stared at the baby. Her young mom was holding her tight!

Bam!

"Freeze! Police!"

"Drop your heat!"

Drop Your Heat

"Ok, we don't want them to breathe! We don't want them to celebrate. We don't want them to score! We want them to die! This is the quarter to pull away in guys! We blow them away in the 3rd quarter, so they won't have a chance in the 4th quarter! This is our game! This is a once in a life time chance. Winning the Super Bowl is a dream that millions will never achieve. Winning the Super Bowl is something that millions of people watch, and cheer for, every year."

"Many great players retire without ever getting the chance to play in this game. This is the game that everybody in America pays attention to. Even if they hate football, they pay attention to the Super Bowl. The world is paying attention to us. So, let's show the world! Let's win!!!" Coach Brown wolfed to his team, beating on his own chest, growling at the team, and bouncing in the air.

"Rooar! Beat New England, up, up, up, up, up!" Coach Brown shouted, and snatched his shirt off. Coach J.L. Brown had all of us hype!

"Look, Coach is right. This is the reason we play the game! To win the ring! We will NOT let them score! Let's go!" D. Wight, a.k.a. D.J. yelled to his teammates.

Running a forty yard dash in 4.2 seconds, standing at 6ft 1 in., D.J. was the best corner back in the NFL, 3rd year vet, and led the NFL in interceptions every year. He had eighteen interceptions in just sixteen regular season games.

D.J. was a beast! And he was not about to let his team lose focus on a chance of a lifetime.

The special team players for each team ran onto the field. Atlanta kicked the ball off to New England. Deon was on the field. That boy played every position. Wham! Deon kicked the ball super high!

"Ebony?!" I thought out loud.

I jumped when I looked up and noticed none of our cheerleaders were there. That's strange. I stood up. I felt cold. Something was wrong! I swallowed deeply. I quickly jogged to where the cheerleaders normally cheered. Nothing! Nobody!

"What?! Nooooooo! Noooo! That's not true!"

I froze. Then looked towards the field, doing a 360 spin. That dang Wonder Boy Wesley was running straight down the middle of the field!

"Catch that nut!"

He zoomed! I watched him cross the 50, 45, 40, 35, 30, 25, 20, 15, 10

. . ."Touchdown, New England!!!!"

Dang. Dang. Dang, I hate ham!

"21-14, Atlanta!"

Where is my wife? She has never not cheered for me. Never!

"Cimeon! Cim! Come on! Let's go! Time to play! What are you doing?!" Coach Pettis shouted at me, waving for me to come get the play.

I walked dizzily, as if I was a drunk slut in the club ready to bone, anytime. Coach spoke, yelled, hollered and chanted, I heard nothing. All I thought about was my wife, Ebony.

Forget this game!

"Bro! Wake up, man! We need you!" my best friend, Sergio said, right up in my ear, like wax.

I snapped out of it. I was back in my kill zone. We ran onto the field, at the 20 yard line. Deon didn't return the kick. We used him as a 3rd receiver. I took my stance behind Elijah. I glanced at the defense, from left to right. It was hard, but I spotted the same linebacker, lined up directly across from my tight end. No way! He can't handle Randy. My tight end was a beast.

"Down! . . ."

I see the pressure coming to my left.

"Set! . . ."

My eyes tighten and zeroed in on the corner backs.

"Red 38 . . . Hut. Hut. Hike!"

I got the snap, and quickly handed it to my running back.

Bang! Bang! Boom!

They hit hard. Fast! Three-hundred pounders! Refrigerator smacks! Banging. Bruising. Popping the powerful running back. Levi broke threw.

25, 30, 35, 40, 45.

Boom!

Number 89 smashed him! A waist line tackle! Hah-hah. Look at Levi. He hopped up like, yeah!

"First Down, Atlanta!" the announcer, commentators, and reffs yelled, worldwide.

I could feel the intensity. We had the momentum again. We had the crowd. Yeah! Ebony was back! Or was she?

"Hut!"

Dang! I took my eyes off the ball! Looking for Ebony!

Boom! Boom! Ooops . . .

I lost the ball. A defensive lineman scooped it up. Kah Pow! Boom! Dive! Jump! Tussle! Smack! Scuffle! Wrestle!

Ten players dived on him, for the ball. Frustrated, I scratched my head, hard and fast, like a Cash-3, scratch off ticket! However, I wasn't winning no lottery! I was losing, big time!

"Don't sweat it, Cim. Our defense will get it back," my best friend said, trying to lighten me up.

Didn't work. Man, I was drunk. I stood in a huddle with my other ten players, awaiting the call. The ref pointed his hands to the right, "Fumble recovery. New England's ball!"

Man, I was beat . . . I walked away with my head down. A quarter back hates to cause a turn over.

"Boooooo!" the furious ATL crowd filled the Georgia Thunder Dome with horrific 'boos.' I looked up and squeezed my eyes in shame.

"Keep your head up, Cim," Coach Pettis said, patting me on the back, without even looking at me.

I know he was upset.

Blip.

I sat down on the bench and stared at the plays that Coach Pettis drew. I was just listening to my offensive coordinator. I couldn't believe it. Wesley had the ball at our 40 yard line, already near scoring position. I watched the play on the field and listened to the coach, at the same time. Atlanta's defense was hungry as starving wolves, to slow Wesley's momentum.

"Down . . ."

Wesley stared at the defense. Instantly, he spotted the elephant end, lined up on the tight end side of his offense.

"Set . . . Blue 42. Hut!"

Hill snapped the ball to Wesley.

Andrew bo-hogged through the offensive linemen! Yooh! He dove over a three hundred and twenty pounder and, BOOM! Andrew peter-rolled Wesley like a bowling ball sandwich! Wesley was not prepared for the pass-rush. The two teams walked back to the line of scrimmage.

Now, it was 2nd and 15. Loss of five yards. Thanks to Andrew.

"Cim!"

"Huh?"

"Muwah!"

I spun my head, as I sat on the bench. Awwweee. I was at ease. It was my sweetheart. My every day of the year Valentine.

"Ebony, not now!" Coach Pettis said, mean and strict.

"What? Hold up, Coach, I thought-"

"Business before pleasure. This is the Super Bowl, not the dang hotel room. You have an entire life to screw, kiss and hug. You only have one shot at the Super Bowl. Wake up, Cim!" Coach ordered me.

I jumped up. Then, I threw my hands up in defense.

"You right. Baby, I got to focus on this game. Muwah," I said, kissing her.

She smiled shyly. "I know. I love you."

"Ok, where are my sister and the cheerleaders?"

"She . . . they . . . It's . . ."

"Noo! Get him! Get him! Stop him! Stop Wesley!" Coach Pettis shouted to his defense.

Wesley was flying down mid field again. Bang! Knocked down at the 20 yard line.

I quickly shook off Ebony's words and focused on the plays.

"Dang it! What is wrong with that idiot! Take him out! Take him out! I'ma choke slam that nit wit!" Coach Brown said, pissed.

"Penalty on the play. Face mask. Defense. Number 25. 15 yard penalty. Half the distance to the goal. First down," the reffs and worldwide announcers said.

Man! Wild, Wild Wesley was about to tie the game! I can't lose to my step brother!

"Hut! Touchdown! Dog!" I yelled with no hesitation!

Bang! Splash! Coach Pettis kicked the water cooler over.

"Pu-wee!" the water boy blew snot out his nose.

Sergio kicked the ground. I cursed out the air!

Wesley ran straight into the end zone with a quarterback sneak, that I didn't even know was coming! But Wesley ran a 4-2. So, it wasn't much we could do.

I stared at the field and watched the extra point, attempt to be kicked.

"Good!"

I heard a few cheers, but it was mostly quiet in the Georgia Thunder Dome.

"21 to 21."

Tie score. Tigers' ball. Special teams took the field and kicked the ball high in the air.

Whip! Scoop!

Dashing Deon scooped the ball up and took off like a jet, speeding through cloud nine! De was gone! Or was he?! Nope! Bang! Yeap! Number 22 missed him! Stop! Deon froze at the 30 yard line. One man to beat. Junk. Shuk. Took off! Zoom! Dashing Deon!

"Touchdown Tigers!!!"

Deon returned the kick for a touchdown, then he kicked the extra point! Good!

"28-21, Atlanta."

"Yeah! Yeah! That's right!"

"Deon! Big Dee!"

"Represent! Baby, baaaby!"

The guys were shouting and patting Deon on the back. De was smiling like the black version of the Joker!

"That's the way to get it crunk!" I told my super, all-star. He played five positions!

"Kill! Kill! Kill! The kill zone! Roar!" Coach Brown shouted, pounding on his chest and ripping his button down, throw back, Falcons shirt off!

Ha-ha. We were high, like Eagles, baby! Gliding like Falcons! Boop! I was in my zone. Blip. I gave Deon a high five.

"Ok, Coach. How we looking?" I asked Mr. Pettis.

"Looking horrible. Our defense is tired. We scored to quick. Wild, Wild, Wesley will make a quick push to score. Their defense is fresh. They will bring a lot of heat on you, Cim. You're all we got at quarterback. You must lean more on Levi, the running back. They coming. They coming, hard. That defense is rested up and hungry, like wolves. We will line up with three receivers in Shot Gun Formation. But, it's a trick! Only running plays. Slant, reverse, pitch, sweep, draw, counter, and off-tackle. Nothing but hard banging! Run plays. We will depend on the mighty strong legs of Levi. Go! Defense!" Coach yelled, steamed up and serious, waving at the defense.

Tigers' defense marched on the field like angry fighters. The defense was ready to viscously destroy Wesley.

"Down . . ."

Wesley eyeballed the blitz and the pass rusher.

"Gold 99! Hike!"

Wesley faked the hand off to the running back. Then ran down the side line, Zipping!

20, 25, 30, 35, 40, 45, 50!

Boom!

D.J. hit him like a pizza! Cold!

Wesley was hurt! He was looking like he just swallowed a bottle of Louisiana hot sauce and ten lemon heads, and got pimp slapped by the Lion King! He was holding and pointing at his left ankle, appearing to be in excruciating pain.

Yeah! Good news for us! Wooh! The reffs waved for the team trainer to run on the field. This is my chance to capitalize on his injury.

"Move!"

What? Wait a dolphin in Dallas, Texas, minute!

"I'm in! Tell Coach, I'm in! I ain't going out. I'm playing in this game! I don't care if I play on one leg! This is the Super Bowl!" Wesley said, surprising the entire world!

He was barely standing on one leg, leaning against his star running back, Jayhlen.

"Time out, New England."

New England's head Coach Mackey, stood up in shock.

Atlanta's defensive coordinator was in a raging uproar!

"Look! Idiots! What is this?! Tackle him! Smack him! Punish him! Hurt him! Good hit, D.J. At least you tried to bam, wham his butt! But what is up with your sorry, big onion heads on the line?! Come on! He is running all over us! Do I have to stop coaching, take off this Polo shirt and show yall how to tackle?!" defensive Coach Manilito Dunlap shouted, angry as a bull with a pig nose!

I was just feeling it. I had to do something. Wesley was wearing our defense out, like sour, bad, prostitute panties! I had to step up to the plate. Like Waffle House after the club. I was about to put the icing on the Super Bowl Sunday cake!

"Ok Warrior Wesley. What's going on with you? Did you re-injure that left ankle?" Coach Mackey asked, confused, but amazed at the courage of his young warrior, Wesley.

"Man Coach, I'm warrior Wesley! I'm graduating from Wonder Boy to King Pettis today! I'm playing. And not only am I playing, I'm winning! I promised my wife I would do it, and man I'm doing it! For you, Akilah! I want in, Coach!" King Pettis, a.k.a. Wonder Boy Wesley said, with fire burning in his eyes.

Coach Mackey stared deep into his quarterback's eyes. This was a tough decision. Cute Akilah was Wesley's high school sweetheart. She was tripping lately. She told Warrior Wesley straight up, "You win the Super Bowl, you win my heart back!"

Wesley took that to the heart like Usher said, "What I gotta do now, to get my baby back?"

Let it burn!

For Coach Mackey, you never want to risk re-injuring your players. If Wesley returns and wins; it's a brave, heroic masterpiece! However, if Wesley goes back in and gets hurt worse, it could end his career, 'cause you can bet your Sunday night Scooby snacks on that. Atlanta was going for the kill! So this will make you or break you, your call. A tough gamble. If he gets injured, Coach Mackey gets fired. Point. Blank. Period.

Coach Mackey pondered with his hand on his chin, during that crucial time out. With the world resting on his decision. History could be made on this call. All the big gamblers, from Las Vegas to Chicago, worldwide were anticipating Coach Mackey's crucial call.

"Go get em!" Coach Mackey shouted, laughing!

"Ha, ha. I believe in you, Wesley! I see victory in your eyes!" Coach said, staring back at him, beaming through the helmet.

Pat!

Coach smacked him on the helmet. The crowd was in awe! Amazed. All you heard were "ooohs" and "ahhhs."

"Bet! Bet! Fifty more, shawty! I like Wesley!" Moonlight Boss Kiki shouted from Atlanta owner's club seat.

"OK, Kiki, you tripping. It's ATL or die." Governor Lawrence said.

"Ha, ha. It's Wild Wild Wesley or choke on one governor! Boop!"

Moonlight Boss Kiki and everyone else laughed.

Eye of a Tiger

Atlanta's defense was tired as a flat tire, breathing like elephants on Thanksgiving Day. Warrior Wild Wild Wonder Boy Wesley took his stance. He was in pain, but his adrenaline rush erased it from his brain. No pain, no gain. His girl was on his mind. He had to get Akilah back. Becoming a Mega Millionaire Super Bowl Star would do it.

"Down . . ."

He felt a little burning sensation.

"Set . . ."

He eyeballed D.J. very hard, playing man to man with his wide receiver, Reggie Brown.

"88 Green. Hut. Hut. Hut . . ."

The center snapped Wesley the ball. Quickly, he tossed it to Jayhlen, the running back. Jayhlen ran! Not! He pitched it backwards to Wesley. The entire defense was running, banging and tussling with Jayhlen.

Too much time for Wesley. The Tigers couldn't pick back up on the razor sharp, laser-armed quarterback. And . . . Boom! Wesley threw a perfect missile, 30 yards to Carnell!

"Touch down! New England!"

"Yeeeah! Yeeah! Yes, baby! Dipsy Due! Wooh!" Coach Mackey cheered and celebrated!

The New England fans worldwide were filled with tipsy, drunken cheers and crying laughter!

You know how good it feels to see your team win? It feels like you're on top of the world! Wooh! The world awaited the extra kick . . .

"Good!" the reff signaled, raising both arms high over his head.

"28 to 28!"

Tie game. End of 3rd quarter.

Uh oh. Money quarter. All tied up. Win or go home. Ride or die! Lie down or stand up! Mildew or bar-be-cue! Be a troop or get booped!

Ebony had her fingers crossed, as she sat down, awaiting on her love to take the field. Yes! She stood up, really trying to shake off her nerves. She just witnessed thirty-six of her cheerleading friends get arrested. The only way she escaped is when, Pow-Kiki shot at her and told her not to leave. She called her bluff. Ebony left anyway! Zoom! Zoom! The cops flew in, the second she crossed the street. Erica, and Cheetara were at the beauty supply store when the cops sped in. Shawn, of course, was sipping Half-time, forty-thousand dollar wine with billionaire, Michael Lackey, in the comfortable, plush seats.

We were at the 20 yard line. Man, I was in kill mode, like never before. I felt like Warrior Wesley had personally called me out. I'm always ready for competition!

"Down!!!!"

I felt the defensive integrity. They had 'eating Cim' on their menu. I was serving a foot sandwich!!!!

"Red . . . 33 . . . Set . . . Hike!"

I snatched the snap and took off! Forget the play call! I just dashed! 5, 10, 15 yards! Then, out of bounds! I just ran out of bounds, quickly to my sideline.

"Good play boy!" D.J. yelled in my ear.

Now, at the 35 yard line, I took the snap and bang! Boom! Tuff! Bam! Levi bruised for ten more yards. First down!

45 yard line, I was in my zone. I didn't care about the clock or the coach. I had to score. It's all in my hands, now. I had to show Wesley who was the man.

"Hike!"

I took the snap, and faked the pitch to Levi! Then I high stepped down New England's side line, into their territory.

Wooh! I was breathing like a tiger. Quickly, I signaled for a fast, no-huddle offense. I was running! No gunning!

"Hut! Hut!"

I took off! The defense chased me down the middle! No sir! I kicked the gears! I was burning them! No turning back! I saw the fans standing and rooting for me!

"Go! Go! Go! Go, Cim! Yes!" Coach Brown yelled, running down the side line with me! He was running nearly as fast as me!!!

Hold up! Ebony was running in front of him! Yeah! My baby was in track star shape! Bam!

I pushed #22 with my left arm and ran into the end zone!

"Touchdown Tigers!!!"

I leaped up to the same little girl, Saniya! She was blushing like Christmas!

Pap! Pap! I slapped hands with two more fans. Then ran to the side line.

"Baby!" Ebony said, jumping in my arms. I swung her around in the air, in circles.

"Good-bad call boy! Hah Hah!" Coach Pettis said laughing his socks off while pointing at me.

"Yea-bro! Kill em! Kill em!" D.J. shouted.

Yea. Yea. I was so hyped. I held my girl's hand, going to my bench.

"Water?" Josh asked.

I just smiled at the silly water boy.

Splash!

"Yea! Water baby! Wooh!" I laughed! After I splashed water all over the water boy!

Then, I snatched the cooler and dashed Ebony with the rest of the water!

"Boy!" Ebony laughed when I splashed a little water in her face.

Then I hugged her.

"Hey. Hey. Cim," Coach Brown said, tapping me on my shoulders. I stopped in my tracks.

"Yeah Coach?"

"Look," he said, pointing in the air.

"Oh, yeah."

"That's right. Too much time on the clock. The game ain't over, until it's over. Don't celebrate yet," Coach Brown reminded me.

He was right. It was much too early to celebrate. Nine minutes to go. Anything can happen. In the blink of an eye. Pow! In one shot gun second!

"What's good, bro?"

"What's up? Man. Look. Danika just got some bad news," Sergio said to Deon.

I just walked in the other direction. I didn't need any distractions. My grandmother's death was enough. I just sat on the bench by one of the practice players.

"Cim. Come on. Look. What's going on? I got this fye, fye, offensive scheme. Ok. Look. On the first play, I want you to hit Sergio on a deep post. 40 yard play, Bam! Touchdown. First play. They will never see it coming! Wooh!" Coach Pettis laughed like the football wizard.

Our special teams jogged on the field, to kick the extra point. I watched Hill hold the ball after Frank snapped it to him. Hill held the ball with his right hand. There goes the kick! And the kick . . . was . . . Good!

"35-28-Tigers."

I studied the plays.

"Facebook or Twitter?" the water boy asked.

I looked in the dummy's green eyes.

"On Instagram just flexing!" I joked.

"Run it!" Josh shouted

Wesley lined up behind his center. In a deep, burning rage! New England was in the West Coast offense.

"Down . . . Set . . . Hike!"

Wesley took the ball, Bam!

"I gotcha Wonder boy!" defensive linebacker Render said, as he stuffed him for the huge quarterback sack!

Loss of 7 yards. 2nd and 17.

Warrior Wesley barely got up. Jayhlen and Reggie had to grab his hands.

"You good?" Pro receiver, Reggie Brown asked.

Wesley didn't answer.

"Ah chew!"

He just sneezed the Subway sandwich out his mouth. Unable to talk from the three-hundred pounder's crushing blow! Render was three-hundred pounds and ran 40 yards in four seconds!

Wesley squeezed his eyes in pain. The left ankle was barking in him. He tried to play through it. Nope! Wesley signaled time out, and talked to Kiana, the team trainer. Pat! Pat! Reggie pat him on the back then ran to take the snap. Reggie took the snap instead of the quarterback. This is the Wildcat Formation. The instant that Reggie received the snap, he took flight! Bam!

He ran 5 yards, then got super banged by a giant war tank! J-B Bennit clobbered him!

"Wooh! Pool creek style, boy!" Big power Atlien, JB barked, as he head-butted the wide receiver a little harder just to send the message, after the play. That there is no more play, in Ga.

Reggie got up after the two-hundred and sixty-five pound defensive tackler decided to let him up. The wide receiver was shaken up.

3rd and 12.

New England needed twelve more yards for the first down or Atlanta would get the ball back with only five minutes left in the greatest game of the year.

"Hut!"

Reggie took off! Bam! To nowhere! J.B. smashed him again!

"Yeeeeah! Yeeeeah!" Atlanta fans cheered worldwide!

4th down and 13.

The twenty-two players ran off the field and both special team players ran on the field. New England prepared to punt the ball. If Atlanta scores now, with 5 minutes left, it's over!!!

I stood on Atlanta's side line, holding Ebony's hand, waiting to stick a nail in the coffin! Best believe, I was gonna score!

The punter stood 15 yards behind the line of scrimmage and whif! He caught the ball after the snapper hiked it. Jayhlen was Ben's personal protector as he prepared to kick us the ball.

"No! What! Hey! Get him! Get him!" I yelled, with every player on my team shouting!

"Catch him! Catch him!" Coach Brown ran, nearly on the field.

Ben faked the punt and pitched the ball to Jayhlen! I shoulda expected a trick play when I saw the running back, pretending to be a blocker! That Seattle boy was gone! Straight down mid-field, after faking out two tackles. Then, he ran through three tackles, jumped over a diving tackle and boom! He ran his shoulders into the next tackler, thumbing him to the ground.

30, 25, 20, 15,

Boom! Jay finally caught him and yanked the star down.

"Yes! Man! Defense! Go! Go! Go in!" Coach Brown yelled, scratching his head, kicking the ground, swinging in the air and cussing like a sailor!

Our defense ran back onto the field. 35 to 28, we were winning. But that ain't worth a green burger on the 4th of July, in a pig's nose! They were going for the tie, with 4:59 left!

Now, I was pacing, but still ready. Really dog, I was too ready to get in the game. Wesley came back in.

"Go! Go! That's my Columbia High School King! Do it, baby! I still love you, Wesley! Do it!" Akilah yelled. She was done fighting the feeling for her first, real love.

Wesley was the only man that kept it 100 with her! He loved her in Real Life. No cheating or beating. She wanted him to win! Wesley was perfect to her. He loved her and himself. He was drug free. They even lived in the same neighborhood as kids, on Columbia Drive. Wesley, however was not clever. He was in too much pain. Actually, he shouldn't be playing because he was too slow. With only one good leg! Like a real warrior on the battlefield or a caveman, fighting off wolves. Wesley had the eyes of a tiger. He wanted this second Super Bowl win more than the first one.

Because he was picked to lose, he wanted to prove the world wrong. Just cause Atlanta had a new billionaire owner, Michael Lackey, best seller author cheerleader, Micki, the best Coach on Earth-Joshua Brown, and a R&B singing cheerleader, Erica Bailey to go along with a team stuffed with pro bowlers.

Wesley wanted to do the unspeakable. Beat the number one defense and the number one offense in NFL history, with one leg! Plus, win his Akilah back! All on one leg!!!! Hard!!!

"Down!" Wesley barked.

"Yellow! 91! Hike!"

Wooh. Wesley hesitated in pain, faked the hand-off to Jayhlen and threw a 5 yard slant pass to Reggie Brown.

10, 5, Touchdown!

Not! Boom!

Oh! Oh! Fumble! Fumble! The ball came loose! Scuffle! Scuffle! Dwight scooped up the ball and sped down the side lines! 10, 15, 20, 25, 30, 35, 40 . . .

Bang!

Dog! Reggie tackled him and with his body, while using his right hand to punch the ball high in the air, backwards! Five players attempted to catch it, as it came with in reaching distance. Three minutes left to play.

Yeah! No!

Dog! Man!

Jayhlen caught the ball. Kah boom! The other four Tigers tackled him at one time! Covered his powerful body like a Polar Bear!

"Stupid! Stupid! How can four players let one man out jump them?! Come on!" Coach Brown snapped, in a rage.

With just three minutes left, at their 30 yard line, this was not good! They could run the clock down, tie, or win! Now, I was bamboozled! I felt dumb as a teacher with no books! I felt dumber than a teacher with no high school education! Tigers' defense lined up on the field. Tired and eager to stop New England's happy, hype offensive. New England had all the momentum though. They had our balls by a string!

Ouch!

Shut Up or Blow Up

It was a little over two minutes left in the game. Right at 2:59.

"Down . . . Set . . . Gold 44 . . . Hut! Hut!"

Warrior Wesley took the snap and he read the entire defense. Quickly, he decided which receiver to hit. The Bullets were attempting the triple stretch, with one receiver blowing straight past the cornerback. One receiver blowing straight up midfield and Reggie ran a simple 5 yards across the line of scrimmage.

Bam!

He hit Reggie and Regg shot for 5, 10, 15 yards! Boom! Andrew smashed him. Dang! Not good. The clock was still ticking. They were eating up the clock like red velvet cake!

We had two time-outs left. We really didn't want them to tie the game. Over time is really just a matter of luck. Coach Brown had to find the perfect moment to call that time out.

"Down. Hut 1, Hut 2, Hut!"

Wesley took the ball and niffed it to his powerful running back who bruised for a long, hard-fought 5 yards.

"What is this? Tackle him!" Coach Brown yelled in panic mode.

The clock was still ticking! Jaguar Jayhlen was still on his feet, pushing for yards, with six-hundred pounds of strong, human flesh in front of him. 6, 7, 8, more yards, then Boop! They wrestled the soldier down.

Not good.

"Time out, on the field. Two minute warning," the reffs and worldwide announcers said.

Man, you just don't know how it feels to sit and watch your team get beat. Have you ever known you're supposed to have something, but you have to sit and watch it slip away? This was the longest, scariest two minutes of my life! I couldn't do anything to defend myself or my team. All I could do is watch and wait . . .

Not being able to do anything was mind crushing. Watching it slip away was literally driving me crazy. On their 45 yard line, with only two minutes left in the game, they HAD to score, or it was over. Our defense had to stop them, so they could not tie it up or win it. A tie would take it to overtime, which meant we would have to flip a coin to see who gets the ball first. Pure luck, and I hate luck! I like to play off skills, talent, and experience. Not luck.

"Wesley win it for us. Two times in a row! My baby has become a mega star! From Columbia High! East Side! Greater Decatur, win for all your haters!" Akilah cheered.

Wesley couldn't hear the brown-skinned love of his life cheering. Neither could he see Akilah, Kiana, Kiki, and Mrs.Pettis throwing up the East-Side, while cheering, jumping, and shouting like crazy!

"Go Wild, Wild, Warrior Wesley! Go! Columbia High Reppin!" Kiki said. Wam! She threw popcorn in the air!

"Weeee! Hah, Hah! That's my son! My baby, yall!" Mrs.Pettis shouted, for her son.

She was nearly in tears-from joy! Naw, she was in tears!

"Oh! Oh! I'm so excited. Lord, let him win! Muwah! I love you Kiana!" Ms.Pettis said, jumping, celebrating, and kissing her beautiful daughter.

"What? You ain't never seen nobody cheer? That's my son!" she yelled at an angry redhead.

"And that's my brother from the same mother! Don't get booped!" Kiana said.

"What?" The girl stood up.

Woof!

She quickly sat back down! Lol. Kiana bull frog slapped her, then kicked her, then picked her up by her nose, and tossed her on the field!

"That's right! I love you, Kiana! Mama loves you! You are good luck, girl. Now that you won the fight, Wesley will win the game! Wooh! Boop!" Ms Pettis shouted, laughing in the expensive, $700,000 end zone seats!

They were so close to the end zone, that they would see Wesley if he scored the touchdown! Straight through his helmet!

Wesley knew what he was up against. The world! Most fans loved Atlanta. He was picked to lose. He limped to the line of scrimmage . . . Two minutes to go.

"Down . . ."

The defense was looking desperate and mean. He glanced at the coverage.

"Set . . ."

He stared into the eyes of his opponents. Three-hundred pounds of mean, thirsty flesh.

"Blue. Green. 45. Hut!!!"

Wesley got the snap. Bam! Boom! Bang!

The big guys pounded each other! The defense tried desperately to pound through New England's heavy, offensive line. No! Didn't happen. Wesley stood in the pocket. All three receivers were covered. He was too slow and hurt to run. The blockers still help up. The clock was still ticking . . .

My heart was still pounding . . . My nerves were still jumping . . .

"Dang!" Coach Brown yelled.

Boom! Raw Render stuff-tackled him!

"Time out! Time out! Too much time off the clock!!!!" Coach Brown yelled, pissed as a baby drinking Kool-Aid and vinegar.

"Defense! Defense! Move quicker! Bennit! Smash through them! Render, D.J., make a play! Anybody that's somebody! Make a play!!! I hate to go out there, with my forty year-old butt!! But, I will put on your uniform and tackle Wesley myself!" defensive coordinator Dunlap shouted! Muscles all in his ears!

Dunlap was short, but his mouth was HUGE! Lol. You could hear him fussing at the defense over all seventy-thousand people in the Dome.

Michael Lackey and his cheerleader, Sexy Shawn, came down.

"Coach, how we looking? A minute and thirty seconds. 2nd down and 15. Two more stops, we win! And I'm the owner of the Dome! We need this money to rebuild this old sucker!" Lackey laughed, like a hyena. A rich hyena! Boop!

Coach Brown was sweating. I stood next to my best friend and star wide receiver, Sergio. Deon stood behind me, rapping Rich Gang, Future, Meek Mills, Tiger and Mystical. I was rapping Drake, Toronto's Representer. The old song, 'We started from the bottom, now we here.'

Twenty-two Super Bowl players jogged on the field. The entire world was watching the last minute of the World's largest game. Now, it was 1:30 left. We had only one more time-out. They could tie the game. If they had the gorilla balls to go for the two point conversion, they would win! Dang! It would be over. All I could do is watch. Don't believe me? Just watch.

The offense and defense lined up and faced off like three-hundred pound cowboys in the old days. We had eight men in the box to defend the run more effectively. We had to totally prevent Wesley or Jayhlen from running the ball.

Our cornerback could cover the wide receivers man to man. They had to get 15 yards to stay alive. Now backed up to their own 40 yard line.

"Cim!"

"Huh?"

"I love you. I'm with you," Ebony said, trying to ease my pain and comfort me.

Didn't happen. All my energy and mind was hanging on this game! It's like, at this particular second, my entire life was football! Nothing else mattered. Man, I couldn't even blink, bark, or breathe! My heart paused, and my eyes were locked on the game.

Wesley and the offense faced off again. With Hungry Render and the biting number one rated defense.

"Down. Set. Hut!"

Wesley caught the snap and bloop! Look at that! He pitched it to Jayhlen. The entire defense came full speed at his head! Whif! Bam! Render ruthlessly tackled Jayhlen. Unn! One second before Render power-slammed him, he pitched the ball backwards, to Wesley.

"Yes! Yes!" I celebrated loud. So did Ebony.

I pumped my fist in victory.

Wesley was bent over, fumbling and juggling the ball on his fingertips. Bloop! The ball fell!

"Yes! Yes! Shoe be do!" I yelled, nearly walking on the field, in unexplainable joy!

"We did it! We did it!" Ebony jumped up and down, holding and pulling me in excitement.

Warrior Wesley looked pitiful. He was on his knees, desperately trying to scoop up the ball, all the way back to his ten yard line! He didn't stand a chance! Everyone in the world besides Wesley saw Owens coming full speed for the game-winning crush . . . KAH BOOM!

Tackle!

"Yes! Lord! We did it! Atlanta did it!" I shouted.

The entire Georgia dome erupted in cheers!

"Hot Lanta finally brought home its first NFL championship! We finally did it! God! I love you, Atlanta!" I shouted to the whole world, representing dat ATL!

"We won! We won! Baby, your dreams finally came true! What we use to play on the concrete, in the middle of the street, football! Football at Perkerson Park and Midway park! Football at Pitman Park and Coan Middle School! Columbia High to Georgia Tech! You finally did it! And I'm here to celebrate with you! I love you, Cimeon!!!! Muwah!" Ebony shouted in tears of happy joy!

She jumped up in my arms. I swung her around in a circle.

"Hold! What?!" Coach Brown flipped.

Coach Pettis held me with his right arm, signaling for me to chill out.

Beep. The whistle blew. The line judge ran on the field, along with the head linesman. The play was? I'm lost.

"Touchdown! Touchdown! Touchdown! What are you nit wits waiting on? That was a touchdown!" Coach Mackey, New England's head coach yelled.

Coach Mackey was steaming! He was yelling at the short, black-haired reff. "Look, man! That was a touchdown! Jayhlen scored the touchdown! The ball was live!" Coach Mackey yelled, spitting all in his face.

He was all the way for New England! Even though Super Bowl winning Coach "Mackey had a Georgia Bull Dogs t-shirt on, under his New England sweater. As the ladies say, he was smooth, funny, womanizing, and to the point.

"No! Get the dang call right, or we gone all fight tonight! And that's on my daughters!" Coach Mackey steamed!

Boy, Mackey was hot! Hotter than an ice burn! Our Coach Brown was shocked, worried, and confused.

The three referees studied the replay. Only seven second was left in the game. However, when Owens power bomb tackled Warrior Wesley, the football came loose! Jayhlen picked up the fumble and ran 90 yards for a touchdown that no one even contested or tried to stop! We thought the game was over! Everyone in the world thought it was over!

"Ruling on the field, the player was down by contact, during the play the ball came loose. It was a fumble. Number 24 recovered the ball. As a result of the play, Touchdown, New England," the referee announced.

"Yeah! Roof! Roof!" New England cheered.

"Huh? What? Man, this can't be real," I said, scratching my head.

My wife squeezed my hand. Man, that was one of the hardest squeezes I ever felt in my life! I've had my hands squeezed by three-hundred and fifty pounders that benched six hundred pounds!

Boy, this little petite one-hundred and fifty pounder squeezed me with the power of hope, hurt, care, concern and love. My wife's love and comfort were the strongest. Her love was the strongest squeeze I ever felt. I even felt it in my heart, brains and veins.

Play began! I looked at the clock, like a hopeless, homeless man with no legs or arms, stranded in the North Pole!

"No, kill them!" Coach Mackey yelled, knowing New England had the momentum.

The score was 35 to 34.

Coaches have a universal chart that tells them when to kick or when to attempt a two point conversion. If you're behind by one point, it's a toss-up.

Going for the two point conversion with seven seconds left can only result in two things. Bam! You win or lose. If you score, you win. If you fail, you lose. Kick it. Tie the game!

If he takes the safe way out, with the kick, it's a tie. If Coach Mackey decides to follow through with the two-point conversion, and fails with a hurt quarterback, he will surely be working at McDonalds tomorrow! Yank! Yank!

"Go for it!" Coach Mackey yelled with all of his might!

The ball was placed on the 2 yard line, very close! However, two-point conversions were successful only forty-four percent of the time! So we are straight!

"Down! Set! Hut!"

Wesley scrambled, but limped! Render came at him at full speed, to end the game! Three seconds, two seconds, one second . . .

Bam!

"Touchdown! New England wins!"

With last second speed, Wesley shot in the end-zone! Sandra, Kiana, Kiki, Akilah and the entire New England nation went wild!!! Cannons were fired! Boo yah! Confetti poured on the field! New England players stampeded on the field! Celebration time! Bottles popping!

"Wooh! Water!"

Smack!

The owner of the Dome slapped Atlanta's water boy! He was so goofy celebrating and giving water to the wrong team! So, the Tigers' owner, Michael Lackey, politely slapped the bull frog dumbness out of Joshua Bell's mouth!

Kah wah yaw!

"Wesley! I love you!" Akilah cried, then hopped into his arms.

He was filled with excitement.

The NFL commissioner presented the Lombardi trophy to New England's owner, Mr. Harper. Harper said his speech, "It's awesome. Two years in a row, we fought through our ups and downs. A lot of smiles and frowns. Through all the injuries, being the underdogs to the ten point favorite, hard flying Atlanta Tigers. They are a great team. I salute Atlanta and the great city of Atlanta. Mayor Brown and Governor Lawrence. However, to my New England Bullets, We did it again!!!" Mr. Harper shouted with joy!

Next, the great, fighting coach of New England, Mackey held the Lombardi trophy in one hand and the microphone in the other.

"We did it! New England! The heart of a champion! Even though we were down, we fought until we got back up! This is for you, New England! I love you, Saniya! Wooh!" Coach Mackey yelled in joy and passed the mic to the commissioner.

"Now, this MVP trophy, the Super Bowl MVP trophy has to go to you. No more Wonder boy. No more Wild, Wild, Wesley. Now, you are king Pettis! You have proven twice that you can handle the intense playoff pressure. Even through an injured ankle. You did it! 200 yards rushing is the NFL Super Bowl record for a quarterback. You, Mr. Wesley Pettis are the Super Bowl MVP!" NFL commissioner C. D. Hood said.

Wesley had on his money green New England hat, with a bullet in the back and a white t-shirt. He had a huge, out-of-breath smile. He was shaking his head, and squeezing Akilah's hand. He took a deep breath, smiled, held the Super Bowl, MVP trophy and began his speech.

"Wow. This one right here means so much to me. It's so much harder the second time around. Now, I have to thank God for giving me the ability to play this game at such a high level. I'd like to thank my entire team. I have the greatest teammates on Earth! The greatest owner and the greatest coaching staff. Most of all, the greatest fans!!!! I love yall, New England! Wooh! We won the Super Bowl, baby! Disney World, here we come!!!"

Wesley and his girl gave each other the highest, high five I have ever seen!

Through all the celebration and cheers, while all the confetti showered down on my face, I held my wife's hand. Watching the celebration, every inch of it. I will never forget the feeling. Seeing the other team go wild, in my home town and dome. I can't explain the pain, shame and embarrassment of losing the game. I felt cold and dead. Something that I thought I had all under control, I lost . . . I looked at my wife. She was biting her pretty, bottom lip and crying on my shoulder, like a hurting child or a sick baby.

My girl had tears streaming down her beautiful face. We held sad hands and watched the other couple hug and kiss, celebrated, take pictures, laugh and smile. They took me and my wife's victory! It felt horrific. We walked out of the Dome in shame. I couldn't wait to start the next season. Suddenly, I had doubts that we could make it all the way back. Odds are against us. Then, if we did, would we win? No! They celebrated on my field! I didn't even get a chance to attempt to win. I had to stand there, with the love of my life, in misery. Just watching New England break my heart into tiny football pieces!

It's hard being defenseless . . .

I popped in the song, 'All That' by the game. I tried to bobb my head, but my head wouldn't bobb. The old remix to De'Angelo, 'You're My Lady' came on. Lil' Wayne rapped. My heart clapped. We cruised through the downtown city. I stopped the red Caddy at the red light.

Then, dog, I flipped the song to the throwback, 'Something Special.' She sung . . . "I need you and you need me. A love like this is very special. All my love is all I have. All my life I looked for you." J-Lo blew it. LL rhymed it.

I felt the song in my heart. All her love was all I had. No ring, no championship, no flashy winning Super Bowl photos. Just disappointment. Millions of upset fans. I didn't even take the field, to defend my skills. No shot of a win. Right now, my wife's love was all I really had. That's how I felt. She loved me regardless.

Why was I driving tonight? I shoulda just . . . "Ahhh!!! Baby what?!" Pow!

You Sleep, You Slip

Blood splattered everywhere! I was beyond nervous, plus I was covered in blood. My wife was frozen, like a rock! I didn't mean to kill! God! What have I done? Man! I committed murder!!! Accident! 'I'm sorry', won't bring a person back to life. Honestly, it was a reflex. I just fired the gun!

Immediately, I felt my world crash like a speeding jet!

"Cim! Pick up the phone! I'm in jail, for robbery! It's your sister, man! Micki!"

I accidently answered my iPhone. I swallowed an egg. Gulp. I felt sicker in the stomach, by the minute. What could be worse than this?

"Freeze!"

"Drop your weapon!"

"Police! Slowly raise your hands over your head, suspect, or I'll blow your head to smithereens!"

I slowly and nervously obeyed.

Click!

"Out!" the big cop shouted, pulling me out of my truck.

Boom! He slung my body into the side of the truck.

"Ahh. Man, be easy. I'm rich."

"Shut up! I don't give a flip about killing a rich black boy!" the seven foot, two hundred and ninety-nine pound, blonde hair, brown eyed cop shouted!

"You have the right to remain silent. Anything you say or do, can be held against you in the court of law," the five foot even, cross-eyed, snaggled tooth, blond hair, black Atlanta officer said.

"Hold up! That's Cimeon Brown from the Atlanta Tigers!" Lieutenant Hill hollered.

"He just committed murder. It don't matter if he played for the Houston Rockets, he flying off to jail tonight!" fine, female officer Detective Walker snapped.

"No! No! No! Leave him alone! It was self-defense! No! Please!" she cried.

"Ma'am, stand down before you get arrested with him for obstruction of a peace officer," Detective Walker growled.

"Forget a peace officer! Ain't no peace! Let my man go!" Ebony screamed in shock, covered in blood.

"You are out of your mind! Cuff her too!" Detective Walker ordered, with her delicious, chocolate, sassy attitude.

"Easy. Put him in the car," Officer Hill replied.

Flash! Flash! Snap! Snap!

Dog Man stood on the corner of Peachtree Street and snapped professional photos of the Atlanta Pro-Bowl, NFL quarterback.

"Got em! Cim on camera! Ten thousand a picture!" White boy Scotty hollered, standing next to Dog Man, snapping photos of the quarterback.

I just held my head down, as the flashing lights shined on my face. I felt so ashamed.

"Why did you kill that man?" Officer Jones asked, while he punched buttons into his computer.

Oh, I was not dumb! Like the supposed to be hard thugs on those TV shows, that always tell on themselves. Even though I had never been arrested, I had enough sense not to tell on myself.

"I have the right to remain silent, so dangit, I'm remaining silent!!! Wake me up when we get to the jail," I told the officer.

I then closed my eyes and prayed. I replayed the entire scene in my head. I was at the light, holding her hands. Snatch! Ahh!! She screamed, and I responded. Pow! With a shot.

Someone opened her door and snatched my wife's $800,000 diamond studded necklace off her neck. It wasn't the value. It was the principle. Before he could run, Boom! I blasted that sucker like World War 10. And, as I play it over, I would do it again! No one hurts my wife. I'm a real man. No matter what, I will kill for my wife, and I will die to protect my wife. We are one. I knew the Bible. Ephesians 5:31-Husband and Wife are one.

Arrrrrrch . . .

"Well, Superstar, you're here. Mr. Football, Rookie Killer of the Year, Super Bowl Murderer," the officer said, laughing.

"Oh yea. I know the mayor and the governor personally. One more laugh, and you won't be getting but one more pay check."

Instantly, his goofy laugh vanished like dinosaur toes.

"Hey! Hey! Cim!"

"Look! There go Cimeon!"

"Tigers, baby!"

"ATLLLLLL!" a semi, tore-up, retarded drunk yelled.

Suddenly, five men in suits and a female quickly approached me. I had my hands spread on the wall as the officer in the jail searched my body with his hands. I was actually sweaty from the game. The air had frozen me clean.

"You have to come with us," the lady said.

Click. Click.

The officer removed the handcuffs.

"I'm Lieutenant Chance. The FBI and GBI want to have a few words with you. Because of your high profile case, you will have five officers with you anytime you need to be escorted. Other than that, you will be placed on twenty-four hour supervision," Miss Chance told me.

She was stupid, sexy thick. With some expensive, gold-framed Gucci shades, golden, smooth, brown skin. She spoke sexy calm, like we were friends.

"Hah, ha. Look Superstar, you will have a bond hearing in the morning. Oh, I'm Captain Evans," the dark skinned, easy going guy said. He had on a Polo suit, tie, and shades. All black.

"When can I use the phone?"

"Here," Warden Brown said, as we walked.

He gave me the cordless, jail phone.

I was six feet, five. Perfect quarterback height. He had to be six feet, six.

I dialed my wife's number.

"Baby?! Cimeon?! Is this you?!"

"Yeah . . . -"

I took a deep breath, as we quickly walked around and down the city jail hallways.

"How much is your bond?!"

"I don't know. They say I will have a bond hearing in the morning. Call my lawyer, Mr. Conley, ASAP. Let him know everything. Tell mom I love her."

"Ok. Your sisters are locked up too."

"Yeah, I kinda got a quick word on it. Micki called."

"Yeah. Kishana called me, cussing like a Candler Rd., cheerleading killa! Ha, ha. That girl is something else. They got a bond, though. You want me to pay it, or wait on you?" Ebony, my wife, asked.

"Pay it," I quickly responded. I care more about my family than myself. I had a million dollar shoe endorsement. Plus the hundred plus million dollar football contract. One hundred million dollar cereal endorsement. Plus the guaranteed million just to play in the Super Bowl earlier tonight.

"Ok baby. I'm down here at the jail now! Going crazy! Your mom, Miss Hannah is out here too. She flew from the TV station, the second I told her," Ebony said, jittery.

"Let me talk to my mom."

My mom was an evangelist. Hannah Sheppard. An anointed, powerful, positive, faithful, holy woman.

"Son? Are you ok? Pray son, pray. Ebony told me everything. WE gonna get you out of there, son. It was self-defense. Everyone at TBN is praying for you too. Rachael said she loves you. So did Liz. I love you, son. Please pray. Know that nothing is too hard for God.

I got your niece, Miracle, with me. Your best friend, Sergio, Shawn, and the owner of the Dome, Mr. Michael Lackey is here too. Coach Brown and Deon pulling up, now. Please pray. Momma loves you. WE paying the bond, son. I love you, son. I love you. Remember, God loves you, and momma loves you, son" mom said.

"I love you too, mom."

It always touched me. My mom's words were always pure, true, honest and real. People would say, Miss Hannah never lies.

"Hey, this is Michael Lackey. The owner of the dome. The second you get a bond, you coming home," Mr. Lackey assured me.

"Thanks, sir."

"Your time is up," Mr. Redd said.

I held out my hand to get more time.

"Ebony?"

"Yes, daddy?!" my enthusiastic wife responded, as they all sat in the jail's parking lot in Bentleys, Porsches, Benzes, Ferraris, and Maybachs.

"Huh! I love you." I told the love of my life. I felt her tears, I felt her crying for me. It took her 60 long seconds to respond.

"I love you too! With all my heart. You are my Best Friend, my Husband and my King. You are my Everything." Ebony said crying.

I felt bad. I hate being in a predicament where I can't help my love one.

"It will work out," I told my wife and queen.

Then I thought about my mom. She brought me into this world, so I bought her the most expensive car in the world, the Bugatti Veyron 11.4. That smoke, gloss, grey car cost three million dollars. That Bugatti is also the fastest, road, illegal car in the world-at 268mph!

Of course, Michael Lackey had the three million dollar Bugatti. The richest man in the world with the most expensive car in the world. Mike had a money green Bugatti. I had a sticky, wet, candy apple red Bugatti, that I only bring out on holidays. Clean enough to eat on. Shawn had a gold, black and platinum Bugatti. Yes, our football team was the Atlanta, Bugatti crew. Erica and Levi had baby blue Bugatti's. Stupid! That's why I'm amazed my sisters would do something as dumb as a robbery. My baby sister, Kishana, is the first high school cheerleader to cheer in professional football while going to high school, and the only eighteen year old with a hot pink and black, three million dollar Bugatti! What's wrong with them?! Micki, she was just crazy! Nobody could tell her nothing!

Bam!!!

She got pissed off at Coach Brown for kissing his wife on TV after the NFC division game, and she beat his entire, 3.5 million dollar Bugatti with her red baseball bat! Micki a.k.a. Red Bone Shawty is insane!

"Now, you just murdered a man in cold blood!" a short, stocky, feet-butt breath detective yelled.

Bam!

He punched the white table like it would scare me. Lol.

I've seen three-hundred and fifty pound men hit each other! At full speed! Plus, he hit me, so I know his 5'3", two hundred pound, Big Mac supersized, French fry body butt didn't think his little fist would scare me.

"Ha, ha. My lawyer should be walking through that door any second," I told them.

Knock. Knock.

"Get the door," the play-play, good-guy detective said to the play-play bad detective.

Boom! Yah!

The entire room froze like jolly ranchers in Alaska, the second my 7' 2 inch lawyer, Mr. Conley stepped in.

"Listen. There will be absolutely nooo further questioning of my client without me or one of my representatives present. So what's the question?" Mr. Conley asked.

Immediately, his powerful size, confidence and cocky smile took over the entire ten FBI, GBI, cop-filled, interrogation room's atmosphere. The energy shifted, instantly! The once police-arrogant room-zoooof—was now bloopy. My lawyer's arrogant swagg and presence let the air out of the police-packed balloon!

Boop!

"Well, we ummm. We want to . . . We wondered . . ."

"Oh, wow?! Really?! Ha, ha. That's funny. Mr. Bad Guy detective, you had a thousand mean, fire, yelling words to say just a few seconds ago. You were punching walls and slapping chairs. Now what, play-play tough guy?" I asked him.

"Shuuuush-"

Lawyer Conley signaled with his hand like a referee with a time-out.

"We won't be talking with you at all until I further investigate the details of my client's charges and the case. Thanks," Mr. Conley said.

Then he motioned for the staff to take me out of the interrogation room. I stood up. One of the FBI agents whispered something to my gigantic, cool, millionaire lawyer, Conley. He blinked his eyes extra fast, then responded sharply, with a powerful, cocky grin.

"Cimeon, I will be in the court room tomorrow. I briefly spoke with your wife. She explained everything. I'll get you released," Conley said.

Cute Chance and Cool Evans helped Warden Brown, Miss McDowell and Mr. Redd escort me to my holding cell.

"Cimeon! You bad! You bad. We woulda won if you had a chance to get back on the field!" A guy yelled from a holding tank. Looking like a monkey trapped inside of a toilet bowl. B00P!

The holding cell had two six inch long benches. It was the size of a bathroom in a three bedroom house. However, there were over two-hundred, angry, funky people packed in that holding cell! Luck of a truck, I had my own cell. But, yank, yank! Boop! Shoe-be-do! I was going crazy. Whif! I swung at the air.

"Dang!" I yelled in frustration. "Why me? God. Why me?" is all I asked. Then, I took a tired, exhausted seat on the hard, steel bench. The bench was so hard, it felt like a two-thousand pound refrigerator was pushing me on the bench. Man, I lost the game, my wife, my sisters and my freedom at the same dang time. Jail and the entire night gave me the biggest migraine headache known to mankind. I was stressing, dog. Hard.

"Wake up, Cimeon. I'm not supposed to give you this, but here," Lt. Chance said.

Clump.

The jail trustee sat the TV down.

"No!"

The Monday after the Super Bowl. This was crazy. They were showing New England's massive parade in Disney World for winning the Super Bowl.

"Man." That's all I could say. I wanted to turn the TV. I had to watch them take my celebration. Here I am, in jail for murder, when I should be in Disney World having fun with my beautiful wife and my awesome teammates, forty cheerleaders and family.

Instead, I have to sit here and watch, in misery. This is very painful. Paralyzing pain. I couldn't move. My mouth was open. My heart was racing. My nerves were biting me.

"Cimeon Brown. Get ready for court, super star."

"I'm not a star. I got a choppa in the car," I rapped, very low of course. I didn't want to brag about having a weapon in my car. I couldn't afford it!

Wow . . . Speechless. Five officers that could easily pass for body guards or wrestlers escorted me to a small, black van with tinted windows. They sped me to court. Actually, it only took about five minutes. The jail and the courthouse were downtown. Click.

Chance opened the door. Where did she come from?

"Let's go, Brown," the biggest of the crew stated.

We walked.

"Hey! Hey! ATL, baby!"

"Cim! Big Cim!"

"Free Cim! Free Cim!"

"We love you, Cimeon!"

"Tigers in da house! Baby, baby!"

Those were some of the chants I heard, while I walked to the downtown, Atlanta, courthouse. I felt a little nervous. Well . . . I felt a whole lotta nervous! What if they denied my bond? Pray. Have faith.

That's what I told myself, as I walked through the large courtroom. Awwe. Instantly, the presence of my beautiful wife in her white, Versace dress eased my pain.

"Hey, hubby. I love you! Muwah!" Ebony yelled.

Then, she jumped up and hugged me. Straight law-breaking! The big guys gave her a no-no, nasty frown. But, under the super-star circumstances, they let her slide.

Cool. Uncool. Cameras were flashing. I felt out of place as I sat down. A huge judge that resembled a dark-skinned, beach whale came out.

"All rise . . ." the beach whale said.

We all stood. I glanced at my mom. She waved at me. It hurt. I hated putting my mom through this pain. I'm her son. I wanted to make my mom proud, not ashamed.

I could only imagine the negative things people said to her.

"Honey. Why yo son shoot that white man? Don't he know them folks don't play that crap in Georgia?!" I could hear Aunt Sallie fussing now.

Mom would probably mumble under her breath in frustration, smack her mouth and twist her lips, then roll her eyes!!!

"In the case against Cimeon Riley on Sunday, February 2, 2017," the judge/beach whale said.

"Your honor. Mr. Riley is a model citizen. His Columbia High School principal is here, Mr. Bailey. He can verify that Cimeon has never been in any form of trouble. He also has his high school transcript. He was a straight "A" student. Never missed one day of school, his entire life. Even won the high school championship game with the flu. Scored two touchdowns, through the game-winning buzzer beater, then fell out!"

"Ha, ha, ha, ha, ha." The entire courtroom laughed.

"His professional Coach Joshua Brown, is here. The mayor of Atlanta, Earl Brown is here. Governor of Ga. Lawrence Rutherford is here. And Author Kiana Pettis and TV Anchor Rachael Miller is present. His mom, Evangelist Hannah Sheppard, who voluntarily works at Christian, global TV station, TBN, she is here. Along with his two-month pregnant, cheerleading wife."

"All sixty of his teammates, and the owner of the Georgia Thunder Dome, Michael Lackey is also here."

"Mr. Riley has never been arrested. The alleged victim was actually convicted of robbery seventeen times! When they searched him, he was found with the eight-thousand dollar diamond necklace, that he snatched off the pregnant, Miss Ebony Riley."

"Also here . . . Those are the photos taken that night at Grady's Hospital of Ebony's neck. As you can see, she had severe cuts from him grabbing her neck. My client felt like his life and his pregnant wife's life was in danger. When bam! The robber, Santana Filbenno knocked out the passenger window with a crowbar, and reached inside Mr. Riley's vehicle."

"We assure you, since my client has a life long record of being an upheld, positive citizen, if you would please give Mr. Riley a bond," Millionaire Lawyer Conley asked while he finally stopped walking around the courtroom, making animated facial expressions, as he described the notorious robber, surprising both me and my wife.

The beach whale judge was silent as a closed library. He was beyond strict. Harry Potter. Hancock the 3rd. The meanest judge in Georgia's history. He sent two of his daughters and his mom to prison! Right in this same downtown Atlanta courtroom!

I glanced at my family, who looked like my supporting offensive line. They always gave their all to protect me from getting hit. I glanced over at the prosecutor, who reminded me of a NFL, mean defense that attempted to smash my head off my body, hurt me, and take me out of the game every chance they got.

Bam!

"One million dollars, cash only, bond," Judge whale body state.

"Yeaaah!" the entire courtroom and all the millions watching worldwide, and even the prosecutor and the camera man shouted.

A measly, million dollar bond? Boop!

"Yes! Thank God!" I added, to the celebration, pumping my fists in victory.

"That's good! You better call me. Ha, ha," Lt. Chance whispered in my ear. She was too cute and funny. But, I wouldn't cheat on my wife, for a zillion dollars, and my own planet and super hero powers!

Real Loyalty and Love, cannot be paid off. I loved my wife for real. In Real Life Action.

"Love you, son." Mama Hannah said.

"Love you, baby," Ebony said, blowing me a kiss, as the five robo cops escorted me out of the excited courtroom.

"Yeah! Cim free baby!"

"ATL baby!"

"Win next year!"

"We need you! Wooh!"

"We need you free, to win next year!"

"Black man with power! Stand-up!"

I just laughed at all the cheers. I loved the love. Downtown Atlanta was crowded with my fans. People were holding 'Free Cim' signs. A lot of cameras and love. My wife stood by my side, until she was forced to leave. She walked with me like I was president! Godzilla's five body guards finally made her leave.

"Love you, hubby. I'm on my way to pay your bond, now," Ebony said.

Mwah.

We lip-locked quickly.

"Ok. Ok. Let's get going," He-man said with muscles in his eye balls. I just stared at him. Then, I walked forward. My eyes followed my fine wife, as my body followed the officers. I had my head turned completely behind my body. My body went one way, my head went another way. I eye-balled each sexy step she took.

Blomp. Blomp. Blomp. I could even hear her hips and booty shake. Each step she took, her booty shook like jelly-dice. I felt at ease. At least I knew I would soon be free. So yeah! That was a slight half-victory. Next step is getting my image straight. To re-catch the Rookie Sensation Repp. You know the media will bury a football player! I'm about to stand up!

Poetic-No Justice

Ebony and Evangelist Hannah Sheppard sat patiently with the bonds man. Ebony strolled through her phone and wrote a poem as her status.

You are my heart
From end to start
Your voice is my motivation
You faith is my determination
Without you, I feel lost
Without you, I feel off
I never cheat
I never lie
I never do you wrong
I'm your ride or die
No other man can ever take your place
I'm faithful, God knows, I only want your face
Love you!!!!
Free Cim, Baby!!!
Sending . . . . Sent
Just Now . . . 20 likes

The tall, slim, grey-haired bondsman grabbed his purple tie.

"Ha, ha! Now, now. I have to say in my twenty years of running Greater Decatur's Bonding Company, Bam! I never got a million dollars! Ha, ha! Weee!" the guy laughed.

He went from serial killer serious, to goofy, jumping jack joy!

Pwah! Snort. Snort. The well dressed, serious-faced, perm-headed guy was spitting. Plus snot of joy was slapping out of his nose onto his thick, chocolate, grey-sliced mustache.

Wham!

The bondsman stood up, like a tree, slanging the wooden chair under the table.

"Listen. Thank yall. Yall come back now! Ya hear?! Wooh!" Slim ran out of the office.

"Lord, have mercy," Evangelist Hannah laughed and prayed out loud at the nut.

"Well, mom, let's go get our baby out of jail," Ebony told her precious, sweet mother-in-law.

They drove downtown, on I-20, listening to the sweet songs of Yolanda Adams. They pulled up, slowly into the jam-packed jail. Even though Atlanta was a city packed with stars, the jail's dirty ground had never felt the wheels of a three million dollar Bugatti!

The two women opened their three million dollar doors, with pure class. They walked into the funky jail from hell.

"Oh! O! Oh! Ha, ha! Yall must be here for the football player, huh?" A stuttering, cute, chocolate officer said at the desk.

Mom and Ebony laughed. Then shook their heads. They exchanged information.

"Cimeon Levi Riley, it's time to touch down and put on your crown," Mrs. Evans joked.

Man. Shoot!

I popped up, like popcorn! Super ready to get out of this crazy jail! Who wants to be in jail? Nobody!!

"Hey!"

"Huh?" I turned around, like a U-turn.

"Take it easy, handsome. Here's my card," Lt. Chance said.

No lie, I smiled. She was hot.

"Naw, I'm Gucci."

She was hot, but not! Boop! Nobody is hot enough for me to cheat! You won't have me burning in hell! Or have me burning in the media as a cheater! I love my wife! That's the whole reason why I married her! Cause I was 100% ready for commitment. Big Cim was a man. If I wanted to cheat, I would have stayed single!

"Games are for lames! Man up!" I told myself.

"Cim. Here's your property. Take it easy. It's a cold world out there. Even in the summer. Them white folks will freeze you, boy!" Captain Riles told me.

I shook my head, then glanced at my diamond-plated iPhone. One hundred and forty messages from my wife, Ebony.

I love you, baby. Cim and Eb for life! Muwah!

I'm always by your side. Always down to ride! My love will never hide! When you hurt, I hurt. When you cry, so do I. I'm here, through jail, freedom, wealth or starvation until the day we die. No lie. I'm your apple pie, and you're the apple of my eye!"

"Awee. How sweet. I got the best girl in the world!"

"Yea, Cim. That was nice!"

"Huh? Oh. Ha, ha. What up, Deon?"

"Nothing bro. Chilling. Making sure you made it out with no harm. You know they will kill you in jail and say you hung yourself!" Deon told me.

"Oh, really? I thank God they didn't kill me. They only made me stronger. Where is my wife?" I asked, stopping the chit chat.

He laughed and pointed towards my wife. "She right there," he said.

So, I walked in the direction of the lady's restroom and waited . . . waited . . . waited . . . and waited . . .

"Umm. Like, where is she?" I asked myself.

It was five in the morning. I've been here since 10:00pm. There ain't a food in the world that can keep you on the toilet that long! I walked into the ladies' room.

"Ahhhh! Get out! You tall pervert!" and older lady shouted, leaning her white wig to the side, pulling up her yellow 1950 polka dot, plaid dress.

Next stall.

"Excuse you," a white, slim officer said, while she sat on the toilet.

Next stall.

"Hey baby!"

"Wrong answer," I told the teenage fan.

Next stall.

Nothing.

I stood in the middle of the ladies' room in my two-day old Super Bowl uniform, scratching my head.

"Where is Ebony?" I wondered.

I nervously called her. No answer. Bam! I rushed out of the ladies' room, in pursuit of my wife. Something was wrong. I knew it! I could feel it in my teeth. She would have been right here waiting on me, the split second I left out of that cell!

"Wooh! Shiii . . . !"

The car was there! "Yes!"

I opened the door.

Nothing. The front seat of the three million dollar car was empty.

"Dang." I just stood in the parking lot, looking in each direction. Up, down, and around. My eyes got a little worried. The worry that a man feels for his child, or mom. His wife, best friend or soul mate.

"What?!"

Another shocker.

The keys were still in the ignition.

"God," I let out a deep, panicking breath.

Nervously and quietly, I drove Ebony's car to our Covington, GA mansion. This palace had ten bedrooms, but it felt like zero bedrooms. My house was empty without my wife. My Ebony, my home girl, my high school, cheerleading sweetheart.

As I sat in the four car garage, stiff, I dialed her number again . . . Nothing. Slowly, I got out. Hold up! Where was the gun?! Her spare gun?! We both were registered gun owners. We had a right to fight for our right.

"Dang!" It was also missing. "No! It's right here!" I said, snatching the red, .38 special from underneath the passenger seat.

God. I ran my hand across my head, then went into my house, expecting the worse. Maybe one of those nasty murder scenes, God forbid!

"Noooo!" I yelled, the second I came in.

There was red everywhere! My white carpet was crayon, paint, blood red. That's when I saw it! Laying there . . . over against the wall. Why? Who?

"Who poured Kool-Aid all over the carpet?" I said out loud, staring at the empty Kool-Aid pitcher. Very strange events.

I jumped and turned around like a tall, Ninja turtle in fight stance.

The phone rang. I looked at it strange. I gave my phone a mean, dirty stare.

"Yes!" Ebony, baby you scared the life out of me!"

"I, I . . . I." Ebony was crying.

"Shut up and listen. You murdered my only son. So, by right, I should murder your pretty, pregnant wife. She is soo gorgeous, too. What a cheerleader-

"Leave her alone!!! I'll kill you! I'll kill you! Leave my wife alone! Eboooony! Ebony! Leave her alone!"

Wham! I kicked a hole in the wall!

"Shut up! I'll kill her! I'll blow her freakin' head off of her body!" the voice barked.

"No! No! Man, if you even freakin' breathe at my wife wrong, I promise, I promise on my life, I will haunt you down and beat you to death. I will knock every teeth outta your mouth, one by one. Then, break every single bone in your body, one by one. Then I'll burn-"

"Cim! Cim!! Help me, baby! Be quiet. Please save me! Be quiet, Cim! Baby, I love-" Ebony started.

"Mr. Wise guy, NFL. Listen. You don't call the shots. You CANT call the shots. I do. You mess up, she dies. You killed my son, so I don't have a son. So you won't have a son. It will die, and everything you say, you will do to me, I will do to your pretty wife. Then, after I knock each one of Ebony's perfect, pearl, white teeth out, one by one, I'ma beat her pretty face with a hammer! Ha, ha. Then, break every bone in her body, one be one. Even her cute fingerbone. While you shout, cry and listen. Then, I'ma cut her unborn son out of her stomach, and cut his small, helpless legs, slap off his body. In your face! I'ma record it, boy! And put the live death of the fallen football star on TV! You think you can gun down my son, in front of everybody and get away with it sky free? This is the Mafia, boy. A Mob boss. You killed the wrong person, superstar. Now you listen, very careful. Number one, I'm Russian, so I hate America. Number two, this ain't the movie, Saw. But to keep your beautiful wife here alive and to see your unborn child born, you have to do one little thing. Go back to the Super Bowl, and lose. If you tell the police, or anybody, the deal is off. She dies. Poof! I disappear. Your choice. I will be following the news very close. If any leak hits the internet, she dies. SO you better have her an alibi for family and friends. You will never find me. It's impossible, so don't try. I'm not even in America."

"If the FBI even blink your way, she dies. Simple as that. My connections are FBI agents. I know judges too. So, keep this simple. I will call you once a month on a Saturday. Saturday is the holy day.

That's the real, seventh day of the week. Sunday is the first day of the week. The day the pagans worshipped the sun. Now, one Saturday, out of each month, I will call you. At 5:00 PM. SO be ready. You miss one call, she dies. You tap one call, your wife and baby dies. So, I've made this simple as 1-2-3. GO to the Super Bowl next year, ha-ha, and lose-again! And maybe you will win the lives of your wife and child. Ha, ha!" he laughed evil as Lucifer in hell.

Those phone lines were gone! This guy had me frozen! Tears were in my eyes, brain and nose. Bam! I punched a hole in the wall. Crying would do absolutely nothing to save my family's life. I must save her. I must find her. With no help? With no police? A Russian? Mob? Probably a big gambler. I must focus. Betting on the Super Bowl. Hmmm. Random thoughts. SO, I killed the son of a Russian Mobster? Ha! Can't be that many Russian Mobsters in the ATL.

I will find him before next year's Super Bowl, and I will beat him for old and new. I will beat him for every sin him and his entire family have committed!

Hold up!

Impossible! What if he really isn't in Atlanta? I'm stuck and out of luck. But, I will never, under any circumstances give up. He could be in Atlanta! I will die, trying to save my wife and baby. The Super Bowl is twelve months away. The birth of my first child is eight months away! So, I have to play football with my family's kidnapping on my mind? Without Ebony's cheer?! Loosing everything I love?

Not being able to see the birth of my first baby? You mean, I have to allow some Russian killa that I don't even like or know, deliver my baby?

"God!" I shouted, as I fell on my knees.

It's so much more to life than football. It's so much more to love than football. But God, I have to block out my loved ones and forget about the danger in their lives, and focus on football? How many teams in history go to the Super Bowl, twice? Why would I be selfish enough to worry about my family? Over the millions of Atlanta families that lived their whole lives, spent a lot of their hard money on, seeing Atlanta finally bring a Super Bowl title to Georgia. Then lose . . . on purpose?

Even with my family on the line. What kind of man would I be to lose on purpose? Who does that? Lose on purpose crap? To look all those other millions of kids in their eyes and lie. Bang! However, my fans won't die! My family will!

That's when it hit me. BAM! Like a tackle. I hopped in Ebony's car and flew! I knew exactly where to look! Like searching for gold in the right place! Screeeeach! The car slid to a screaming stop! Then I hopped out the car to confront her.

"Boy, I love you. When in the world was you gonna call me, and let me know you was ok? Awwwee. I know, you and your Ebony been smooching. Oh well, God said the bed of marriage is blessed in all ways! Pure! And Honored! That's Hebrews 13:4, paraphrased. But sex without marriage, will burn in hell! I Corinthians 7:9, paraphrased.

"Mom," I said cutting her off.

"What son?" Mom asked with care in her eyes.

"Ain't you been to Russia?" I asked Mom.

"Umm, yeah. Three times, why? I have been to Africa, New England, Jamaica, Japan, and Israel too. Even been to Jerusalem, what's up?" Mom asked.

I smiled; yeah, of course Mom, aka Apostle Hannah Jeanette Sheppard, have been all around the world. That's enjoying life. Oh back to the subject!

"Mom, when you were in Russia, did you see anything strange? Like gangsta people?" I asked, hoping for the best.

"No, I didn't and couldn't see any gangstas, boy, shoot! If you weren't with the supervised tour group, you couldn't go no-where! You couldn't even get off the ship. Most places allow you to leave off the cruise ship and walk around downtown and stuff: Not Russia. It was really beautiful. It was back in 2006. It was nice, the places they let us see. The Kiek in de Kok Tower in Tallinn, Estonia, was the name of one of the ports in Russia; I went to."

"Ok mom, I love you. Give me a hug." I said.

Mom smiled, then gave her son a big hug. I reminded her of my dad, the Jamaican Kool King. Out of all his children, I'm the one that looked like Earl's twin.

I got back into my car frustrated. Still at ground zero, where is my wife?! I just sat in my car, reminiscing. I remember our first hug, right here in front of my mom's house.

Hah-hah, she was so cute. We were 5 years old when I hugged her. She took off running! Lol. She was laughing so hard! Ebony fell down in the grass, laughing.

"Eb, you crazy. Let's play throw up tackle." I said.

Then . . .

She jumped up! She was a tom boy. She was tougher than me and taller than me, back then. Shusssh

She could even beat my butt, when we were little. But don't tell no body! Boop!

"Let's go!" Ebony yelled. Then she grabbed the green nerf football, and threw it in the air for the catch. Well, I had to catch it!

Blip!

She hit me in the head with the ball! She threw it up right above my head!

Boom!

Ebony rushed me! Like a hard NFL tackle, she went straight for my legs! Ebony picked me up in the air and ran with me.

Then

Bam!

She slammed me!

"You just got BANGED!!!" Ebony yelled, in her faded blue jeans and white t-shirt.

Her long hair was in a pony tail. Wooh! She was tuff.

"Cim!"

"Wha—what?"

"What's up boy? Where Ebony at?" My homeboy from Pimp City, Big E asked.

"What's good?" I replied.

Hey, if you don't have answers, answer the question with a question. Lol.

"Oh, I'm just chilling bro, Shoe-be-do. Getting it in, taking care of my kids. Working. You and yo girl hold it down." Big E said. Dapping me up, he was my 7 feet tall East-side homie.

Cheer Leaders Verses The Cop

"Man. Look, I can't sleep in this nasty junk! I'm rich! Get me out of here!" Kiki shouted.

All 37 cheer leaders were in the ATL jail. 18 in one cell, and 19 in the other. The feisty sisters were too much, together. Kiki and Micki had to be separated.

"Call my brother. He out! I just saw it on TV, Don't play me. I will have everyone in this jail, standing at Avondale Train Station, in the food stamp line.!" Micki told the 6 feet tall, pretty Captain Bussy.

The captain didn't even look at Micki.

Zip!

Micki was up in her face, like skin!

"Look, I'm about to beat a chick up, every 5 minutes! Where is my bond?!" Micki screamed.

"Calm down."

"What! Calm down! Who gonna calm down in jail?!"

"Miss,—" The officer grabbed Micki.

What on Cabbage Town, Howard earth, did she do that for?!

Smack!

Micki swung on the police! Popped her right, dead in her juicy nose!

Her nose got more juicer from the blood!

Micki was outside the holding cell, by the phones. Rolling her pretty brown eyes.

Then! Ten super sized female officers attacked the petite, feisty red bone.

"Naw! It ain't going down like that! That's my home girl!" Akilah yelled!

"Get off my sister!" Kiki shouted.

It was on like live boxing, karate, and wrestling, all put together! Pow! Boom! Bam! Slap! Kicks! Hair pulls! Body slam! Shove! Bang! Bang!

"Ouch!"

"Hold up!"

"Tiger stomp!"

"Hold up. Move. Let me stomp her!" Micki yelled.

Boom!

Micki held both of her hands on the two cheer leaders shoulders. Then she jumped up in the air and landed on the cop's head!

Boom!!!!! Micki was gone!

"I'm in my zone! I'm feeling it! Beat a cop up, up, up, up!" Micki shouted.

Officer Jackson caught her slipping. Red Bone Shawty fell to her knees. Blood skeet out of her pretty head, like rainbow Skittles.

Bam!

Shay tackled the 260 pounds lady!

"Nobody beats up an ATL Cheer Leader!" Shay Shay yelled.

"Oh, I'm good!" Micki yelled, popping back to her feet.

Bam!

One right hand elbow to her jaw, knocked Officer Bryant into the middle of next month! Micki stood over the officer, she just knocked out. Then she smiled like the light skin female Joker!

Now, it was 37 on 37!

Cheer leaders against the cops! Who wins?! A battle to the finish! Like popeye spinach! Advantage cheer leaders! All the ATL cheer leaders knew karate! Boop!

"Time out!!!" The owner of the dome shouted, out of nowhere! Man, Michael Lackey had mad pull in the city to get inside the jail!

Wham!

Two cops tossed a cheer leader clean across the room!
Whap!
A cheer leader broke a phone on a cop nose! Kiki, of course!
Bang!
Two cheer leaders dropped a cop on her head! Shan and Veronica!
"Freeze!!!" Mr. Lackey yelled.
All 74 females froze! Hair messed up.
Officers adjusting their breasts, sitting on top of cheer leaders punching them, they froze their punches in mid air.
Cheer leaders were sitting on top of officers smacking the day lights out of them! The girls were hot! Their hair was wild, but still swim suit sexy! Their bodies glistening! Some of them were top less! Their stockings were torn so you saw some of the finest, physically fit legs, known to mankind!
Everyone stopped in their heated sexy battle when the owner of the dome spoke! The Governor, Lawrence Rutherford; the Mayor, Earl Brown; professional boxing champion, Mr. Purvis; and Coach Joshua Brown all entered the jail together.
"Look ladies, this is insane. All of us want to see Atlanta win that Super Bowl next year. All charges are dropped. It's all on me, $100,000 for everyone in the room!" Michael yelled.
"Wooh!" Officer Walker shouted! Even with a busted lip.
"Yeah!" Cheer leader Jalisa shouted, even with a broken jaw! LOL.
"Come on baby." Coach Brown said, grabbing his girl friend's arm.
Micki just smiled and leaned against his strong shoulders. The top of her head was a little red.
Coach Brown was a retired NFL star. He won two Super Bowls with the Saint Louis Hound Dogs. He had the highest contract in quarter back history, 200 million, the year after he won his first Super Bowl in 2015. Coach Brown held Micki with real protection of a husband, you can tell he loved her by his expressions. Even though he was so good and she was so bad. Opposites attract. It made their love a steaming hot topic on millions of TV shows world wide. He held her close to his muscular frame.

He was in his Rookie year as a coach with a rookie quarter back and a rookie wide receiver, Deon Riley. That's fye!

Plus, he made it to the Super Bowl! However, Micki was his main concern. With her secret one month pregnancy! Boop!

"$100,000 ain't enough for me, Mr. Lackey." Captain Bussy whispered in his ear.

"No problem Captain, $200,000 for you."

"Cool, I ain't seen a thang!" The caramel cutie yelled, laughing.

Cross Roads

I was confused. Nowhere to turn to, I stayed closed up in my house for months: Working out, praying, on my lap top, and I couldn't eat. I went from 225 pounds to 190 in two months, not good. I was getting thinner by the seconds.

Future and Kelly Rowland's 'Never End' was my ring tone, cause I didn't want our love to ever end.

"Hello?"

"Hi my good buddy. Here's your cheer leader!"

"Ebony I love you. Are you ok? I'ma save you, I promise. How is the baby, are-"

"Shut up! You heard her voice. She's alive. Bye."

Click.

"Wait! Noooo!" I squeezed out through so much hurt and pain, too much to explain.

God, all my prayers can't go in vein. The way I was losing weight, I would lose the Super Bowl any way! Heck! If I even made it there!

"Jesus, He will fix it.
Jesus, He will fix it."

The Mississippi Mass Choir song. Like faithful angels, on TBN.

I had the TV in my bedroom glued on gospel. I kept the other ten TV's on CNN. I was thinking that only faith in God, will find my wife and child.

Plus, any breaking news, may find my family. A Russian arrest or God forbid, a dead body. Something had to give. I didn't want—

"Cim!"

"What? How in da world did you get in here?"

"Duh. You left the door wide open. I need a break from Coach Brown. Can I chill with you for a few days?" Micki asked.

"You have 3 houses and a condo in Jamaica. Why you want to chill with me?"

"So! I don't care if I had ten houses and a hotel! I only got one big brother!" My sister said, very dramatic.

"Hah-hah. True. True. In my 2-Chainz voice." We both laughed. Actually, I needed the company, to cheer up.

"Where in the football, sweaty boxers earth, is Ebony?" Micki asked, the zillion dollar question.

"Who knows," was all I said then I threw my hands over my head.

"Bro, I know. You know lil sister don't miss jack!"

What? How?! Oh. Dang. I forgot she was there!

Beep!

Beep!

"I know this sucka didn't follow me! What is he gonna do next?! Sniff my drawls! Dog!!!" Micki snapped, running off my pretty pearl porch. Even the dog, Cup-Cake, laughed at that one.

"What is he gonna do next?! Sniff my drawls!" Pookie, the parrot repeated.

I stood up, scratching my throat and my head. In two months, I wasn't expecting company. Not this kind of company!

"Fool! Why you following me?!" Micki snapped, running off my pearl porch.

"Look. I don't got time for your games Red. Why did you burn my house down?!" Coach Brown demanded!

I never saw coach this mad. You could strike a match on his forehead, and fill up an 18 wheeler's gas tank with his breath!

Whap!

Micki punched him. Nope! Wrong answer coach! I just lost one of my main girls. I wasn't losing this one. I blocked his punch. That punch would've knocked the red off Redbone Shawty!

Whap!

Micki swung around my left eye, and caught him in the lips. Instantly, it bled!

"I'm tired of love!"

Pow! She fired the gun, the real gun!

Oh my God. I couldn't, in no way believe this, not here and not her. I froze. God, what in the world did I do to deserve this much death, hurt and pain?

I just held my chest. That chest was once so strong. Strong enough to pound through thousands of pounds. Strong enough to bench press 300 pounds. Strong enough to do 1,000 push ups in ten minutes. That once strong chest of mine was losing strength, fast. I fell! Hand first, catching myself on my money green Porsche.

"Gloria!" Coach Brown yelled. Then he took off, running to her car. Her face was completely blown off. She committed suicide, in front of my house. Coach Brown was out of control, for a second. His wife was dead.

"Look, I don't need this kind of drama at my house! What in the hot sex, world is wrong with yall! Man! This can't be good for our team! Take yall love fights somewhere else!" I shouted.

Loud! Sirens! Blasted within minutes! Maybe seconds! After Coach Brown wife's suicide! Ten, eleven, twelve police cars zipped in front of my yard!

Micki just laughed, low. I saw her silly, crazy butt with that wicked red bone grin. I just shook my head.

Flash! Flash!

Oh Lord. A thousand cameras; all eyes on me, and I ain't 2 pac or 3 pac! My Future and Kelly ringtone went off!

"Hello?"

"Cim R. My man, drama at your house is not good my boy. Keep that suicide thang to a minimum."

Click.

The Russian said.

I swear. If I ever get my hands on that punk! Hold up! How did he know, that fast? I looked at my watch then looked at the commotion. He found out in 7 minutes! Where was he?! Who did he know? I was puzzled once again.

"FBI Agent Walker, what's the deal?" The chocolate, no-non sense looking, petite sexy female asked; flashing her badge in my face.

"The deal? It is what it is." I said, then looked at the suicide scene, as if it was self explanatory. Then I walked away.

I didn't want to risk losing my wife and child's life by talking with the FBI. Surely, the Russian would know. Hold up!

I stopped then spun around, that's when it hit me! "Where is she?"

No one paid me any attention. They were flashing pictures of the crime scene. Then they zipped the once pretty lady into a black bye, bye bag.

"Where is she?" I asked the two Atlanta police. They just ignored me, after giving me a 'what the heck you talking about look'.

I jumped in my 3 million dollar car bumping 'Future' by Rick Ross and Ace Hood! "I woke up in a Bugatti!"

Where did that lady go?! I couldn't see her Jaguar. I was flying through my once quiet neighborhood!

In pursuit of my wife and child, I felt like I was part of the movie 'Taken'! Things like this just don't happen to black folks!

Zoom!

The car almost tilted and flipped when I did 130, flying around a curve! Bingo! My Ebony!

Now I mashed the gas like potatoes, 220 miles an hour! I pulled right next to her.

SReeeech!

I slammed on brakes then I decided to pull in front of her.

Bam!

Her car flipped over. Bam! Bam! Boom!

"Dog!!!"

I jumped out of my ride to see if my wife was alive! The car was upside down, plus on fire!

"Help! Help!" She cried in the passenger side.

The driver was crying too. I didn't know what to do! I was rushing, having a panic attack!

Bang! Crack! Break!

I kicked the front wind shield open and pulled both of them out.

"Are you ok?" I asked the female, Russian driver. Her neck looked broken, like she couldn't move it. Tears just rolled down her pretty face as I carried her to my car.

Then I quickly, grabbed my wife.

"Thank you, thank you baby." She cried, in my arms.

I was so happy. Now we can get back to football, After Love.

"I love you." I told her as I held her in my arms, in the middle of the street.

The car was still in flames.

Boom!

"Whoa!"

5 feet away from me, the car explored! I just held my baby, and walked away. So much for love and joy.

Relief. Belief. Disbelief. Grief.

Man, I felt like a thousand pound weight had been lifted off my back.

"Thank you for saving me," my Ebony said.

"I love you. Are you ok? Did he hurt you?" I asked her.

"Cim!"

I turned around, still feeling teary eyed.

"Huh?"

"What happened to Sharonda?"

"Hmm. Sharonda? How would I know?" I replied, not trying to be rude about my wife's sister, but all I cared about now was my wife.

"Fool! You are holding Sharonda in your arms! What happened to her?" Micki asked me, looking at me like I was a lion in the projects!

"No! No!" I couldn't believe it.

"Hold!" Coach Brown and Micki caught Sharonda. I almost dropped her!

"Man! I'm losing it!" I admitted then jumped in my car, and pulled off!

"Why in the world did you run me off the road?" Akilah asked.

"Huh?" Dang! I forgot she was in my car!

Ebony and Sharonda were sisters. They actually played a trick on me on Halloween, last year!

Knock.

Knock. Knock.

"Who is it?" I asked, peeking through my platinum peek hole.

"It's your sister-in-law fool! Duh!" Sharonda said, with a Jason mask on.

"Oh, hah-hah. Come in."

Sharonda took off her mask, sat down in the living room, and played Grand Thief Auto for 3 hours! I didn't pay her a bit of attention.

Ring!

Ring!

The gold, antique house phone rang.

"Who is?" I answered.

"It's your sister."

"Oh, Micki?"

"No!"

"Shawn?"

"No!"

"Kiki?"

"Sharonda! Funny!"

"What? Wait, I'm looking at you play the video game."

"Boy shut up. I'm outside," she lied.

Well, I thought; until I went to the door.

"Sharonda!" I yelled, like I saw a ghost! Well, a pretty ghost is still a ghost!

"What? Silly?" Sharonda asked, walking into the mansion.

"Well, who is that?" I said, pointing toward the 80 inch flat screen TV.

"Boop!" Ebony said, laughing and kicking her feet in the air.

Dang! They got me again! Only this time it was Ebony instead of Sharonda. I coulda sworn that was Sharonda and a foreigner, sneaking in the car during the commotion! However, it was Akilah and Sharonda!

"Um. Are you buying me a new car?" Akilah asked.

I didn't respond. I couldn't. I felt too stupid and embarrassed. I just kept on driving, feeling like a fool!

"Yo, Cim."

"Yea." I answered, flat as a bicycle tire.

"What's up with you, man? You ain't the same energetic, funny, silly Cim. You are losing your coolness. What's up with you?" Akilah asked me.

"Nothing. Nothing you can fix anyway."

"Oh really, you never know, I may be able to ease your pain." Akilah said, like a seducing question and a sexy answer at the same time, letting her words float like a boat.

For a long two seconds, we just stared into each other's eyes.

Snap!

I had to snap out of it! Akilah was fine! Lust was not even the thing, though. It was like I couldn't see clearly anymore. All I could see was Ebony. Everyone I looked at, looked like my wife. When I picked up my Holy Bible, I could see Ebony's picture on the front.

"Hah!"

And I know my wife wasn't the Cover Girl for the Holy Bible! No female have ever been or could be a Cover Girl for God's Word!

I was tripping. Everything looked like Ebony to me! When I was staring at Akilah, she looked just like my wife, even though Akilah is a shade darker! I was losing it, hard and fast.

My entire life, I never went more than a day, without seeing her. Since the day I was born on Jan16. I don't know, man.

How can I find her like this?

How in the world can I make it to the Super Bowl, the Sugar Bowl or even the dang Salt Bowl!

I don't even know if I could play football in the Dirt Bowl! Even the football would look like my wife!

Hey, in that case, maybe I should switch positions: from quarter back to wide receiver, cause if someone threw Ebony, I would surely catch her head before it hit the ground!

I would be the only receiver in history, to NEVER, miss a ball!

"Cim, umm. When are you leaving from this stop sign?" Akilah asked.

"Oh. Hah, I'm just in a zone."

"Yea, a good one too! What drug you on boy, some new stuff?! What kinda pill you pop, a dinosaur Molly?" She said, laughing.

"Hah-hah, that's a good one. Let me put the underground CD 'The Single Get That Cash' by my home girl, Veronica Ash, in. I said while shaking my head to Veronica and Weezy's CD.

"That's Fye!" Akilah shouted, dancing as I pulled off slow, like a pimp in my fire red Bugatti.

"Where you going?"

"My Cousin Akilah answered.

"Cool; hey. Do you know anybody from Russia?"

"Huh oh!" She snapped!

"Cim!"

"Akilah?"

"Man, I live in Decatur, Georgia. Do I look like I know a Russian? Hah-hah, you on one, you are really on one." Akilah said, rubbing her pretty legs.

"Hah-hah, I guess."

"But you know what, I met a Russian in Vegas, name Zumbiania."

Scccreach!!!

I slammed on the brakes, and reached for my gun.

"Where is he?!" I shouted.

"In Neptune, I guess, I don't know! It's been 10 years! Take me to my sister's house. Get off that dope, and give me my money for a new car!" Akilah said, and rolled her eyes.

"Yea. I'm tripping, my bad." She just looked at me and shook her head.

"O.M.G. Drugs kill." She said, looking upset.

"Cim! Cim! What's up?! Can I get your autograph and picture?!" A slim, familiar, extremely beautiful female asked.

"Sure, and do I know you?" I asked the baby doll.

"Duh! That's the Super Model, Destiny Brown!" Deon said, pushing me, looking at me as if I should know!

"Oh. Hah. Yea! I should be asking for YOUR picture. I saw you on the Tara Banks Show."

"Yea. Lol. I saw you at the Super Bowl." Destiny said blushing, shyly. She was tall, slim and extremely pretty. She had to be 6 feet, cause she wasn't too short under my 6 feet 5 frame.

"Come on, take this million dollar picture of these two stars." I said, holding her hand, looking too cool and famous while Destiny put on her billion dollar, beautiful, Top Model, ATL finest, smile.

"You know, when I was young, around 15, I always wanted to be a model, and my dad asked me from prison, what I want to be. And I told him I want to be a model. He made it happen, from prison! Man, that's what's up.

Your brother is so real." Destiny, Top Model Brown said.

"What? My brother?" I asked, to another surprising strange event. I looked at her even harder now. No, I know what it is!

"Yes, we never met. I'm your big brother's daughter." Destiny said, to my surprise.

"Wow. I'm so lost."

"Listen! Get found. Come with me, quickly! I got to show you something!" My niece said, pushing me into her glistening new ride, dog of puppy chow!

Destiny's car even looked like a model; a shining, Spanking new blue Hummer. It looked like the ocean, in the sun. She backed out quick, putting her arm around my seat, looking backwards.

"Erica Wheeler! I'm wheeling this ride, gotta go!" Destiny said, as she pulled out of Erica's driveway.

"Where we going, brand new niece?"

"Hah-hah, I'm not a baby. I'm grown now. I got to show you something, Top Model style!" Destiny said, laughing and speeding with her tongue out.

I just sat back, fastened my seat belt, and braced myself for the ride! I just lean back, like the song! Even though I'm rich and famous, I wasn't accustomed to being a passenger: Especially, to a speeding female, Top Model!

Destiny blasted the old smash single 'Bad' by Wale and Tiara Thomas. Man, Destiny could sing!

"Yea. LOL. I got my voice from my momma."

"Who?" I asked, noticing her name on the photo hanging off the mirror, inside the car, Number 1 Mom.

She didn't answer. She was in a zone, a very deep zone. So I didn't know if Destiny mom's name really was Tracy! Screeeach!

"Get out!" She yelled.

"Ok. Ok.!"

"Come on! Don't you play football?! Run!" She yelled, running and holding my hand. The slim model was nearly pulling me!

We ran through some back alleys, through nasty trash, behind a stankin dragon bootey smelling dumpster!

Suddenly! We stopped! It was now blackness, quietness, and it was very creepy.

"Shussh." Destiny said with her index finger over her lips. Destiny placed her right ear on the steel back door. It appeared to be an old warehouse.

She waved me over to listen. "No!" I was about to go off!

"Shussh. You can't blow this. It's life or death." Destiny warned me.

I regained my composure. I heard it! I couldn't help but be fidgety. I felt death, victory and worry in my throat, as I continued to listen.

I heard a foreigner: Maybe French, no, Russian! Bang! Bang! KaBoom!

I burst into the door. He spun around and smiled, the 7 feet tall, Russian giant.

"I wasn't expecting you this soon. How did you find me?"

Bam! I leaped ten feet with one giant step! I ran over and punched the snake! He flew backwards, stumbling over his size 20 feet. However, he didn't fall. He was dazed. He shook it off!

"Try it! And die!" A voice yelled from behind me

I made a weird facial expression, then spun around!

Then!

I stared straight in the barrel of his shot gun.

Boom!

"No! Cimeon!"

He shot towards my head, but Destiny kicked him in the back. Bingo! It was just enough to mislead his aim. I grabbed him and snatched his gun.

"Where is my wife?!" I demanded, on top of the giant, choking him.

"Right here" he yelled, through choking words.

"Huh?" I froze. Everything inside of me got weak as Kool-Aid with no sugar. I was on top of the Russian. I looked up, over my head, I couldn't believe my eyes.

"Umm! Umm!"

My wife was wrapped up like a mummy, her entire face! I didn't know if she had bruises on her or not!

Destiny really came through! But . . . how did she know?

Bam!

Wake Up Call

I was cold and shivering like a snake in flames. Where am I? I was lying on my stomach. I felt my forehead. Dang! Dried up blood, what else is wrong? Could I move my legs?

"Yes." I slowly sat up, trying to remember the former episode.

"Cimeon!"

"Whaaaat . . ." I answered, drooling my words. Who was that?

"Man! What's up bro. Get up and take a pic with yo boy!"

Snap!

Too late, oh boy, he just snapped a picture of me with his cell phone.

"Dude . . ." I said, trying to pull myself back up. "Umph," I fell back down. Now I felt a little embarrassed, in front of what seemed to be a fan.

Boom!

"What you do that for?" The dude asked.

"Man, I'm a little weak." I admitted.

He reached his hand out and pulled me up.

"Good look." I said, dusting myself off.

"God, what brings a NFL Star, Super Bowl Quarter Back in a downtown Marietta alley?" The stranger asked.

"Man, bad night." I admitted,

"Ok, I'm 3P. I won't Boop you."

"Ok, man. Don't Boop me." I told the dude, hating my predicament.

We walked from behind the building.

Zoom!

Zoom!

Two cars rolled up on me, red Cadillacs.

Panic?

"Get it!!!"

"Yea, right." I said then looked at 3P Who looked at me like, Huh?

"Cim, it's Mookey and Micki, nicca.

"Get in!" Mookey shouted.

I got in.

"What? How did?—I mean—

"Word travels bro. I was coming through to pick up some birds from Diamond and Porsche in Baby Land. I got word from 3P and Two Brain that you was drunk in an alley. You trippin. But I had my people to keep an eye on you, till I got here." Mookey explained, counting so much money, it had to be illegal.

Mookey was Micki's old boy friend. They were like Bonnie and Clide, the new Bonnie and Clide.

Rumor was, Mookey and Micki robbed 10 banks in every state in America. And! Never got caught!

That explains how Mookey got a 3 million dollars car, with no job!

"Cool, so you and Micki hooked back up?" I asked.

Mookey seemed to be focused on the crowd of teenage thugs at the gas station. He pulled in, quickly!

"We never unhooked." Mookey said then hopped out the car, like a running back!

In high school, we used to battle, hard. Mookey was undefeated at Washington High. And I was undefeated at Columbia High. 4 years in a row, we were the best quarter backs in the state.

Of course we won, but truth be told, it wasn't because I was better than Mookey. It was because I had better players. Ced was a hitting Beast! Ohh!, especially Deon! That boy, been bad!

Sergio and Mookey were a raw one two punch: Quarter back and Receiver.

But Deon and Lou killed them!

"Suwooo!" Lou yelled, in our 12th grade State Championship Game, to win in overtime. It hit me!

"Yo, what happen to Destiny?" I asked.

"Who is that?" He asked, cool but confused. After collecting his money from one of teenagers, and beating two of them up, for being short five dollars.

"The Model. Destiny Brown!"

"How would I know, last time I saw her, was today." Mookey replied, cool as ice.

"Where? Is she ok?"

That's my niece! I didn't-"

Mookey cut me off, stopping the car.

"It was on TV, man. Cover Girl lipstick commercial, the one where she puts the lipstick on at Miami Beach and says 'A pretty smile is worth a thousand words'."

"Oh," I said. So I guess he never saw Destiny in real life, action.

"Bro, Deon gone pick you up. Coach talking crazy . . . I don't want to hear that crap," Micki said. Then they walked into Mookey's red, 15 bed room, pearl driveway, Cobb County Mansion.

I sat in the Cadillac and everything slowly came back to me. Destiny was gone too! They tied her up! Right before that big Russian knocked me out with a bat!

"Man! Now I got a double kidnapping! My wife and my niece, cheer leader and a model!"

I wonder how Destiny knew! Bingo! Her dad was in that jail too! So Destiny probably saw the entire episode! Knowing my niece, she probably trailed him and came back to tell me. Destiny is smart, I could see that! Destiny is in trouble! I got to find her! I took off!

"Cim! Bring my car back, boy!" Mookey yelled, standing in the middle of the street, with Polo shorts and Tank Top on (all white). Too late!

I was gone! Back to that old warehouse!

"Cool, I see why pimps, like Snopp, like Cadillacs!" I laughed to myself.

This baby could fly, and float! "Cadillac CTS! Fast, fly, and funky fresh!" lol. I shouted, with my tongue out, zipping through Baby Land in Austell, Georgia.

Boy, the Germany made BMW and Mercedes may have a rival! This Caddy is a hot, luxury car! Batman, Pimp Mobile! Boop! It accelerates fast and it's light in weight! I got back to Marietta in 5 minutes!

I jumped out of the car, reached under my seat . . . grabbed Mookey's gun . . .

I was ready, this time. I'm not fighting fire with Ketchup! I'm fighting fire with fire!

"Come on!" Bang!

I kicked the back door down, like a sand castle!

"Give me my wife and niece!" I yelled with gun aimed dead at the Russian's back.

"Hah-hah, you didn't expect me back, so soon! Never mess with a man's family!"

Pow! Pow! Pow! Pow!

I blasted him like I was the first shooter in the Civil War in April, 1861! He fell like a sidewalk sandwich!

Splat!

"Ebony! Destiny! Daddy is home!" I yelled to the girls, my hearts. I looked up! Hold up!

"A trap!" I shouted, and took off running with all my might! Faster than a daughter running from her father, trying to molest her!

I ran faster than a slave running from his master with nasty wounds on his back! After a brutal beating, just for reading his Bible!

The ceiling was collapsing! The Russian I shot was a giant manikin!

I ran faster than a prisoner with two life sentences, escaping through the woods!

I was gone! To the door! Not!!! I dove like a running back with a football, stretching the ball out for the touch down!

"Touch down!"

Ka Boom!

Boom! Boom!

The entire building collapsed! I was holding the gun in front of me, like a football! When I dove out the door! Quickly! I hopped onto my feet, like a bull frog on steroids!

Boom! Kah-Boom! Dark smoke!

The building exploded! The rapid but hot release of energy was electrifying!

"Dang it!" I had to run to the Cadillac! Fast!

"Sorry Mookey!" The smoke cloud and debris were moving towards me fast!

I had to leave Mookey's CTS! I took my chance on feet! I believe I broke the record in the 40 yard dash today! I ran it in 3 seconds flat!

Boom!

I heard another roaring explosion, as I ran onto the street.

Boom!

Two more buildings exploded. It was hot and darker than an eclipse at midnight, in the country part of Mississippi!

Time To Chill

"I knew it! Get in! I know my brother!" Micki said, whipping the CTS Luxury car up to the sidewalk, kicking the passenger door open! Wham!

I hopped in!

"You owe me." Mookey said, from the back seat.

"Yeah, for the car." I replied, exhausted. Almost at my breaking point, but I couldn't give up. Not ever.

"You owe me for introducing me to Joe! That nut got me locked up! That's why I'm not a star quarter back like you! I shoulda been beating you in the Super Bowl this year, instead of Wonder boy!" Mookey joked.

"Hah, hah." We all laughed.

"Shut up! Wesley is good." Micki checked Mookey in the mirror, giving him the evil, funny eye.

"True." Cim admitted.

"Yea, he fye. Wesley fye. But what is a Super Bowl Quarter Back doing setting fire in Cobb County?" Mookey asked me.

"Yeah bro. Why are you blowing the city up, instead of working out in Summer Camp? You beginning to look like a high school basketball player in rehab; instead of the Professional Football Rookie of the Year!" Micki snapped on me. She was laughing but serious.

"Yea bro. You're drug dealer skinny! Nicca. What you weigh, 150? You look like one of those teen age drug dealers at the gas station in the neighborhood that sales dope all day long for 5 years straight, and still riding a bike!" Mookey said, laughing and weighing up his cookies.

I smiled and shook my head. Mookey and Micki were letting me have it.

"Oh." I jumped. What was that? I wondered, now what? Uhh . . . My phone.

"Hello?"

"Hi. Football idiot. Lovebug, dummy. Next time I'ma kidnap yo mommy!"

"Don't you talk about my MOMMA! I'll kill you ten times!" I yelled, forgetting all about Micki and Mookey.

"Oh really? Mr. Lover Boy. Like you killed that dummy? You're an idiot!" The Russian Master minded mobster wolfed.

Whap!

"Uncle Cimeon! He hit me!" Destiny screamed.

I balled my fist up real tight. Blood boiled in my fingernails, green smoke came out my nose. Hot sauce came out of my toes. You could fry a Quarter Pounder on my forehead! Zzzzz!

I was furious at this Dumb Maniac! This man was teasing me. Threatening my family; snatching them up, one by one, and enjoying it! Guilt plagued my mind like a deadly disease.

I can't let him win. I can't let him draw anyone else into this! I just met Destiny, and now she's gone!

"Bro. What's up? Who Micki and Mookey gotta kill? Who talking about my Momma Sheppard?!" Micki yelled.

Scccreach!

Smashing the brakes in the red Cadillac and sparking red flames out the tires.

"Nobody Micki. That was Nick and Peaches messing with me." I lied, for a reason.

"Ok, cause you know, Mookey and Micki will take a hit, quick!" Mookey said in the back seat.

"Hello . . . What!!!" Micki said, answering her $19,000 platinum iphone. While holding the steering wheel with her left hand.

"Baby, just come home. She is dead and gone. Leave that thug and come back to me." Coach Brown said, on his speaker phone.

"No."

"I'll kick that thug's butt!" He yelled, out of control.

Micki hung up, shaking her head and smiling. Then she pulled up at Levi's mansion.

"Cim, what's up bro? Let's go to the gym" Levi said, in his Atlanta Falcons Wife Beater shirt. Standing next to his gorgeous wife, Erica, who had on a matching Atlanta Tank Top, white; God forbid.

Slap myself!

I cannot stare at her breast.

"Hey Cim." Erica said smiling.

"What up?" I said, playing cool. Hungry as an elephant in Grant Park, on a spiritual diet! Suddenly, as I stood in the driveway, I got dizzy.

Bam!

I fell down, hard!

I passed out.

I was too weak to fight. No food and water and too much worrying, can kill you!

"Mr. Riley. You have to drink more fluids and eat some food." RN Bailey told me.

She was standing with her back turned, reading her chart. I looked up. I had IV in my arms. I could not believe I woke up in the hospital.

"Son, leave your worries to God. Pray. Put God first. You are trying too hard and doing too much. Let God fight your battle." My always encouraging Mother, Apostle Hannah Sheppard told me.

"Hey Cimeon. How are you doing?" Rachael Miller, from the TV station, asked. She was a beautiful, excellent, saved TV Host.

I nodded my head for fine. However, I was doing terrible. Mom was right. I was doing much too much, bye myself.

Jumping the gun, I lost my niece. Her dad's in prison, so now, that's on me too!

I have to find Destiny! Because her dad, Shoe Be Do, will have the whole Pimp City going off!

"Son, God has a plan. Everything happens for a reason. Let go and let God. You are human. We all are, no matter how successful we are on earth. You can run like a cheetah, but die like a fly. We still return back to the earth. So let's focus on the prize: That's God and our souls." Mom told me, with the anointing of God in her eyes, words and spirit.

Jennifer Harvey walked up with her son. Ced, my line-backer, stood next to her with Erica.

"Brother, God loves you. Heal up, and play ball!" Ced shouted.

"Let's pray for my son." Mom said, and we bowed heads.

"Yes Father." Jennifer prayed.

"Amen." Destiny added. I jumped! Like I saw a ghost!

"Dear Father God, we love you. Forgive us for our sins, in the human flesh. We know we are not God. But we are created in your imagine. Help us to be more like you.

And God, whatever Cimeon is going through, let him know You can handle it. You can fix it. Mark 10:27 let him know: All things are possible with God.

The Super Bowl, The Sugar Bowl, The Soul Bowl, and/or The Life Bowl, God can fix it. In Jesus' Name, remove his worries and fears, on this day. Heal his mind. Amen." Mom, Apostle Hannah Sheppard, prayed.

Aunt Elouise Gleaton, Miss Millsap, Aunty Liz Ward, Aunt Connie, and Aunt Jolly all were in the room, when I opened my eyes. Even Destiny, now I was stunned.

How did she get away? Was I dreaming? Where was Ebony? Why did she leave Ebony?!

"Cimeon Riley! Why are you looking at me like that?"

"Huh, like how did you get away?"

"Get away from what? Oh. Hah-hah, he let me go." Destiny replied, with a huge Kool-Aid smile.

"Why did you leave Ebony?" Now I was angry as a lion that got pimped slapped by a tiger!

"Why not?!"

"What you mean? Why not?!" I hollered.

"Cim, calm down." Mom said.

"No! Why did you leave Ebony?! Destiny?!" I demanded an answer, immediately. I sat up. Snap! Snap!

I snatched the IV's out of my arm. I stood up.

"Hold on—" Nurse Bailey started.

"No! Destiny, why would you laugh about leaving my wife? And why would you laugh about the man letting you go?" I said, calmer, because I did love Destiny. After all, she was my niece.

Oh. Destiny was ready! The 6 feet tall model stood her ground to my 6 feet 5 body, of muscles and mean swag.

Destiny got right up to me. She shook her head then looked around the room at all the saved people. Then Destiny bit her lip, looking at me like; oh, it's about to go down!

Did she know Karate? Boop!

"First of all, I left Ebony because I didn't rob banks or whatever her, Micki, Kiki and those crazy cheer leaders did. Second of all, Michael Lackey let me go, because I'm a grown woman. 3rd!!! of all, my name ain't Destiny!" She yelled, with an extra thundering roar!

"What?" I said, scratching my now, nappy head.

"My name is Shawn, idiot! Hah-hah, what have you been drinking, boy?" Shawn said.

The whole room laughed at me! Even mom and Aunty Liz! Now, I felt silly as a turtle with a pink and purple sweater!

"Oh Lord, is he on any kind of anesthetics?" Rachael asked RN Bailey.

"Yea, he's a little out of it. He passed out, so he may have a short memory loss. To go with those hard bruising hits he take in football, add to the injury.

However, don't worry. The Quarter Back will be fine, in a day or so." RN Bailey told the crowd of open mouths and big, concerned eye balls.

"Magnificent!" Governor Lawrence 'Pop' Rutherford said, entering the room in his money green pinstripe, Jacquard stitching, $4,000 Dolce Cabbanna suit.

Looking like money, with a Godly smile, and with swag; next to his beautiful, stunning wife, Kishana.

Kishana was dressed like she was going to the wedding with the president! In a money green silk and taffeta gown adorned with 750 diamonds, a 30 million dollar dress!

"Cim! Heal up boy! We just signed Jayhlen from New England!" Levi shouted. Running up in the hospital room like New Jack James!

"Yeap! We going up through there! Like the Atlanta Falcons when they almost won the Super Bowl with Osi Umenyiora and Stephen Jackson! We winning it for show! This year!" Micki added, like a female football wizard!

"What! Wow! I'm so ready!" I shouted, shocked as a platinum mop bucket! I got two of them!

Boop!

Then! Erica! No she didn't She had a 30 million dollar dress! Cheer leaders don't stunt like that! She had platinum and 750 diamonds in her baby blue silk and taffeta gown.

"Plus! We just picked up Christopher, perfect kicking Barrett!" Erica added, smiling.

"Whoa! He has made 80 field goal kicks in a row! Do you smell what the Tigers are cooking?! Super Bowl! Baby!" I shouted.

Everyone laughed.

"Amen." Mom added.

"I'm leaving! I'm fine now, Nurse Bailey. I gotta go!" I shouted. Hyped from the two key additions. I was back in my football mode!

"Yeah! That's the Cim I know!" Sergio yelled.

"Bad news." Mr. Lackey added.

"What's that?" I asked, not knowing what in the Christmas China, to expect.

"I had to let Coach Pettis go, personal family issues." Mr. Lackey stated, with an honest stare.

"Man." I mumbled. That was hard. Coach Pettis was my mentor. Him and Coach Brown were the best motivators in my lifetime.

Micki looked a little sad, so did Sergio.

"But! The Super Bowl winning Coach Mackey agreed to fill in!"

Michael Lackey shouted in victory!

The entire room erupted in cheers!

"Whoooh!" Everyone shouted. Pumping their hands in the air!

Now, my motivation was back. My focus zoomed in on the upcoming season. Mom was right. I was losing weight.

I was killing myself. It was no way I could get Ebony back, if I wasn't healthy! Or if I killed myself with starvation!

Now I even got Destiny involved! I shoulda prevented her from that. I shoulda sensed something wrong and stopped her. Yeah! I shoulda stopped her from coming in!

I shoulda never jeopardized my big brother's oldest daughter! Now he's in prison going crazy! Probably beating prisoners up, for nothing!

Bang!

Hitting them in the head with locks! Oh No! I won't let him find out. I will find her first. However, Number one, I must get back to Football! To seal the deal!

Back To Football

"It's in your blood to win!
It's in your soul to compete!
This is our year! To bring the ATL Heat!
No Falling! No Tripping!
Just a Super Bowl Victory!
And every opponent will get a
Tiger whipping!!!
Cause this year!
No fear!
We up in here!
'1-2-3—We Ready!!!' (All shouted.)
Ahhh! Rooar"

Coach Brown growled at the team! Snatching his shirt off! He was still built like the 200 million dollar quarter back, he once was! At 37, he still didn't look a day over 27!

He was super crunk! And oh yeah! Atlanta was winning the Super Bowl this year! Even if Coach Brown had to play his dang self!

"You're in great shape; excellent shape actually." My new, favorite personal trainer, the beautiful, sweet, Alyssa informed me.

She trained Beyonce, Rock, and even won an Olympic gold medal! Also trained Saniya in gymnastics! Saniya Brown did great! Alyssa was awesome!

"Hey! We going all the way! Give it to me! Turn Up!" Alyssa shouted, pumping me up, while I did my sit ups. My stomach muscle screamed! I brain washed myself to think ONLY, about football. I had to, that's the only way I could win my baby, wife and niece back.

The owner already built this team for a championship. Now I had to do this; I had to get there! And . . . sadly . . . loose on purpose.

But! I had to first, focus on getting there, because he may be there!

Our first pre-season game was this Monday night. It was our big game against New York!

Can you spell . . . Beat down?!

We put in forty hours every week! In our conditioning programs, 5 days a week!

I went extra hard! I had weight lifting periods, classroom work, and on-the-field work.

The draft was over, so our OTA (organized team activities) had started. This gave our team 16 practices, most teams only have 14. Coach Brown was determined! Plus, Super Bowl Coach Mackey preached that, "Practice Makes Perfect!"

Michael Lackey built a real, experienced, talented Super Bowl team. Atlanta, Georgia, was determined to win a football championship. Maybe! Build a dynasty! I'm in!

Bingo!

"Get in, bro! Get it in! 4 more mini-camp weekend practices to go! Turning you up! Got you in Perfect Ready to play Football shape!" Alyssa shouted, looking like an exercising Halley Berry!

Boop!

Coach Mackey had plenty new schemes. He had cooked up a great recipe for winning! Plus. He won two Super Bowls coaching, and two rings playing!

Coach Brown and Coach Mackey were teammates. Coach Mackey caught everything, but a cold and the flu or any kind of sickness! But, boy ole boy! When Brown threw it, Mackey caught it! Now, I was ready to test my new rookie target, Danny Lyons, who we drafted in the first round out of Alabama.

So now, the regular season was about to begin. The 53-man squad was paved in stone!

The road to the Super Bowl was set! And it meant soooo much more to me! To get there! Sadly though, to loose . . .

"Hello?"

"Cim! I love you!" Ebony yelled, through tears.

"Uncle Cim! Save us!" Destiny screamed, then the line disconnected.

A-Town Down

September 11 A day with so much meaning to me and the entire world,9-11. The day those cowards crashed those planes.

9-11, the day Luda was born.

9-11, the day they falsely arrested my little sister, Red Bone Shawty.

9-11, the day with so much personal meaning to me.

This is a big day, for Football Fans, worldwide.

9-11 was huge for Atlanta fans.

9-11 was our opening day, the first Monday night Football game of the year.

Plus, it was against a new improved New England team! Our get back game! 9-11 was even more painful to me. Because it was the first time, in my history, I played professional game. Without my wife cheering for me . . .

Still, I stood! I was amped up! I had a lot on my chest, and a lot to prove! To my city, to myself, to my family, to my haters, and to the world!

Bam!

Johnson kicked the ball off with a screaming Atlanta crowd! Home in the dome! I was really mad, that Levi got traded! Kool! We got Rah-Rah and Jayhlen, two good players, for one! Rah-Rah was my personal, talented homeboy from Columbia High! Now he is our Full-back.

Bemp!

Deon caught the ball, and took off! Straight up the middle!

Bang!

He got . . . nowhere . . . Fast! New England's gunners, gunned him smack in the ground!

Man. New England already looked better! Two Super Bowl wins back to back. Let's see what's up with that.

"Cim! Go get em!" Our new Offensive Coordinator, the one and only, Super Bowl winning coach yelled! Right in my ear! It's kinda funny, Coach Mackey was now on our side. After winning two Super Bowls with New England.

The crowd roared and cheered! Louder than thunder! I ran on the field. I glanced at my two new running backs. They both looked hungry and ready! Both Jayhlen and Rah-Rah. Then I super mean mugged New England's defensive line!

Bonner growled at me! Ok!

"Down!"

The crowd was on their feet.

"Set!!!"

Miss G, my grandma was cheering like a cheer leader! She looked 21! Columbia Drive is in the house! She and Kiana was jumping with joy!

"Hike 1!!! Hike 2!!! Hike!!!"

Dang! New England was too fast! Two Defensive Ends stormed through my huge, healthy offensive line!

No Ebony, to cheer me on! No Micki and Kiki to cheer me on! All new cheer leaders! All new defense! In my face! They hit me, HARD!

Kah Bam!

I fell back into Rah-Rah! No! Raw Russian Rat Rug! I bounced off Rah-Rah's shoulders like a 6 feet 5, ping pong ball! Then I took off! I instantly, snapped into my beast mode! I ran! I ran! And home boy, I ran! I heard the crowd! I moved the crowd! I rocked the crowd! Worldwide and televised! Like Monday night Raw!

The cornerback was fast as me! I thought about my wife, baby, and niece! The love I have for them was uncountable!

I had a flashback of that warehouse, collapsing on me! I sped up! Faster than a real life tiger! Mixed with a horse, a cheetah, and a rocket! I turned it up! One man to beat! I saw him out of the corner of my right eye! I couldn't avoid the tackle from the side line! One little push, would slang me violently, out of bound! Smack into the New England players!

There! There! I saw the Ruthless Russian in the end zone! He was laughing at me! With my wife, newborn baby, and my niece! All tied up, to a wooden chair! No one noticed through the excitement and anticipation! He was heartless, cold, and bold!

He hit my child! Whap! Whap! Oh no! I'm coming now! Straight to the end zone! No one was catching me!!! Bam!

The safety dove at me! Zoom! I dodged him. Then turned up faster! He missed me! Boom! The safety flipped over the bench! Taking the referee to the ground! The water cooler and two more 300 pounders all fell backwards! I was gone, in the dome!

40, 30, 20, 10, 5

"Whooo!"

"Town Doooown!"

I stopped like my feet were a new pair of brakes! I looked around, ignoring the screaming, happy crowd. They were shouting and jumping. I searched for my family. Man! It was all in my head! My mind was playing tricks on me!

I looked up at the end zone crowd. With a stare meaner than murder! Then I aimed the football towards the cheering crowd!

"Yeah! Wooh!" I shouted. Releasing a much needed smile. Then I ran to my fans! Now, the tone was set! 49 to 0 half time!

"Cim! I love you! You spanked their butt!" Porsche yelled, hugging my neck. Porsche was a cover girl and our new cheer leading captain! Mr. Pruvis, the new NFL Commissioner, fired my sisters! Well, he fired all of the cheer leaders from last year's squad! Now, Lexi, Nu-Nu, Aaliyah, and Saniya, were 4 of the new top Super Model Cheer Leaders!

"Cim! You represented! You ran for 2 touch downs! Then threw 3 touch downs! You a beast!!!" Lexi shouted, congratulating me with a hug.

"I just want a picture?!" A gorgeous white nurse asked.
"Ok. Cool." I told Nurse Mickens.
I saw her name tag. Nurse Mickens actually had a body like a cheer leader. Well, I posed for a picture with her. Then, I continued to walk through the tunnel.
"Donte! Rookie of the year!" I yelled, giving him a high five. Donte was my Tight End. He was awesome! He caught 3 touch downs! Rah-Rah ran for one and Jayhlen ran for one!
49 to 0!
"Wooh! Feels good to get revenge!"
"Yeah! So sweet!" Coach Manilito A. Dunlap aka Shawty laughed.
It hit me. Bam! I thought about how happy Ebony would be. I thought about how she gave me poems at Half Time, of every game. I thought about her charming, caring, encouraging smile. Even in a loss, she cheered me like a boss!
I missed her. However, I was very pleased. Because I was one step closer to the Super Bowl. Plus, I was beating the team that beat me, in the Super Bowl.
"Water?"
I looked up. "Yeah. Shan. Thanks."
"Wooh! Defense. Shawty love that Defense!"
Coach Dunlap jumped on the bench in the locker room. Dancing. Then, he started doing jumping jacks. We all laughed.
"And offense. We looked gooder than good. Knock on wood. However, don't let up. Don't relax. Don't slack. Don't lay back. This year, we will destroy everyone!" Coach Brown demanded.
I could see the fire burning in his eyes.
"True. True. Last year yall had a big lead. You had all the momentum. You had the crowd and the game. So you thought. So, you gave up. You thought you won the game, before the game was actually over. It ain't over, until it's over.
You started playing soft. So yall laid down! Like pillows! Then! New England caught on fire, like a forest! Yall couldn't find any water, to

put out the fire! I told them. Hang in there. Keep fighting. Don't give up. They will relax. And when they do . . . Hit it! Turn up!

So now, I'm your coach. And we both know from experience. Experience, is the Best Teacher. Remember. It ain't over until it's over!"

Coach Mackey preached. Nothing but the naked truth! I felt every word. I remember how we celebrated the victory that we thought we had. I remember how happy Ebony and I were. The look in her eyes . . . man . . . I know now. We must fight, till the very end! Getting back to the Super Bowl, won't be easy. But I'm in! Just in case you want to know, the final score was 75 to 0!!! We crushed New England!

I was exhausted. After the up north beat down, my body was beat up. I finally won a big one!! Usually, the up north teams crush us. Not anymore! I was making a statement, this year!

"Awe, that feels good." I mumbled out loud.

Two Asian masseuses were giving me a full body massage.

"No!" I stumbled off the table. Wham! I hit the ground.

"Hey! Hey! What's wrong?!" Shan, the sexy slim, caramel owner of the Platinum Spa of Atlanta shouted. Shan ran in to save me.

"I'm ok. I' ok. I stuttered, pulling myself up.

"Are you sure? You know we take care of our people, especially you." Shan said, smiling.

"I know. I was just dizzy." I lied, truthfully.

"Naw. I know what it is! You can't fool me. You miss Ebony!" Shan shouted, like she just solved the hardest murder case in history.

I scratched my head, confused. How did she know? Was I missing something?

Yeah. I missed seeing Ebony. We always got a full body massage at the same time, in this very room. We would stare in each other's eyes, as we received the great relaxing pleasure. Shan probably just noticed Ebony wasn't here.

I gathered my composure and laid back down. Receiving the best massage the human body could ever receive! The Asians were perfect, pretty, and precise. I love it! But I hate it! I really hate that my wife is missing—

"Sir."

"Huh?"

"Here."

"Hello?" I said, grabbing my iphone.

"Baby, I miss you. I need you. This is too much for me. I can't wait for you to rescue me. This man is horrible. He feeds us like birds. He yells at us. Baby, he talks to me like a wild animal. I love you so much Cim. Baby I—

I could hear her. Ebony broke down in tears.

Whap!

The Russian slapped my queen with a banana. Rage burned in my brown eyes, turning them fire red.

"Enough! Cut the pity party. You pitiful American girl, you make me seem like a bad guy! Hah-hah, we are very hospitality people. But you took something very special from me. So I took 3 very special people from you. But hey, who knows, maybe if you can't make it to the Super Bowl and lose. I will just take your wife to Moscow. It's extremely beautiful. Your wife and niece would love it! Most of the Russians in Moscow speak English. So they want miss a beat!"

"Twah!" Ebony spit in the monster's face. If she could only break free. She woulda beat the big guy up!

"Hah-hah, you're so adorable." The mobster slash abductor said. Whap! He hit her in the forehead, instantly knocking her unconscious, from his huge and powerful fist.

Blip!

Ebony fell on the floor. Her neck slumped to the side. Destiny was tied to a chair. Crying, fast and hard and scared. The model was breathing like a boxer. Having no idea why she was even there. Who was he? Why was he doing this? Her body was completely wrapped to the steel chair, like super glue.

The rope was 4 inches thick and 12 feet long. All she could do for defense was pray. Destiny knew, prayer could carry her through. Her body was shocked with horror chills, not knowing how her future would unfold. She stared at her aunt, as she hit the floor.

I jumped to my feet! I ran out of the spa. Like it was on fire! Then jumped into my candy apple Porsche! Usually, my red apple Porsche glistened like a real candy apple, when the Georgia sun beamed on it. However, it was rusty dusty now!

My car was yelling, "Wash me! Wash me!"

I was yelling, "I can't! I can't!" I barely had the strength to wash myself! I had to force myself to shower without my wife. Maybe the shower pounding against my face would hide my tears of angry pain. Real men don't cry, I guess. That's what I always heard. But I know, I could beat the average tuff guy in less than 5 seconds! You hurt a man's family. You have real problems! And this mob dude had a HUGE problem! 6 feet 5!

As I sped in my fire hot ride, I received a text from my lawyer. The state of Georgia dismissed your murder charge. "So what?!" I shouted in frustration.

I mean that one man's split second sin caused a life time of pain, for me and my family! Even caused pain for his own family!

Like momma said, "Trouble is easy to get into, but hard to get out of."

I was doing 110 miles an hour. My wife was heavy on my heart. Her tears, her fears, her crying in my ears, and I'm not near. I wanted to hold her, comfort her, protect her, and tell her everything will be alright. Tell her that no one will ever hurt her again. Even her own father hurt her. Then I came, and I have never let her down . . . until now!

I hate that she couldn't defend herself. I hate hearing my wife plead and beg for my help. Then, she got hit, by another man. However, I have never hit my wife, a day in my life. He will pay, somehow, someway.

My baby! God will not spare anyone that hurts a child. That's the worst thing on earth, a person can do. That child never even had a chance or a choice.

No lie, a tear of revenge, bubbled up in my left eye. Visions of my wife, niece, and baby crowded my brain. Right now, the only thing I

can control is myself. So with my all, I'ma strive to win every game. I must play Football, to save my love. Not only play, I must win! Every game! That's next to impossible. Having back to back, undefeated seasons. In the NFL, that has NEVER, happen!
God knows, through Him, humans can make the impossible, become possible. So the impossible, is what I'm pushing for! I'm on a mission, a drive, a fight till the end!
A fight for my wife!
A fight for my child's life!
A fight for my niece!
Until the day I see them free, there will be no peace in me!

Dreams Come True

"Married!? What!" I almost crashed.

"Yea, she didn't tell you?" Grandma G asked me.

"Hmmm No. I had no spaceship idea! Who's getting married?" I asked.

"Micki! Yo sister, boy!"

"Wow. To who?"

"To your coach!"

"What?" I asked, baffled. His wife just committed suicide last week! I just saw Micki with Mookey yesterday, shopping! Oh well, I guess that was nothing. I scratched my head, extra hard!

I looked at my platinum Rolex: April the 3rd. Destiny's B day. Ok, what else is gonna happen! A flying hamburger from McDonald's!

"Come and talk to me, I really want to meet you . . ." The sounds of Jodeci played inside my car.

"Cuz! You coming!" An excited female asked. She sound super happy.

"Hah hah. Sure. When?"

"Now!"

"What? Now. Well . . . I guess . . . Where?"

"Where else! Candler Rd! Ray Of Hope International Ministries Church!"

"Hah hah. Of course, the best church in the city. Wait! Who is this?"

"Jamiesha!"

"Hold up. So you came all the way from Washington?"

"Duh! Yea!" Jamiesha shouted, in joy.

"So, when?"

"This morning, Micki told me last week."

Wham! What a slap in my face!

What planet had I been living on? Neptune or Mars!?

"How in the Jolly Rancher . . . ok, I'm on my way." I disconnected. Now I was even more shocked. Last week, Micki told Jamiesha. Then, she came all the way from Washington?

Was that before his wife died? Umm. Ok. Never mind! I don't have time to try to figure my sisters out! I have a game tomorrow. They will be fine. Joshua and Micki want each other any way! Mookey might be a little upset! Boop! Blood is thicker than water, so I'ma support my family.

"This is like . . . my dream come true!" Micki jumped up and down like a cheer leader. She was crying tears of joy.

"I know! Kool-Aid smile!" Kiki laughed, excited for her sister.

"You deserve to be happy, blessed, and married Baby." Miss G told Micki, hugging her.

"How do I look, grandma? Kiki? Momma?" Micki asked, turning in a complete 360 degree circle.

Everyone eyes were stunned, and blinded by the bright brilliant beauty. Micki had on a beautiful lavender wedding dress. It was more like a floral lavender. It closely match the color of the lavender flower.

"Oh God, I want to cry." Mrs. Pettis said, holding her hands over her mouth, in disbelief. Micki just gave her the biggest smile on earth.

"It's gorgeous. I love you." Mrs. Pettis said, unable to hold back her tears.

"Yes, Joshua and Micki are a perfect match!" Kiki said, smiling.

"Why are you still crying?" Grandma G asked Mrs. Pettis.

"I'm just so happy for her. I never show her how I really feel. And to actually be alive to see Micki and Joshua finally get married. It's just a blessing." Mrs. Pettis said, smiling and looking Micki up and down.

"Ok. Mom, yall. How do I look?" Micki asked again, blushing in tears.

"Girl, you have on a 20 million dollars Diamond Wedding Gown. How else could you look? Besides beautiful!" Momma Sheppard said, laughing.

Micki's dress was laced with 200 carats of diamonds. Making her look like a humble bride and pretty princess. This was the most expensive wedding dress on earth! In real life!

I was tongue on a hot frying pan shocked! As I walked into the already planned wedding, that everybody in the world knew about, but me!

"Come on bro. Come chill with the groom! Coach is happy as a dog in a bag of bones!" Levi said, pulling on my arm. Laughing like he was at a comedy show.

While I'm still dizzy and shocked, getting dragged by my arm!

"Cim! My man, glad you could make it on such a short notice. Hah-hah. What's wrong boy, Ebony's cat got your tongue? Boop! You didn't know the old man had it in him, did you? Yeah! Kah bam! I still got it boy." Coach Brown joked.

I was still stuck and speechless. He went all out for my lil sister. In his million dollars tailor made, gold plated, diamond-encrusted suit. Coach Brown's suit had 480 single cut diamonds in it. Studding the Cashmere cream colored wool suit, with a lavender silk blend on the sleeves.

"Hold up boy! Look at the tie!" Coach Brown yelled like a hungry kid. Slapp.

Man, coach was killing them. In his lavender Ferragamo World Gira Ffe-Print Silk tie with 50 diamonds encrusted in it.

Seeing all of this made me forget my current situation. All the laughs and smiles. I was anxious to see my sister's face. I know Micki would be so happy!

"Whoa! There she is!" A voice yelled. Instantly, I turned around to a smiling Erica.

"Who?" I asked.

"Bre' Shauna! Who else!" Weezy shouted. I was stunned. My favorite singer in the world was about to perform! No one could sing and hypnotize a crowd like Bre'shauna!

Then! Bre'shauna sung the Whitney classic like no one I ever heard! "I Will Always Love You . . ."

Bre'shauna sung, in her royal blue $20,000 silk gown. It was entrusted in diamonds and trimmed in platinum.

Wow, I may be the richest person in here, but I didn't feel like it! Everybody had on million dollars clothes!!!

Then, the crystal confetti rained down on everyone. It rained down as Ari and Minnie walked down the aisle, two beautiful flower girls! Wait! Now, Ari and Minnie were only five and six years old. Even they had on $5,000 white gowns! There were 50 diamonds in each dress!! The sisters looked good!!! Too much money on some kids! Oh well, you only live once. Better enjoy it!! Minnie and Ari, ball till you fall! Boop!

Snap!

I turned around, quick! My Quarter Back instinct kicked in! I was trained to be alert! Always quickly prepared to dodge 320 pound hits! Like bullets!

Now! I saw him standing behind me, like King Kong! I knew everything was going a little too good. This Russian was bold! He really got me messed up! This chump had the nerves to show up at my little sister's wedding! I'm about to beat him to a pulp!

Bam!

I jumped up and dove into his jaws with my powerful knock out punch! One Hitter Quitter! I laid him, as if I was the Black Rocky!

"Chill cuz! Chill!" The governor of Georgia, Lawrence Rutherford yelled. Governor Lawrence grabbed my arms. I yanked my arms loose. He saw the desolate look in my eyes.

Pop calmed me down.

"Bro! What in the world is wrong with you!?" Levi asked me, in his million dollars money green suit.

I snapped again, just thinking about why I was so angry. Suddenly, I charged him again.

"Stop!"

Instantly, that voice calmed me down. I froze and looked up. My left leg was in kick mode. I saw my sister running at me, in her million dollars dress.

"I'm sorry." I said, feeling ashamed.

This was not the place to show out. Micki and Josh were getting married. I could handle this later. I felt 3 inches tall.

"Why did you knock out the water boy?" Michael Lackey asked, with a confused facial expression.

"What?" Now, I really felt like an idiot. Everyone was looking at me weird. I was accustomed to being the center of attention. However, I was not accustomed to being a clown.

I had too much anger towards the Russian. Even in happy wedding bell time, he slid into my mind. How in the Fruit Loop, ice sucking world did I get a chubby white guy confused with a 7 feet tall Russian!

"Hah-hah! Love you bro! I knew you would set this sucker off! Leave it to my brother, to bring some funny action to this dead, dry, rich wedding! Wooh!" Micki yelled, hugging me.

"Huh? You are crazy girl."

"Really bro? You are crazy too! Nothing like a good old wedding fight! Wooh!" Micki shouted.

"Hah-hah." Everyone laughed.

All the tight faces were now loose. Thanks to Micki's sense of humor. I smiled, looking at my sister. She refused to let anything spoil her day. April the 3rd, belongs to her. And boy, did she let it be known! She was unpredictable, just like me. After all, life is unpredictable. If it wasn't, no one would make mistakes!

"Cim! Wake up! We are next!" Levi shouted, kissing a beautiful Erica. She was right on his side. That's when I saw it. The sight was shocking.

Levi was fresh as the winter air, in Alaska! He had on a money green suit with real hundred dollar bills in the suit!

"Levi. My homie. I will be there dog! The second you and Erica get married! I'm the best man!"

"Yeap! You betta be there!" Levi said, hitting my shoulder. Levi was holding his beautiful, brown fiancée tighter than a homeless man with a hot cheese burger! Erica was smiling in the arms of her strong king.

"What is that!?" I spun around! Then, I looked up and down. I was frisking my pockets and body, like I was arresting my own self!

"No!" It was my phone.

"Hello?"

"Enjoying your wedding? Micki Brown is so beautiful. What I . . . let's say. What if I kidnapped Micki?" He said on the phone.

"I'll kill you!" I shouted, with no hesitation.

My sister was totally off limits. Even though, Micki was very street smart. Even though she never trusted anyone, and gave nobody any space. I had to watch my family, EXTRA close.

"Hah-hah. It's the computer in you. You want to win. You want to protect. You can't win them all, I'm not touching your sister. Your wifey here, however. Hmmm. And,

I may take your niece to Russia and marry her. Your wife and niece are so gorgeous. I don't need your sister! I'll let your coach have her. He may be on my team, you never know. Hah-hah!" He laughed, like the devil.

"I'll destroy you!" I growled. The cold hearted coward, disconnected.

"You may kiss the bride." Apostle Hannah Sheppard said to the bride and groom. The handsome Joshua held his beautiful wife Micki in his arms. He gave her the longest, loving, passionate kiss on earth!

With all the revenge and anger in my heart, I was stunned, and I forced a smile on my face. When I saw Joshua and Micki kiss to seal the deal to their marvelous marriage. Beautiful.

"I'm next!" Erica shouted, kissing Levi.

"Wooh!" Sandy shouted in tears, watching Micki and Joshua get married.

"Got it! Erica shouted.

"Hah hah," everyone laughed when Erica reached out her hands and caught the pretty orange bouquet.

"Told you! We next!" Levi shouted, kissing Erica.

Bre'shauna kissed Erica's left cheek as Levi kissed her right cheek. Micki and Joshua were still kissing! I felt empty, alone and unloved. I wasn't next. Actually, I was first! Sadly, no one knew that me and Ebony had already married . . .

Football For Love

The next day, the wedding cake was gone! The game was on!

"Booooo! Booo!"

I ran out the tunnel in New Orleans to a rowdy crowd of boos. Most of them booed me cause they hated me. Most of them really booed me cause they wished, I played on their team! "Nope! ATL baby!" I yelled to the ruthless crowd, as I ran out and pounded on my chest.

The New Orleans Lions were tough!

"Ebony look at your man. He's so cocky, and arrogant, Mr. Macho, like me. He looks like he can't be beat! Gotta love his attitude and confidence. He's super competitive. I bet he will lose! He looks like he could get away with murder! Well . . . did he?! Guess what though? Even if you get away with murder with the law of people. You will never get away with murder in the law of God! For now, I can get away with murdering all of yall!

I could just murder you two pretty, innocent black girls in cold blood! And, 'Boom!' end this whole ludicrous deal!"

While Ebony and Destiny sat chained to a steel pole, he would switch them from a pole to a chair. Whatever he felt necessary to torment the beautiful women, he would do.

The girls were on their feet, hungry, crying, and weak, watching the Football game in misery.

Ebony cried so hard, till all the tears were cried out. Then, she glanced over at Destiny, her niece, and winked her eye. She was trying to encourage the young model, to just hold on.

Ebony couldn't and wouldn't give up, under any circumstance. She kept praying. She kept hoping and believing. Ebony kept quoting the Bible verse in her head: 'No weapon formed against me, shall prosper!' (Isaiah 54:17)

Like Minister Joshua would preach every Saturday. "No matter how many weapons, sickness, problems, or worries rise against you; they won't defeat you as long as you have God in your heart, mind, and soul. Believe!" He would preach, even when life is dry, dull, and cold.

Ebony was a real black queen. She knew even in death, the victory belongs to God. 'Death . . . where is your sting?' (1 Corinthian 15:55)

She was a real woman with hope and a vision. She tried to assure Destiny and herself that some way, somehow, God would save them. Because God knew His plan for your life, before you were created. Cimeon would come running through that door! Now! Right Now! Bam!

Cimeon Riley was running! He was running with force, hope, revenge, and speed! He surprised him!

Boom! Bam! Crack! Push! Punch!

Break!

Cimeon jumped over him, then pushed the other villain to the ground! Then stiff armed the assassin.

"Touch Down! Tigers!"

Cimeon stopped! He looked at the crowd, looked in the sky, then kissed his wife's tattoo on his arm.

"Oh, I'm coming!" Cim shouted through the 72,000 boos! He was shaking his head at the camera.

Wham!

With no remorse for the opponent, Cim gorilla dunked the football on the goal post! While Ebony watched, unable to prevent her huge smile for her man, who scored, soared, and shined yet again. Like an awesome author that continued to drop best sellers; despite his circumstances in prison, or a single mom raising a child to be successful with no help, Cim continued to pull through!

And baby, please know through sickness or death; Ebony is still pulling for you!

50 to 3 was the final score. A-Town stomp, the comp, like chumps! No disrespect to the team, it's just no play, in Ga.

I MUST win every game. I MUST play every game as if it is my last; because it very well may be for my wife, my baby, and niece. And . . . . Pow! Pow! Pow!

They could be already dead . . . .

We zipped through the regular season. Our last game was against Seattle. Believe, Seattle was going hard.

Every team we played, we stomped! We were 15-0. This was the last game of the season. Seattle was in a must win situation, tied with Saint Louis. If we win, Saint Louis is in. We lose, Seattle is in.

Wham!

They kicked the ball off like a rocket! Deon looked left to right, then took off! Bam!

"What!" Jayhlen shouted, pushing Coach Brown out the way!

Man!

Bailey bomb tackled Deon! The ball came lose! It was a small tussle, fight for the ball! Harper dove on it!

Bimp! Deon tackled him 5 yards shy of the touch down!

"Man! Come on! We got to stay undefeated!" Jayhlen shouted! He shouted like he was madder than me! My mouth was just rock star open.

All year, for 15 straight games, we NEVER Trailed! I was sweating, and I was not even hot! Tigers defense soared on the field! Donte looked mean and serious, like a man on a mission.

"Down!" Donte shouted. He was thinking about his big sisters Nu-Nu and Lexi who were fighting in the Navy; and cheering for him and his Seattle Bulldogs to win.

"Hut one! Hut two! Hut!"

Donte tossed the ball 5 yards backward! He tossed it backward to Levi. Yeah! That Levi! "Go! Levi!" One of our own cheer leaders yelled.

"What!?" I spun around. Oh, it was Erica cheering for her man. Her man that we stupidly traded! Render wasn't having that. Boom! Render hit him hard! Sike!

Levi matched Render's 280 pound shoulders hit. Shoulder hits shoulder! Two dump trucks! Levi won!

"Touch down! Seattle!"

"Oh no." I complained, in super serious shock.

Seattle won! The Seattle fans went wild! The score was 31 to 0. Levi scored 3 touch downs! Pushing his team into the play offs, for the first time in 10 years!!

"Good game bro, no hard feelings!" Levi shouted through the nerve rattling cheers.

"Man, they act like yall just won the Super Bowl!" I said, stressing.

"Hah-hah, we beat yall. We are in the playoffs. Plus, we are the only team to give yall a loss. We crunk!" Levi shouted, all in the owner's face.

Michael Lackey laughed. "It's cool, good game. But, believe we will be there." Michael Lackey told the player he traded.

"Baby!" Erica screamed, jumping in his arms1 Mike was visibly upset. Mike was wishing he had fired her with the other 37 cheer leaders! However, she was innocent as a new born lady bug! Boop!

I was still shocked. You can win 1000 fights. However, that one loss . . . will CRUSH your pride like a rotten egg!

"No . . . Hello."

"Your two pretty princesses are starting to sweat. They were just cheering their happy black butts off, 15 weeks straight, thinking their super Cim was really unbeatable. They thought he was on his way to the Super Bowl. But!!! My Black American Friend, you looked very rusty tonight, and very VULNERABLE.

Yall may have a rematch against Seattle in two weeks, in the play offs. A team you visible have a problem with. You lose, they die! No questions!"

"No!" Too late, he hung up. For some reason, I knew he was serious as a 99 years old man, having a heart attack. We lose that playoff game, my family is good as dead. Then, we have lost five straight games to Seattle!

"It's Football . . . For Love . . . .

It's Football . . . For Love . . .

It's Football . . . For Love!" I shouted, as I BENCH pressed 500 pounds.

"Come on Cim! Give it your all! Work! Work! Push!" My foxy female trainer cheered me on. I listen to Alyssa and continued to pump; pumping, pressing, sweating with Ebony on my mind.

"Come on Cim! Win this game for me baby!" Alyssa shouted, walking in circles in her skin tight red stretch paints. She was sexy but professional at the same dang time. With a sexy, real woman swagg.

"Squats!" She shouted, like the first female ever to train Rocky!

"A thousand straight! Let's get it!"

She pushed me to the limit. Naw . . . Alyssa pushed me pass my limit. I was determined to overwork every muscle in my body, for a week straight. The Halle Berry look alike, Alyssa, was a great help!

"Run!" Coach Brown shouted, as I sprinted 40 yards in 4 point 2 quick seconds. I was still the fastest player in the game!!

"Throw it!" Coach Brown shouted, as I nailed Deon on 40 yard bomb! To complete the missile pass, in our wildcat offense against the mean 3-4 front.

I over worked. I over studied. I spent hours watching films on Seattle. Donte was a beast! I studied his moves, his arm strength, his speed, his natural quarter back instinct, his quick release, his competitiveness.

The light skin destroyer! Is what they called Donte. I watched the chemistry of him and his favorite wide receiver, also his little brother, Malik.

Bam!

It was like magic, Donte always found Malik, and Malik nearly, ALWAYS caught the ball! Then Levi pushed this 13 and 3 team over the top! Levi had 2,000 rushing yards and 18 touch downs, to lead the NFL this year!

Levi was making Atlanta PAY for trading him. For the younger, quicker, Jayhlen who was just one touch down behind Levi for the lead.

I was ready, man, believe that. We lose this game, I may even die!

Bam!

Saturday morning, the Georgia Dome, the heat is on. It was the playoffs and a National televised game. Atlanta was picked to lose by 3!

Brad was dogging us on Sports Center! Vick picked us to win, by a touch down. The foxy female commentator, Sandra predicted us to win by ten! Tiffani, 'too pretty Tiffani' picked us! Wesley predicted us to lose by 20! Hulk said Seattle would body slam Atlanta! Nature Boy said Atlanta would fold like paper! Wooh! Hah-hah. We will see!

They interviewed Levi before the game.

"So is this personal?" Liz Ward asked, with an anticipating, thrilling, beautiful smile.

"It's very personal!" Levi yelled, in a very determined voice, with a serious, charming, handsome smile.

"Erica, you cheer for Atlanta, who lost 39 cheer leaders in a Super Bowl robbery last year. How do you feel? Split decisions?" Miss Liz asked, making the interview very spicy, dragging her words.

Erica smiled, no comment. She refused to jeopardize her job with Atlanta, her hometown, or to talk against her man. However, her smile, said it all.

"You lose, they die!" He said.

"Ugh!" I shouted at my phone.

Kick off!

Chris, our new, raw kicker, nailed the kick! The ball sailed in the sky. Dunlap caught the ball! Our gunners hammered him IMMEDIATELY, at the 20 yard line! No gain!

The crowd went wild! Oh, ATL came to play! No more play in Ga! Our defense jogged onto the field.

D.J. pumped the Atlanta crowd up with his fist. The dome loved D.J. He was the hype man, plus a gangasta! D.J. took off his two million dollars Dolce and Gabbana gold and platinum glasses. Then, lined up with Malik, man-to-man. Yeah! Money making Malik! He didn't miss a beat. D.J. pointed his fingers at Malik, as if to say, "I'm going to shut you down!"

Donte got in his proper player position. He glanced at the defensive alignment, instantly, knowing which offense would work. He read the free safety position. Donte breathed hard.

"Down-

"Set!"

"Hut!"

Donte eyeballed Malik, then danced three feet backward. Then , . . . Bam! He nailed Malik for the ten yard slant pass. Boom! Scott tackled him. First down, Seattle.

I wasn't sweating yet. I was sitting next to Rah-Rah, studying the plays that Coach Mackey was drawing up.

Seattle raced to the line of scrimmage! Donte spotted the corner backs eyeballing the receivers. He handed the ball to Levi! Oh God, now I was sweating!

"Stop him! Stop him! Got, dog it!" Coach Mackey shouted, in a mad rage.

Cheers!! Some people were wearing Levi's old Atlanta jersey! Levi power, pushed a defensive tackle!

Boom!

He shoulder shoved another player. Then, drug two Atlanta players for 10 yards! Then, he drugged another player across the 50 yard line, 30 yard gain!

Boom!

Timothy saved the touch down, with a powerful, hard, Bush wick, Chocolate Thunder tackle!

The Atlanta crowd went wild! Wooh! We were all on our feet, afraid that Levi would score.

"Levi is so sexy!" Ivory told Debra, laughing.

No Huddle!

Donte spotted a weakness.

"Down! Hut!"

He took the snap, and Bam! He hit Malik for a quick ten yards!

No Huddle!

Donte and the Dogs raced back to the line.

"Down!

Set!

Hut!"

Quickly, Donte ran for 10 yards himself—out of bounds, untouched, to the Atlanta sidelines.

"Yeah! I'm coming!" Donte told me. Then, he ran back on field.

"Time out! Time all the way out!!!" Coach Dunlap yelled! Man, Coach Manilito A. Dunlap, aka Shawty, was in a rage! "Look! Play Defense! Tackle! Tackle! Tackle! Idiots!" Coach Dunlap shouted, like a short, strong warrior!

"Ok, ok." Render agreed.

"Not ok! Stop them! Atlanta can't lose!!!" The Hard Nose, defensive coach, shouted. Dunlap was all up in the defensive players face. Shawty demanded! Defensive!

I was nervous, sweating, but anxious to get on the field. Deep down inside, I knew Levi and Seattle were trouble, big trouble! They burst Atlanta's bubble!

The 22 players ran on back the field.

"Defense! Defense!" Lovely Lexi and the Atlanta cheer leaders cheered!

Nu-Nu did a split! Lexi hit a split! Aaliyah jumped over both of their head, and hit a backward flip! Asia ran and hit two flips in one! Porsche, the team captain hit two front flips and a split! Super hot!

"Defense! Tigers!" The 40 foxy, fabulous, fine Atlanta cheer leaders yelled!

Both teams lined up. Donte spotted something! He noticed we were using two nickel backs. He figured our defense would be weaker against the run.

"Down . . . Red in your head! Hike!"

Donte backed up! Big Ben chased him like a bomb chasing a slow frying cheeseburger!

Ben had him! Almost! Ben chased him all the way back to their own 30 yard line!

However, Ben was too slow to catch Donte, who stopped. Then, he tossed the ball 5 yards to Levi. The ball touched the ground.

"Incomplete pass. 2nd down." The line judge announced.

Seattle fans could breathe again. Donte wiped the sweat from his eyes.

"Down! Hut 1! Hut 2! Hut!"

Boom!

Bonner bulldog tackled him! The dome was on their feet rocking! One more step, and I'ma bring the play off pain! Levi and Malik helped Donte to his feet. He was OBVIOUSLY shaken up.

"Hut 1 . . . Hut 2 . . . Hut!"

He wasn't able to throw the ball. His right arm was in screaming pain. He tossed the ball softly to Levi, who dropped the ball!

Yeah! Atlanta turn baby! No! Levi didn't drop it! The ball hit his shoes, he kicked the ball up into his hands! UNBELIEVABLE!

He took off across the 50 yard line. He leaped over the diving nickel back, whose pinky finger touched the heel of Levi's shoes.

He was gone!

45, 40, 35, 30 . . . .

No! Levi wasn't blue jeans! Levi was a running machine!

"Touch down! Seattle!"

The dome was silent, only a few cheers! Levi stunted, he pointed at me! He did the butterfly dance. Then, tossed the ball in the end zone seats!

"Revenge baby." Levi mumbled to Donte, as everyone on his team gave him love. Donte said, "Kool, I got this."

Seattle kicked the ball off. Deon patiently waited . . . He caught the ball! Then he took a knee.

Ok. Now I made my way on the field. I got in my stance behind the center. Coach Mackey gave me the play, in my head phone device. I didn't agree.

"Blue! 22! Hike 1! Hike 2! Hike!"

I took the snap, then back pedaled like a quick moon walk.

I aimed the ball at Rah-Rah, then Bam! I nailed it right in his chest! The rookie from Decatur took off!

Rah-Rah's first time to shine! Yeah!

"Go! Go Rah-Rah!" His wife, Jasmine, and Melissa cheered! They came all the way from Virginia Beach, to see this game! He was gone!

"Touch down! Tigers, 7 to 7!" Sandra and the announcers worldwide stated, after our new perfect kicker, Christopher nailed the extra point!

This game was a great game to watch, but a horrible game to play! We went tick for tack!

Levi ran 3 touch downs! Rah-Rah had the play off rookie record, with 3 rushing touch downs in one quarter!

"Half time, 21 to 21"

I was exhausted as we walked back to the locker room. Pat on my back, I looked up, it was my guardian angel.

"Hang in there. We will win this game." Alyssa assured me, handing me a new, red Atlanta towel.

"Lord . . . Something isn't right." She said, as she prayed inside her room. Apostle Hannah Sheppard could feel it. God gave her a vision in her sleep.

A vision but more like a dream. After praying 3 times on the prayer line Friday night, God showed her something. Cimeon was fighting, shouting, and crying. Her son never cries, not since he was a baby of course.

However, in this dream two females were tied up in a house, in the middle of nowhere, and crying. They were not able to scream, because their mouths were tied up.

In her dream, two girls appeared to be Diamond and Liyah. In real life, she knew it was Ebony and someone else. The other girl was a mystery.

"God, I knew it! After all these years, I've never gone this long without a visit from my daughter-in-law, not even a phone call! Lord, something is wrong with Ebony!" Apostle Sheppard yelled.

Apostle Sheppard was in her 15 bedroom mansion in Decatur, Georgia. Everyone thought momma was hilarious, but they knew she was anointed. Yolanda Adams ringtone went off. "Hello."

"Grandma, where is Ebony?" Bre'Shauna asked. Ari and Minnie stood next to Bre'Shauna, waiting on the answer.

"Yea, where is my sister?" Sharonda asked.

They were all in the restroom at half-time, inside the Georgia Dome.

"I have no idea. I was praying and wondering the same thing. Ask Cimeon after the game. Don't bother him now." Mama Sheppard said.

"What's wrong mama?" Micki asked, while dying her wavy hair red. Coming out of the bathroom in a glamorous $3,000 robe with gleaming emeralds in it, Micki swore she was Queen B.

"Something is wrong with Ebony. I mean, her birthday is in two weeks. She'll be 22. In the 22 years of her young life, I've never went this long without seeing her." Mama Sheppard said, confused, in deep thought, and in a lot of worry.

"Bingo! Super Bowl Sunday is her birthday too! You are right mama!" Micki yelled, then ran out of the house, in her robe.

"Micki!"

"Mama?"

"Here," Apostle Sheppard said, handing her daughter a red Atlanta Hawks Jersey dress.

Micki stopped. She thought for a split second, then slipped the dress on.

Zoom!

Micki took off in her red Benz!

"I have been quiet. I got to step up." Jayhlen said to Coach Brown.

"Make it do what it do." Coach Brown said to his new Super Bowl winning running back.

Ebony and Destiny watched the game in tears. They were visibly worried that Cim might lose. Their kidnapper was getting meaner by the second! He was yelling and hitting on them. Destiny's eye was black. Ebony's nose was bleeding.

"Y'all are dying! Dying in approximately 30 more minutes! The Russian mobster yelled, with literally the largest gun in the world aimed at their heads. A 264 pound Kaiser Wilhelm Geschutz, it had 131 feet barrels. One bullet would totally wipe the house off the map!

Boom!

Start of 3rd quarter.

Seattle cannon kicked the ball off! James waited for the kick. He caught it, and took off in a flashing speed!

Boom!

Immediately, they dropped him like a bad habit! Two gunners smashed our return man!

Cool.

I have to stick the nail in the coffin, vampire in Brooklyn style! Baby! Boop! I gave Coach Mackey the thumbs up, then, said a quiet prayer. I zeroed in on the defense, like Superman. Once again, they played man-to-man with my receivers. Their strong safety musta swallowed an elephant sandwich! I knew he wasn't stopping our new tight end, Pop Rutherford.

I scrambled out of the pocket! No one was open! Well, I couldn't see anyone! Two 300 pounders were instantly in my face like pimples!

Boom!

"Ouch." I hit the ground hard, like a jet. I laid there, silent and still. I was hurt. I knew it.

I lost this game, man! I felt bad. Naw, bad wasn't even the word! I felt horrific!

"Get up!" Jayhlen shouted, yanking me up with his strong grip.

"Cool!" I was surprised, I was ok. I stretched and shook it off.

"Ebony!" I yelled when I saw her on the sideline!

Yes! I knew it! She and Destiny had escaped! She was cheering like never before! I changed the play!

"Red! 35 Hut 1 Hut 2 Hut!"

I gave the ball to Jayhlen. No! I faked it and aimed the ball at Donte! Bam! He was wide open on the sideline. He got it! I saw fire blazing out of his shoes! He zoomed across the 30, 40, 50 . . .

"Touch down! Tigers!" The referee said.

"Yeah!" I took off running to the sideline. "Move," I mumbled to the players who tried to congratulate me. I just wanted to hug my wife!

She gave me the extra umph! I grabbed her and picked her up in the air, swinging her around in circles! Man, I was so happy.

She was smiling and laughing like a kid, reminding me of Ari and Minnie on Christmas! When Kiana and Mayor Earl Brown gave the kids their own zoo!

"Boy! You must be happy, to swing Alyssa around in the air like that!" Jayhlen said, laughing.

"What! Alyssa! My bad!" I said, putting her down, and shaking my head.

"Touch down Seattle!"

Man! That was quick. I spun around, and Donte was running in the end zone! Untouched!!

Well, our tight end name Donte scored. So I guess their quarter back, Donte had to score! This game was too crunk! Every time we scored, they scored: "28 to 28."

"I'ma un-wrap you skinny girls' mouth for this. It's the last quarter ladies. Hopefully, the last of yall lives."

"Where is my baby?!" Ebony yelled. She was very weak, hungry, and tired. She had given natural birth, last October. Now it was January.

The second she gave birth to her son, instantly, they took him away. He didn't even have a name! She was in excruciating pain; having her first child, natural.

More pain though, was the fear of dying and dying without ever holding her baby. She cried every day and every night. Ebony cried because the only man she ever loved, couldn't be there to see their first child be born.

No cute pictures and no holding her baby. No laughing at the father's reaction during the birth, no grandmother present or NOTHING!

She loved Cim so much. She didn't know her real father. For 17 years she was lied to. Her mom told her that this other dude was her father.

She never told anyone, he tried to molest her. Ebony ran away. She moved in with Micki when she was 15.

Cimeon's family showed her love. Instantly, Miss Sheppard treated her like she was her real daughter.

Ebony missed her man. Ebony missed her baby. Ebony barely knew Destiny. But she knew it was her fault that Destiny and her son had to suffer.

She even felt like it was her fault that Cimeon was losing the game. It was her fault that Cimeon killed the evil man's son. She felt like it was her fault that he would never complete his childhood dream.

Ebony was a black girl in pain. It was two weeks away from her birthday.

Boom! I fell on my butt! The ground felt like a brick floor! Rah-Rah and Jayhlen picked me up. It was 3 minutes left in the game. We were down by 7, at their 30 yard line.

A field goal would be worthless. We had to score a touch down! This was our last chance. 4th down, and we needed 5 yards.

"Down!"

I grimaced in pain, holding my left shoulder.

"Set! Hike!"

I couldn't throw the ball. So I just underhand tossed it to Jayhlen.

Bam!

Destiny and Ebony's eyes got wider than the Pacific Ocean!

Jayhlen got crushed, immediately! The game would probably be over.

The Russian put the gun in Ebony's mouth.

"This is for my son . . . Pow!" Her heart stopped. Then he laughed and said, "Not yet African American females, 3 more minutes and pow, pow!

I'm either blowing both of yall head's off, or I'm burning the house up, or both!"

Now I was afraid. Now, I felt like dying. I was helpless. I didn't play defense.

If Seattle scored, even a field goal, we were dead. We would be literally dead. I would never again see the love of my life.

Atlanta punted the ball to Seattle. Jackson caught the ball.

"Man! Stupid!" Coach Dunlap yelled.

Then . . . Bam! Dunlap kicked the water cooler out of the water boy's hand!

"What kind of kick was that?!" Coach Mackey complained. The ball only went 20 yards! Chris obviously slipped. We lost!

They were already in field goal range! Oh no! They was about to score! Boom! We tackled him at the 30 yard line!

"Time out!" Coach Purvis shouted, to the side judge.

Both teams ran off the field.

"One play, we need one play to put Atlanta away! Then we kick the field goal. They will be down by 10, with under 3 minutes left. They will be dead and stankin'!" Coach Purvis told his Seattle Bull Dogs.

"Listen, it's 2 minutes and 50 seconds left on the clock. We MUST stop them. Our season is on the line. We win this game. We go back to the Super Bowl in two weeks. And we can straighten our face.

I don't care how it looks. We are winning this game. And we are winning the Super Bowl. We will never give up! Make something happen!" My favorite coach slash brother-in-law, Coach Brown shouted to the team. He was possessed by a Faith Angel!

I really prayed for a miracle. It didn't seem possible though. My wife, baby, and niece are 2 minutes from a bullet.

"Hah hah! I miss my son. I'ma blow your son's head off right in front of your face! Boom! The baby dies first! I loved my son!

Since your stupid, super star husband killed my son, about a dumb necklace. I'ma show you how it feels. Bring that baby!" The Russian shouted, looking like the devil, with red hateful eyes.

"Anny!" The baby cried. He held the baby upside down, by his legs.

"He dies! They lose! He dies, in 2 minutes and 50 seconds!" The Russian yelled, aiming the gun at the beautiful, innocent, crying baby boy.

"No! No! Give me my baby! Leave him alone! Please! Just kill me! Leave my baby alone!" Ebony yelled, struggling to get out of the thick ropes that had her bound to the chair. She was losing it; crying hysterically and cussing at the monster mobster.

"Why are you doing this? You won't get away with this. God will pay you back" Destiny told the man, in tears.

Boom!

Donte got the snap and nailed Malik for a 20 yard pass! The game was over. Touch down Seattle! They was up by 14 with 2 minutes left!

Boom!

Wrong answer! The second Malik caught the ball, Bonner, our line backer, super strong head tackled him! Bonner head knocked the ball loose!

"Get it! Get it!" I shouted. I was jumping up and down on the side lines and running nearly onto the field; as the players all fought for the fumble!

Bam! Bam! Dive! Splash! Smack!

Ten players jumped on top the ball. No one knew who recovered the ball.

"Cross your fingers." Coach Brown said, in a determined hopeful voice.

Everyone was quiet.

Sergio and Deon stood beside me. Jayhlen was sitting down, praying. Rah-Rah had his hands on top of his head. Coach Dunlap had his shirt off, like a cartoon coach! Shawty was mad! Dunlap was always animated! Everyone in the dome of 70,000 people were quiet as a dead mouse.

Both teams left the benches to wait on the call. Radio, Television Stations, Prisoners, Bars, Homes, and every Football Fan in the world were standing by, waiting on the call. The cheer leaders were quiet; some cried.

The line judge and side judge ran on the field, pulling the players off each other. They were looking like a huge human sand castle. Now the last two guys were on the ground: Levi for Seattle and Bonner for Atlanta.

"Atlanta Ball!" Female ref, Meka Mackey shouted.

"Yeah! Yeah! Yeah!" Coach Dunlap jumped in the air, kicking over the coolers! The fans went wild!

I shouted and pointed in the air!

"Yes! Yes! Super Bowl bound! We got a chance!" Sergio yelled in my ear.

"Good. Go! Listen for the call!" Coach Brown yelled, patting me on the back. Oh, I was more than ready. We had a very long way to go: 95 yards to be exact.

My mind was set. The whole play, I was going to Sergio, period. My main target in crunch time, when the money was on the line!

"Down!"

I eyeballed the defense.

"Set!"

Sergio was ready, but Seattle wasn't ready.

"Hut!"

I took the snap, faked the hand off to Jayhlen and threw a deep rocket prayer of a pass down field to a running Sergio!

He ran with his hands out in front of him. He didn't even look back! The corner back ran toe to toe with him.

Boom!

"Yeah! Baby! Wooh!" I shouted. Sergio caught that sucker. The corner back dove on his legs. Sergio ran with the defender: five, six, seven more yards; then hit the ground! 37 yards gain!

First down, I signaled for the players to hurry to the new line of scrimmage. I didn't give Seattle any time to adjust. Both teams only had one time out left, with 2 minutes and 5 seconds left in the game. Atlanta was down by 7. "Can I stop my family from going to heaven?"

I prayed out loud, though no one heard me; no one but God. The entire dome was on their feet shouting, cheering, hoping, pumping!

My new biggest cheer leading fans Lexie and Nu-Nu: the prettiest, coolest sisters on earth, Cobb County cheer leading cuties were shouting like crazy!

"Down!"

I noticed they had two nickel backs in.

"Set!"

I can run this one myself.

"Green! 33!"

"Hut!"

I took the ball, and started to run.

Boom!

The line back nailed me to the ground.

Bam!

I punched the artificial turf. This was an automatic time out.

We were at the two minute warning. We had 12 more yards to go, for a much needed first down.

Ebony and Destiny were shaking in fear, staring at the evil man holding her baby like a toy. The baby wasn't crying anymore. It was as if the tiny toddle didn't have no worries!

However, like a super model walking on glass with no shoes on in 120 degree desert! Ebony and Destiny were worried.

The timeout was over.

I'm on the line of scrimmage in the biggest game of my life, the game to save my child, niece, and wife.

"Down. Set! Hut!"

I was determined. I took off!

"What is he doing?! I told him to throw the pass!" Coach Mackey shouted, hot as Africa in July! The crowd was on their feet! The cheer leaders were jumping and cheering!

I zoomed cross the 50 yard line, too fast! I nearly tripped over my own feet! So what! I ran across that Atlanta Tiger on mid field. As if I could see my wife and niece cheering for me this very second!

Bam!

I slammed the ball on the ground. Then jumped in the air, beating on my chest in the end zone with tears of joy in my eyes, while the dome rocked with uncontrollable cheers.

"Touch down Tigers!"

We were down by one. Chris came out to kick the field goal to tie the score. With 1 minute and 10 seconds to play. 35 to 34 score.

"No! Time out!" Coach Brown yelled, to everyone's surprise. The whole world was shocked! Like electric chair sex! Why did he waist our last time out?

Seattle could score, and we couldn't even stop them! A minute is enough time for a game winning field goal!

"Listen, we are playing for the win! Period! No tie! We are going for the two point conversion. Forget a kick! We lose. We lose. Ride or die! My job is on the line! So score!" Coach Brown shouted, to a pumped up team.

Man, this was a very bold call! Life threatening call! It would be safer to kick the field goal, and tie the game. Chris never misses a crunch time kick.

If we didn't score the touch down, for the two points, it's over! The fat pig and man, will be singing! With a singing grim reaper! I shook off all my doubts. I had to!

I ran to the 2 yard line. This was a hot situation. The two-point conversion was added to the NFL in 1994. It fails about 57% of the time!

"Down!"

We had the momentum! This was still a huge gamble! A ride or die, all on this one play! Let's get it!!!

"Set!!"

"My new born baby is riding on this play! I love my unseen child!!!

"Hike!!"

I yelled then ran sideways looking for an open receiver. Where is Sergio! Nowhere! Nothing! No one was 0pen! Good, boom! I couldn't risk the throw!

Oh God! Man! No!!!

The two fastest line backers in the NFL started chasing me! I was ten yards behind the original line of scrimmage!

No one was even close to help me! I ran backwards like I was in the hood, running from the cops!

"Hah-hah! You dead!" The Russian growled, like a ware wolf on crack!

Ebony's eyes were bigger than the Titanic! Sinking in the ocean!

I had to try! They were coming too fast! I just tossed the ball to the closest player! Praying he would catch it! The throw was too low! It was 40 seconds on the clock!

Bemp!

Jayhlen reached down to his left foot and caught the ball! The football stuck to his hands like glue! He turned around, and immediately saw he had ten yards to run for the game winning touch down.

Bam!

They both hit me hard! I was on my back like a tramp!

Jayhlen, the Seattle born native, danced and tricked the two defenders that faced him. Then he ran up the middle with the speed of light!

He was one yard away from scoring the touch down, when a defensive tackle hit him in both legs! Jayhlen leaped high in the air and stretched the football into the air.

Bam!

The football came loose, in the end zone!

"No! No!"

Jayhlen knee hit the ground!!! Everyone stood still like death . . . Kelly, the head ref, made the call . . .

"Touch down Tigers!"

The crowd went hysterical! I was hype and jumping! Pumping my fist, too excited! Jayhlen saved my life! The owner of the dome ran to hug Jayhlen!

"Good run! Good run son!" Michael Lackey told Jayhlen in exciting joy!

I was too hype and happy! I gave Jayhlen the biggest hug I ever gave another man! "Wooh!" I shouted, as he smiled, with too much happiness.

"36 to 35 Atlanta!"

38 seconds left.

"Yeah! Yeah!" Destiny and Ebony shouted. Like they were cheer leaders in the dome!

Boom! Kick!

"Ouch!" The Russian kicked the table, hurting his huge toe!

Chris, the Muslim and master kicker, launched the ball, Immediately after the referee blew his whistle.

Chris was perfect! He kicked the ball squarely in the lower quarter and got the proper distance! The ball traveled a long 71 yards, hanging in the air for 4.5 seconds!

Hood scooped up the ball, then bam! He tricked our players by back passing the ball to another player!

Sutton caught the lateral pass and took off! Atlanta chased him! 37, 36, 35, 30 . . . 20 . . . 15 seconds left on the clock!

Sutton was still running! Crossing midfield to the 40 yard line!

Boom!

Render brought him down, finally at our 39 yard line! Already, field goal range!

Offensive Coordinator, Coach Hill gave his quarter back the play. 14 seconds left and was down by one.

One shot, then go for the game winning kick! If anyone caught the ball, they would have to immediately run out of bounds to stop the clock.

"Hut!" Donte yelled, then gave Levi the ball! Levi ran toward the side line to go out of bound.

No! Hold up! Levi changed his mind! He saw he had an open shot for the end zone! He took it! Pay back a mother!

25, 20, 15, 10, 5.

"Noooooooooo!" I yelled, dropping to my knees!

Zero time on the clock!

"Touch down Seattle!"

Levi scored the game winning touch down! Killing his old Atlanta team, and killing his friend's wife, baby, and niece! Killing them without even knowing!

Erica was the only laughing cheer leader. "Hah! Hah! Bam! In yo face!" Erica shouted! "0ops! Sorry." She caught herself. She stopped dancing.

Micki sat inside the bar in Stonecrest Mall and cried.

Ebony, Destiny and my baby cried. The Russian limped in pain to grab his gun.

In shock, once again, history repeated itself. Atlanta teams failed the fans. Levi slammed the ball, and laughed at the owner, Michael Lackey, for trading him; pointing at Mikey.

The Seattle cheer leaders, lead by team captain Daja, cheered with joy! The Seattle team cleared the bench and disrespected my city! Running on my field to celebrate. I stood frozen.

Coach Dunlap was pissed. Coach Brown ran towards the refree! For what reason, I didn't know.

Jayhlen held his head down in frustration. He had given his all, as always. Sergio closed his eyes. Deon squeezed his twin sisters hand. Shawn cried, squeezing her brother's hand.

Lexi, Nu-Nu, and the rest of the cheer leaders were in tears. Alyssa shook her head in despair. Coach Mackey was shouting.

"Ok. Say bye bye to your baby!" The Russian said, holding the gun to the baby, one inch away from the mother's face.

Ebony was trembling and crying. Her last moments on earth were her worst, watching her first born baby's head explode in her face. The best way to die would be in your sleep, not like this! Not to suffer. Not to hurt.

I was still on my knees, on the side lines, with my hands folded on top of my head.

The Russian smiled, then committed the horrific sin of murder. The sin Cain committed against his brother Abel.

In the Bible, the first murder recorded on earth (Genesis 4:8).

I repeated Cain's infamous words to God in Genesis 4:9. "Am I my brother's keeper?" I asked God out loud. Knowing I had to protect my helpless beautiful wife, my new born child, and my gorgeous sweet niece.

"I was my brother's keeper; I failed." I mumbled on my knees.

"Time to die!" The Russian barked.

"No! Look!" Destiny shouted.

The Russian turned towards the 70 inch TV; holding the baby upside down in one hand, and the pistol in the other.

The referee was blowing the whistle to silence Seattle's celebration. Two officials were pointing at a yellow penalty flag that was on the field. Identifying and marking the exact location of the penalty.

The yellow flag was wrapped around a weight of sand. As usual, to be accurately thrown great distances. I have never in my life been so happy to see the yellow flag!

The yellow flags were first colored white! Until 1965, when they turned yellow! Thank God for Mellow Yellow!

I stood on my feet.

"Micki! Micki! Look!" Kishana yelled in her crying big sister's ear, at the bar, in Lithonia.

"What?" Micki answered, as Kishana pointed at the TV above the bartender's head.

The ref spoke: "There were two files on the play. Chop block number 52, offense, 15 yard penalty. Unsportsmanlike conduct number 23 . . . offense. 15 yard penalty. That's 30 yards on the penalties. 2 seconds will be added on the clock. Repeat first down."

The entire dome stood and cheered!

"Get up! Get up!" Jayhlen and Sergio yelled in my ear, picking me up in the air! You shoulda seen the expression on Levi's face. A fan stuck his tongue out at Levi.

Now! ATL was crunk! 2 seconds was nothing!

"Yeah! Owner of the Dome! Boi!" Michael Lackey shouted, in his super County voice!

"Hah! Hah! There is a God!" Coach Brown shouted

"Thank You Jesus!" Coach Mackey shouted.

"Hallelujah!" Apostle Hannah Sheppard shouted, in tears of joy!

The Atlanta Tigers took the field with swag! Up by one little point, with 2 little seconds left!

Back to the Super Bowl.

Donte called the play. One last desperate throw!

Atlanta used 7 players in pass coverage. We played the prevent defense. They would not do a desperation, Hail Mary play on us!

Donte tried the Hail Mary last second, touch-down play! He scrambled and ran from Atlanta defenders. Can Donte do it?! The crowd was on their feet.

Bam!

Bonner ended the game with a thundering, Georgia Dome shouting, quarter back sack! "Wooh!" I cheered, pumping my fist.

"Atlanta wins! Atlanta wins! Back to the Super Bowl!!!" Ms. Pettis and the worldwide announcers shouted!

Boy, the words in a dictionary or even Google, couldn't describe the size of my smile! Or the excitement I felt! We were right back in the Super Bowl!

Splash!

"Man! Yall got me!" I laughed, in my Tigers T-shirt. Sergio and Jayhlen dumped a cooler of Gatorade on me!

"Yaaay! We live! We live! Losing is the easy part!" Destiny taunted their abductor!

Ebony had the biggest Kool-Aid smile on earth! She knew her man would come through!

No doubt!

"Yeah. Your king is a winner and a competitor. Losing on purpose won't be easy for the American. It ain't in his blood to lose. Plus your team is so good. If he lose, it will be obvious . . . So, let's see how good your winner is, at losing! Hah-hah!

Then, I might kill you anyway!" The abductor said, laughing like the devil!

I skipped all the champagne and parties, in the party capital of the world, Atlanta, Georgia, aka ATL.

I needed this week of rest, and prayer. Also needed a full week of preparation for the Super Bowl.

Ebony's birthday was Super Bowl Sunday . . . .

I prayed and read my Bible with my mom and two sisters.

The Last Dance

Super Bowl Sunday, 6:30pm on Feb. 8, 2017. It's kick off time. I'm as ready as I ever been in my life . . . to lose! Hah, hah. Not funny. This is weird. Plus harder than I thought. I was in the tunnel, standing next to Sergio. He wanted to win this very bad. I could see the fire in Sergio's eyes.

Then I looked at Coach Brown. He felt like winning this Super Bowl would be his biggest accomplishment. Of course, he figured it would give his hot head pretty young wife, some extra bragging rights! I can hear Micki now. My brother and my husband won the Super Bowl. At the same dang time! Boop! Then I looked at the rookie Rah-Rah. I knew this would be special to him. For a rookie to win in his first year. I looked at the owner, Michael Lackey who sacrificed so much, putting this team together.

He took a lot of negative heat, even death threats, for trading Levi. Levi is a Zone 6, Atlanta born thorough bread. He's also a fan favorite, that was traded for the younger and quicker Jayhlen and Rah-Rah.

I thought about the little kid in the tunnel that ran up on me. "Hey! Cim! Please win the Stuper Blowl. For me"

"Awwee." I smiled at the beautiful little girl name Jada. She touched my heart. She couldn't even say Super Bowl. lol (lol mean laugh out loud.) I had to lose this game on purpose. Atlanta will be so hurt, if we really coulda won the Super Bowl.

Finally, every city needs a good story. I could almost bet my life on it! I could feel it in my stomach. Either way, it won't be good. I took a deep swallow, and thought about all these Atlanta kids.

Kids I drove pass at Grant Park, Crim High School, Columbia High, Washington High, Harper Archer High and Cedar Grove with Kishana my super star baby sister.

I had to lose this game on purpose; hurting the hope of all those little kids and my fans.

Boom!

The cannon sounded off!

We ran out of the tunnel, behind Porsche and the cheer leaders.

Everything was a flashing repeat of last year. Except this Super Bowl was played in Seattle, Washington, a Beautiful City!

"Head or tale?" The referee announced.

I couldn't look my teammates in their eyes.

"Tale!" Jayhlen shouted, anxious to take control of another Super Bowl decision. Sergio swung his head from left to right and started bouncing on his toes.

"Head!" The reff yelled.

"Yeah!" Keith, the Portland Dolphins quarter back shouted.

I watched Chris super kick off the Super Bowl Kick!

Out of nowhere: "Somebody told me to give you this," Alyssa said, handing me something so tiny I couldn't see it. She had it inside her pretty small fist.

"Huh?" She secretly put the device in my hand; shrugged her shoulders, and walked off.

I held it up and stared at it. What is this? Bam! That's when it hit me like a paralyzing tackle! The Russian was here or he had football connections! How else would Alyssa get this ear device?

This is a NFL quarter back ear piece. It fits perfectly inside my helmet! However, this device was newer and more advanced. I snapped it in my left ear.

"Hi Mr. Football, you make sure you lose this game. And I will drop your wife, baby and niece out of a helicopter, Alive! So catch the one you love the most! Hah-hah. Forget the baby. Your wife is gorgeous! Catch her, and yall can make another baby tonight! Hah-hah. I'll be pushing them out; one by one, oldest to youngest. They will land on top of the dome, immediately after the game. Don't worry, I do have the decency to use a parachute, for one of them! Hah-hah.

I told your pretty model niece, Destiny, she was just out of luck!" The evil Russian said in the ear device.

Snap!

I snatched it out. I didn't want to hear that non sense! If he was going to kill them anyway; I might as well win! Atlanta have been wanting this, for too long! I put on for my city!

Number 22 for Portland picked up the Super Bowl Kick! He was gone! No—where! Fast! Bam! We hit him RIGHT when he picked up the ball!

Then, he was hurt! Automatic time out, off the top! The Tigers wasn't playing today! Cooper, our new cornerback, bee stung tackled him! The medical cart rolled on the field. This was a devastating lost for Portland! Cause Petterson was the number one return man, in football! Oh well, pop goes the weasel!

"My boy hit hard!" Titiana, the new pretty cheer leader, shouted.

"I know! Hit em hard cuz!" Shay-Shay yelled, cheering after doing a new dance video with Bre'Shuana and Weezy.

Cooper and the Portland Dolphins ran on the field, like they were really ready! lol

The Atlanta Tigers ran on the field like they KNEW they were ready! The crowd in Seattle was maybe split: Half Portland, half ATL; well, more ATL! They were loud! Plus President Harold Purvis the 3rd was here with the first lady. All the rappers alive were present! Every actor in Hollywood was here! Country and Rock Stars were present! The King of the South was sitting right behind our bench. All the Hall of Fame players were in the house!

Time to show out! Keith

Cooper eyeballed the meanest, toughest, hungriest defense on earth! He looked nervous. However, he was ready.

"Down! Hike 1 Hike 2 Hike!"
He took the snap. Boom!
Our defensive end, Tiquavious, hit the quarter back soo hard, the number came off the back of his jersey!
"Yeah! ATL!" Shay, Titiana, Erica, Kenyatta, Lexi, Nu-Nu and all 40 of the stunning Atlanta Top Model cheer leaders cheered!
"2 and 15" The referee announced.
Fat Daddy's hard hitting tackle, made them lose 5 yards! Another sack!
Two players helped Cooper up. He shook it off. The Tiger girls were cheering! Everyone was cheering except my wife!
Well, she was probably somewhere cheering for the first time, for the other team!
"Score! Sore!" Ebony and Destiny yelled; as the baby cried.
The baby probably cheered in baby language!
"Shut up!" The rude Russian shouted.
Cooper ran from left to right, pointing at his tight end. He drew back three times to make the throw.
"Forget it!" Keith blew Africa a kiss and took off running like a train was behind him! He crossed the 20, 25, 30 . . . Bam! D.J. pulled him down by his shoulders!
Now, the Portland fans showed up! They were standing, talking trash and cheering.
It didn't matter to me. However, I still caught myself cheering for Atlanta!
Keith was breathing harder than a boxer in the 12th round. However, he was in a zone and feeling it. He took a deep breath . . .
"Down!"
Beeeeep! Whistle blew.
"False start, number 19. 5 yard penalty. Repeat 1st down." The line judge said, then ran to the side lines.
Number 19 cussed at himself for making a rookie mistake. Keith didn't know, he was playing a game to save the lives of 3 innocent people: A loving couple, a new born baby and a top model niece!

"Down! Set!
Hike!"

Cooper back pedaled 5 yards then under hand tossed the ball to Neal. Neal took off! Two Tigers grabbed the powerful running back's leg, dragging him down! His left hand hit the ground, but he bounced back up. He kicked his right leg! Then he broke the tackle! Neal was gone! 35, 40, 45, 50, Boom!

Taylor drugged him down by his legs. Yes! No! Oh!

The ball came lose before Neal hit the ground. Taylor knocked the ball out of his hand!

Tiquavious scooped the ball up and took off like 2013! He was gone! The crowd in Seattle, went 2wild! I was jumping up and down cheering so hard, I didn't notice.

"You dropped something." Jayhlen said, handing me that stupid device. I nodded my head, in a frown. The Atlanta team bench was in a cheering up roar!

I placed the device in my ear.

"Baby! Baby! Please! Do something! You can't let Atlanta win, please! He has a knife to our baby's throat!" Ebony cried. I felt the worse pain ever. I cussed at the air then put the ear piece in my socks . . . No!

"Cimeon Riley, listen, rule number one; keep that ear piece or the deal is off! They die! I'll cut this pretty brown baby into pieces. Then drop him off in the middle of the dome!

However, your team is too good! Hah-hah. Even if you do nothing; your defense can win this game without you!" The devil laughed, then the device went mute.

"Yeah baby! You see me? I'm up in here! We bringing the trophy to the A!" Taylor shouted in my ear.

I faked a smile. "Good go! You made the first tackle in the Super Bowl, Bio!" I shouted at Taylor. Now Cooper was extra excited!

"I know! The first tackle of the Super Bowl! Plus, the hardest tackle of the game! Wooh!" Taylor shouted, then pointed his fingers at the cheer leaders.

The ATL Tigers kicked the ball off, once again! A new, rookie tried to return the kick. Not good! Bam! They smashed him at the 15 yard line!

"Go get em!" Coach Dunlap shouted, patting Taylor and Render on their backs. "Make em eat dirt! Big Ben!" Sergio yelled.

Our defense jogged back on field. The big boys have to be tired, Keith thought to himself.

"Down!"

Someone was out of place! Free play!

"Set! Hike!"

Keith quickly took the snap and threw the ball with all of his might! D.J. and Vick were side by side, in the middle of the field!

The entire world watched the football float high in the air like a rainbow. Then it fell! Bam! Right into D.J.'s hand! D.J. flew all the way back, like a Mac!

45, 40, 35, 30

"Touch Down!"

Beep. Beep. Whistle, the reff blew the whistle. The yellow flag had already been thrown.

"Before the play, off sides defense, number 59—Portland ball 1st and 5." The reff announced.

"God!" Ebony yelled. She almost had a heart attack! When she saw D.J. Mac flying down field, untouched! Scoring that touch down.

"Thank God." Destiny said, praying. She was happy that the play was ruled dead.

Portland got the ball on their own 25 yard line. Keith glanced at the 3-4 defense. He knew Evans could burn their strong safety.

"Down . . . Set . . . Red . . . 55!

Hut!"

Keith took the snap from Jones. Eyeballed his running back, Neal, who ran a slant.

Bam!

Keith nailed Evans for a 10 yard gain.

The teams ran to the new line of SCRIMMAGE.

"Down! Set! Hike!"

Quickly, Keith zipped the ball 10 more yards to Evans then ran back to the line. He was killing Atlanta, with the no huddle offense! He didn't give Atlanta enough time to adjust. Keith was a very smart vet. Evans was a big, strong, fast receiver at 6 feet 5 inches. Evans beat the man to man coverage, fighting off D.J.; knocking him to the ground!

Bam!

Evans caught another pass! Keith rocket launched a 40 yard streak pass! Evans caught the pass on the side line; with no one to beat, but his feet!

"Touch down. Portland!"

Franklin kicked the extra point, straight down the middle!

"7 to 7"

"Uh oh." I mumbled, nervously.

My turn to mess up on purpose. This was something very new to me. I hate to lose. All I do is win! My entire life, I've been a winner, a fighter, and a competitor. It's hard for me to just purposely lose. Seattle power kicked the football. Deon took the ball off the ground and ran like a horse!

I just squinted my eyes! Atlanta was on a mission; cause Deon was gone!

40, 30, 25, 20 . . .

"Touch down, Atlanta!"

The crowd erupted with cheers!

"Yeah! You see our bro!" Serio yelled, shaking me in joy.

"Yeah! Atlanta ain't going out bad this year!" Coach Brown shouted.

"Go Tigers!" Kiki shouted in the bar.

Chris nailed the perfect kick.

"14 to 7, Atlanta."

I was scratching my head: in my head, or should I say, in my mind? What on earth? I ain't never seen a Super Bowl like this; where the quarter back goes the entire first quarter without touching the ball! Yet, we still got the lead! Plus 14 points!

The second quarter would started after the break. The Atlanta crowd was outrageous!

"Yea! Blowing money; stay clean. Michael Jackson Billy Jean!" Deon rapped in my ear, laughing. I faked a smile.

"Ok, wezzy future. Wooh!" I shouted.

"Listen, we winning. We ain't toe sucking around! Defense! Pen them to the ground!!! Taylor, go break some bones!" Coach, Shawty Dunlap barked at his mean Atlanta defense.

Atlanta kicked the ball off!

Bam!

The ball soared like a bald eagle, smack in front of the rookie's leg. Moody scooped up the ball and ran, straight up the middle, stopping them, faking out two defenders. Pushing one to the ground. Then! He turned up his speed like a jet! Five people were chasing him! No one was even close! He left them like a race car against 11 Cadillacs! Portland fans were on their feet!

"Touch Down Portland!"

Moody spiked the ball in the ground; snatched off his helmet, and did the old dirty bird! Rubbing his bald head.

"14 to 14"

"Lord, not the kind of game we need." I mumbled.

"Ok, Cim, you just might be able to take the field. Take a shot down field on the first play. They will never expect it!" Coach Brown told me; standing next to Coach Mackey. He fully agreed. This was a perfect game plan.

Portland kicked off the ball.

Boom!

Deon, once again picked up the ball. However, this time he tripped, slipped and fell! Wham! The ball came loose! There was a tussle over the ball. Number 25 for Portland picked it up . . .

"Touch down!"

"Wow." Is all I could say. What a fast, zipping game. I have yet to . . .

"Cim, you ok? Hah-hah, I know you ain't tired. You ain't even got in the game." Alyssa joked, handing me an ice cold cup of H2O.

I smiled at the cute, pro trainer.

"True, I might as well join you." I replied.

"Hah—hah, I know that's right." She joked.

We laughed. I actually felt better, going into the game from behind. At least now, I could do me. I can score, and just tie the game; make it look good.

"21 to 14—Portland" April announced, wavering her silky hair out of her face.

"What a game; lest see what the ATL does!" April added.

Portland kicked the ball off again, to Atlanta.

Boom!

Deon was hurt! They rolled him away! Not good at all, even for me! Now, I may lose any way!

Heck, without Deon I will struggle even to tie the game. Plus, Deon is my people. I was hurting even more.

Our back up, 3rd string rookie, Danny Lyons, aka Bald Head, was back; ready to return the kick.

He awaited the long, 75 yard kick. Then . . . he stumbled. He fell, catching himself with his hands. Rookie mistake! The entire Dolphin team was on D. Lyons like fleas. Boom! Boom! The entire team tackled the ATL native, Bald Head!

Kah Boom!

Knocking his helmet off! Bald Head flew backward! 5 Yards! Butt! He didn't

hit the ground! He landed on his powerful right hand! Bald Head stood back up, then sprinted like a flash! The boy was gone!

All you could see was a greasy, skinny, round Head! Danny Lyons AKA Bald Head was gone!

"Touch down Atlanta! What an awesome, unbelievable Super Bowl!!!"

Miss Pettis the cute Decatur girl was really into the game!

Heck the whole world enjoyed this game! It was unbelieveable!

"21 to 21 Half Time."

I scratched my head, as we went to the locker room. Huh? Someone patted me on the back. The Russian!

"Nice game my friend, but lose. I got a ten million dollars bet on this game! If you let your stupid, dumb, talented teammates win this game; I'ma kill your family ten times!"

Bam!

"Cim! Cim! Wake up!"

I was drolling and swinging! Then, I noticed it was Halle Berry's twin!

"Calm down. You were lying in the tunnel with a bloody nose. However, Doctor Holloway said you are fine." Alyssa said, smiling.

The Russian came up on me, dressed like a player! He had on a uniform! What number was it? I couldn't remember. Boy! He was slick as ice!

I do remember. He knocked me out! Caught me off guard man . . . Won't happen again!

The crowd went crazy, the second Bre' Shauna hit the first note!

"If I . . . Should stay . . . I would only . . . be in your way . . . And I . . . e . . . I . . . will Always Love You . . ."

Bre'Shauna was the only one on earth, who could duplicate Whitney's song! The entire world was standing, rocking, attempting to sing along. Bre' Shauna ate the song! Bre ate that song up, up, up, up!

Boom!

Then smoke appeared and the entire dome became dark! What was happening?! Something went wrong! Everyone was quiet. Even the air was still and dry. Someone had sucked the air out of the building! But who . . .

Flash!

Then, suddenly, the lights flashed back on. 40 of the baddest, finest dancers on earth hit the stage! Lead by Saniya Brown, the cheer leaders all danced to 'Billy Jean' then they danced to Chris Brown's 'Transformers.'

Saniya did the robot, then slid straight across the stage!

The Tiger cheer leaders all hit backward flips then dove in the swimming pool. Splash!

Then Bre'Shauna came back on stage Bang! Kicking through a life size, 6 feet high, ice cube. Bre'Shauna did every dance known to mankind plus some new dances! Decatur was surely in the house! The wet cheerleaders joined the dance!

Even the president and Governor Lawrence were dancing! The crowd was full of laughter and hype. Then Bre'Shauna moon walked off the stage; smiling, singing like an Illinois angel, and waving at the crowd!

The Russian paced his crystal clear floors in his 10 bed room mansion.

Ebony and Destiny were nailed to the wall; not in their skins, the nails were in their clothes. Their hands were down by their sides and tied. All the girls could do, was watch the 70 inch TV.

There was a time bomb sitting on top of the TV. The second the Super Bowl ended, the bomb would explode! The Russian would collect his 20 million and disappear to Moscow, without a trace!

The gamble continued to go up with the mob members.

"Double it! 40 million!" The Chinese yelled.

"80 million!" The confident Russian said. He was sure Cim would find a way to lose this game.

Maybe Cim would throw a last second interception on purpose. Who knows?!

He didn't care if Cimeon ran a touch down back himself, in the wrong end zone! He just needed to lose! Because just as sure as the ocean is deep, the second he cut that TV off, the family was dying! The TV automatically would cut off, ten minutes after the game! He planned on blowing everybody up, and taking Ebony for himself; maybe Destiny too!

"Yeah! Yeah! Yeah!"

The Tigers yelled, running back on the field to finish the game. The start of the 3rd quarter was on!

"Atlanta has to win," Kiana told her husband, the Mayor of Atlanta, Earl Brown.

"They will!" Their son, Malachi, shouted.

"Hi, this is Miss Pettis from ESPN. I'm here with Cimeon Riley and last year's Super Bowl winning Coach, J Mackey. So Cim, strange game, huh? You have yet to even touch the field." She smiled, then held the microphone toward Cim.

Cim smiled and took a deep breath then spoke.

"Well, very strange game. That's for sure. But I commend my teammates on one of the greatest, entertaining Super Bowls ever. We are still a team, and we will win as a team."

After Cim said all the right things, Miss Pettis spoke to Coach Mackey.

"Coach Mackey, you're here again., hopefully; to win. What's the status on Deon Riley?" Miss Pettis asked, looking concerned.

He shrugged his shoulders.

"Well, unfortunately, Deon won't be returning. But we have a team filled with competitors. We will win." Coach Mackey said, then jogged away with Cimeon to start the 3rd quarter.

Boom!

The kick soared high into the air. Danny Lyons stretched and waited. He scooped up the ball, running behind Bonner; holding the back of his jersey. Boom!

Bonner made a ground eating, big man block, shooting Portland's gunner dead on his back.

Once Bonner made that block, that's all Bald Head needed to make a name for himself! The rookie was now flying straight up the middle of the field!

His first time ever playing in a game! He was shinning; Super Bowl shinning, where it counts!

"Go! Go! Go boy! Go!" Coach Brown ran and yelled, running down the side line like he was blocking!

"Touch down! Tigers!"

The world went wild!

"That's my baby!" Miss Jeanette shouted.

"Yes, that's my son!" Jamaican Earl added, cheering with his wife, in the end zone seats. Proud that their son had come in the game and scored TWO quick touch downs!

Danny Lyons, aka Bald Head, instantly went from an unknown, to a Super Star in 20 seconds!

"Wooh!" Bald Head shouted.

Bald Head leaped up and dunked the football, ten feet! Hold up! Bald Head stopped, looked at the ground, pointed at his son 'Steve' and started dancing! Doing the bird!

Aunt Velma went crazy, laughing and cheering! "We made it from the bottom, now we are here!" His Aunt Velma shouted.

"Oh God!" Ebony cried.

"Shut up! I'ma kill you twice, if these Atlanta idiots win this game!!!" The Russian Roared!

"Man. Wow. What kind of game is this? Alyssa I swear I'ma go to your home town in Seattle, and swim!" I joked with my pretty trainer. She smiled and gave me a high five.

"Hah-hah, you will get to play." Alyssa told me.

Actually, I don't know if I wanted to play or if I could play! I was rusty!

"28 to 21—Atlanta." Miss Pettis and the world announced.

I couldn't believe this game!

"Hey buddy, do we even need a quarter back?!" Coach Dunlap joked.

I didn't even attempt to smile. I just looked down at the short little, big mouth coach. Boy, I was getting mad!

Atlanta kicked off the ball! Portland waited . . .

Portland's rookie got the ball . . . He was gone too!

"Battle of the rookies!" Miss Pettis yelled.

"Touch down Portland!"

Not! Devin 2 Fine Boyd ran on the field in her skin tight white pants. Looking sexier than a stripper in a swim suit outfit! The other 6 referees had on black pants. Devin had on white, because she was the Head Ref.

"Illegal low block. Number 35 recieving team. 15 yard penalty. Ball on the spot of the foul." Devin announced. "Touch down no good! Punks!" Couch Brown yelled as the crowd cheered. Portland got the ball at their own 5 yard line. BAM! Burke County immediately turkey stuffed tackled the quarterback. Bam! Render super crushed the quarterback. Boom! Howard rammed Cooper inside the ground like an ant!

"28 to 21."

We forced Portland to kick the ball off. Once again, Danny did his thing. He picked up the flipping, turning, rolling ball. Danny was gone! Boom! Nowhere! He got crushed at the 20 yard line.

"Finally! Go Get em boy!" Alyssa shouted. I hugged her! Almost! Wait, this ain't Ebony! I caught myself. She laughed.

"Come on Cim! Deon is gone. We got to do this!" Sergio yelled, almost pulling me on the field.

I looked weird. I felt weird. It was almost like playing football on the moon! Was I in Seattle or Pluto? Let me see.

"Come on baby! Let's buss these suckers!" My offensive blocker, Tucker shouted.

I looked at my dark, mean, cool teammate.

I gave him that look. Quickly, I stared at the cheer leaders. No wifey. No sisters. No Glory!

I want it. I felt the crowd. I felt the vibe and the atmosphere. Everyone was silent and wondering how would I react.

Ebony eyes got bigger than a football! To actually cheer against her husband was hard. Forget it!

"Go Cim!" Ebony shouted.

"Huh?" Destiny said, shocked; looking at Ebony like she was crazy.

"Forget it! If I die; I die! I'm not cheering against my man! No way! His entire life, as a kid when he was 5 years old in kindergartner; his dream, watching the Atlanta Falcons, playing on the playground was to win the Super Bowl. Cimeon's dream was always to win the Super Bowl for Atlanta.

Our city never won it! Our parents, our families, our friends want this too bad.

When my baby lost the Super Bowl last year, it took a lot out of him. I was there by his side. It was like all the air just disappeared out of his body.

I love that man, that's my heart. To live is him, we are one. I want him to win! Even if it means I have to die. You have to die for something! I'm dying for my man! My life belongs to God! Not you! Win! Win! Cim! I'm cheering for you! Ride or die, baby!" Ebony shouted.

The Russian was shocked. He looked at her and shook his head. Then walked away cussing.

Destiny exhaled . . .

"Well, I guess you got a point. We might die anyway." Destiny added, with tears in her eyes as she watched Uncle Cim with the football. She looked at the pretty baby with no name. The baby that would die, never knowing what life was like, to live. An innocent baby that will die, before his famous father ever saw him; Cim's first born. He was Cim's first born son.

A first born son, was even important in the Bible. He would automatically become king.

Cimeon would never get to see this pretty baby; his pretty baby with no name. Destiny looked at the baby. He was so happy.

"Cah—cah." The bay looked at Destiny and laughed. He didn't have one care in the world.

"Go! Go!"

Destiny quickly looked back at Ebony. She was a real cheer leader! A cheer leader by nature! She was in her zone cheering for her man!

Bam!

"That idiot! What is he doing?" The Russian shouted.

I took the snap then rolled to my left. I aimed the ball at Steve. Then I pointed at Sergio.

Wham!

I pushed a 300 pounder out of my way. Bam! He hit the ground like fish meat. I was going fast backwards. Two line backers flew at me!

Wham! Wham!

I quickly stepped out of the way. Not only did they miss me; they hit each other! I took off! I ran. Man, I ran! No one had yet to go up by more than two scores.

I love my wife and child, boy or girl. But I was winning this game for the world!

50, 45, 40

I looked backed . . . No! I thought about it, but continued to look forward and run down the middle of the field!

Ain't no looking back! We made it too far to go out bad, Atlanta!

ATL! We here! Home of M.L.K., I'ma represent!

"Touch down! Atlanta!"

"Yeah! Yeah! Yeah!" Micki and Kiki shouted.

Bang!

Micki was so happy and crunk; she knocked her steak on the ground!

Zzzz. The steak even cheered! The well done steak was still sizzling!

Blazing hot! But not as hot as Micki!!

"Told yall! Told yall haters my brother would shine!

We ain't going out bad! Peace up! A-Town down baby!" Micki shouted.

Wham!

Micki jumped on top of the bar table, cheering! 90 percent of the East Atlanta Bar at Stonecrest, was cheering! Kiki was smiling too hard.

"And yall thought my brother was nervous! Never that!" Kishana yelled, to the Atlanta doubters!

I ran straight to the crowd, then leaped up and tossed little Jada the football. Her Aunty Jasmine smiled and cheered.

"We up through there!!!" I yelled.

"35 to 21 Atlanta." Ms. Pettis shouted, super hyper. "What an unbelievable way to answer! For all those, watching worldwide and wondering how Cim would react. Now you know! He showed out!!!" Miss Pettis shouted as she commentated the national Super Bowl game.

"Yu wah!" I jumped in the air and gave Sergio a high five!

"ATL Shawty!" Sergio yelled, laughing in the air.

I was fueled up. I was gassed up to the max! Like a Navy Battle Ship!

I was on one!

Wham!

Chris kicked off the ball. Portland took off.

Bam!

Nothing! Atlanta had the crowd and the momentum. Keith winked his eye. He knew what he had to do, something big!

"Down! Blue 22! Set! Hike!"

Portland was running the run-and-shoot offense.

Keith had the ball, standing in the pocket. He had 4 receivers to choose from.

Bam!

He nailed Lou for 20 deep yards!

Boom!

D.J. pulled him down. Portland rushed to the line. A no huddle!

"Down. Set! Hike!"

Keith got the ball. Bam! He hit his running back, Neal, for 5 yards! Neal flew! 10, 15, 20 yards, Bonner yanked him down!

"Down . . . Set . . . Hike!"

Keith took the ball; faked the hand off to Neal, then aimed down field. He threw it! Zack was running toe to toe with Grant . . .

Bam!

Grant caught it and it was a foot race!

"Touch down! Portland! 35 to 28." Miss Pettis cheered and announced. "What a game. Let's not count Portland out yet." Miss Pettis added, to the television world.

End of the 3rd Quarter. Now . . . It was the 4th and Final Quarter . . . for Ebony, Destiny and the baby to live.

It didn't seem like Cim was losing. He looked zoned out, like a Football Zombie.

Ebony thought to herself, when the camera zoomed in on Cim. Ebony knew her man. She knew that look. He had on his game face. The same look he had when he made Columbia High School win the State Championship. The same look he had when he made Georgia Tech win the National Championship. Cimeon wanted to win the World Championship.

Portland kicked off the ball. The last quarter had begun! Lyons scooped up the ball! He ran 15, 20, 25, 30, Boom! Tackled at the 35 yard line.

"I'm ready!" I yelled, as we jogged on the field.

One more touch down would kill them. I got to win. I just have to win. I don't know how to lose. Boom!

Franklin hit me Hard! I was slipping. I lost the ball! I felt everywhere. I tried everything I could, to get the ball.

Franklin beat me to the ball! I was on my knees trying to get it! Franklin landed on top of it!

"That's my uncle!" Franklin yelled from the stands. She was too hype. Her gold teeth gleaming, brown smooth skin as silk. The pretty girl was jumping for joy! Miss Franklin sipped her $20,000 champagne, then continued to watch the game.

"They still gone lose." Kiana said, with a whatever facial expression.

"Hah, hah. We will see about that." Franklin replied.

Portland's offense ran back on the field.

"Score!" The Russian shouted.

"Score, Portland! I want to live!" Destiny shouted.

"That's right! Top Model!" The Russian said, smiling at Destiny.

Ebony just shook her head. She knew they were dying regardless. She stared at the bomb, then the baby. Then she stared at the TV. She would rather die, seeing her husband fulfill his dreams, winning; than to die seeing him lose.

That would make him lose twice! Ebony would rather die seeing her man make history, and see Cimeon bring joy to the city.

Cooper got the snap, then tossed it to Evans . . . Evans tossed it back to Cooper. Cooper slung it down field.

"Touch down!"

Franklin caught it; leaping over a fighting D.J.Mac, in the end zone. Franklin ran out of bounds.

"What?! Here lil sister! We up in here!" Franklin bragged, tossing his sister the scoring touch down. Franklin looked at Kiana and laughed.

"My brother and uncle bad! Tie game!" She yelled in Kiana's face.

"Whateva! Ties are made to be broken!" Kiana yelled back, smiling.

"35 to 35, world: we got ourselves a show!" Miss Pettis shouted into the microphone.

Whap!

Ms. Pettis gave Matt Ryan a high five.

"Atlanta still looks good." Ryan added, as they sat behind the table.

Portland kicked off the ball. It skipped into the end zone. Danny tried to pick it up. He fumbled it! So he took the knee.

"End this shoot out." Coach Brown said as serious as a lion on a piece of meat.

I read their defense. A 3-4 blitz. I got em! I said to myself.

"Down . . . Green . . . 44! Hike!"

I tossed the ball to Jayhlen. Jayhlen was happy to touch the ball!

Bam! Bam! Bam!

He lowered his shoulders and knocked three big guys on the ground! For a rough 5 yards.

I grimaced and walked to the line. It was 2nd down and 5. We were in a shotgun formation. Meaning the defense wouldn't even attempt to touch me. They knew I would pass the ball.

Not!

I took off! 5, 10, 15, 20 yards then ran out of bounds. Now I was in my kill zone.

My family was completely blocked out of my mind. Once I get in my zone, it's nothing else on my mind.

The center snapped the ball, chest high 7 yards. I took the snap then nailed Sergio. Sergio faked out two players then ran mid field.

Boom!

20 yard gain, and they hit him; knocking him out of bounds. I came to the line.

I could see the end zone. I glanced at the score board; 7 minutes left in a tie game. I've waited my entire life to win this game.

"Down!"

I really want to win.

"Set!"

But I want to see my baby.

"Hike 1"

Kill zone.

Hut!"

I took the ball and tossed it to Jayhlen. Boom!

They hit him immediately! Franklin knocked the ball lose! The ball was getting kicked around by D.J. and Tumlin.

Tumlin, aka Westside, scooped the ball up! He ran, ran, and ran!

I dove at the short, fast defender . . . Boom! Knocking him out of bounds.

"Yes!" Ebony cheered.

The Russian looked at her crazy. They cheered at the same time.

"Who side you on?" Destiny asked her.

"Both sides." Ebony said, confused with her own answer.

"Oh, it must be two sides!" Destiny yelled.

Portland was already in field goal range, at the 39 yard line. Man, Franklin was tough on both ends!

"Now what?" Miss Franklin asked Kiana, smiling and clapping, knowing Portland would score.

"We will see". Kiana replied.

Keith eyeballed the Tiger Defense.

"Go for the touch down! Disregard a field goal! Put them away!" Coach Hood yelled. Keith took the snap then tossed it to Alfred.

"Go Ooh Wee! Go!" Alfred's family cheered, hoping that Ooh Wee, Aka Alfred, would score . . . He did.

"Touch down Portland!"

Alfred did a crazy, Ooh Wee, Hot dog dance! Now, I was nervous. I could easily lose the game. If I threw an interception on purpose; it's over. 6 minutes to play.

Portland kicked off the ball, up 42 to 35.

Danny scooped the ball up. Bam! This time he got nowhere fast! Roscoe smacked him. "Oh no! The ball came lose!" Coach Dunlap yelled.

"Man!!!" Coach Brown hollered!

Bang! Coach Brown kicked the bench, hurting his right toe. He was too mad to feel it.

Portland recovered the ball, at the ten yard line!

"Dummy! Dummies! Nut cases! Idiots! Fools!" Coach Dunlap, aka Shawty, shouted!

He was so mad, Shawty got naked!

"Coach, what are you doing?" Alyssa asked, laughing.

"No! No! No! We lose this game, I don't want no clothes or a job! It's over!!!" Coach Dunlap, aka Shawty, shouted; standing on top of the bench with no clothes and a clip board!

"Get the naked coach!" Butler, the 7 feet tall and 375 pounds officer, shouted.

"Coach Naked, you have to leave!" Officer Johnson said, as they handcuffed the short angry, butt naked coach.

"Cover him! Kids are out here!" Officer Paige shouted.

Alyssa tossed him the towel.

I just smiled. I knew the game was over now. It was nothing nobody could do. Great! I didn't even have to try to lose. I laughed.

"Cim!"

"Huh?"

"Why you laughing man? We done lost again!" Sergio yelled.

Then, Bam, he punched me. I leaned to the right then rubbed my chin. He was standing up, and I was sitting.

Sergio had lost his football mind! Boom! Bang! I tackled him, legs first. Then I got on top of him and knocked the football sense out of my best friend!

"Stop!" Jayhlen yelled.

I froze, surprised that the new comer saw this. I was embarrassed. Why did I allow myself to fight? Jayhlen and Rah-Rah pulled me up.

"You good?" I asked Sergio.

He looked at me like Satan, mixed with a pet bull.

"No! We lost!" Sergio yelled, then walked off.

No one saw the fight. Everyone was staring, stuck and stunned! The fight was too quick! The pain was too hard!

"Hah—hah, Portland won!" Miss Franklin bragged to the Mayor of Atlanta's wife, Kiana Brown.

"Not yet dear. Not yet, it ain't over, till it's over." Kiana replied.

"Hah-hah," Franklin laughed and slugged her wine down her throat!

"It's good. We will burn the clock, trying one play. Then we will kick the field goal." Portland's head coach told his offense.

"Have faith baby." Michael told Shawn. Shawn just frowned.

"I do. I got my fingers crossed." Shawn said, holding his hands, standing.

Portland fans were shouting, standing—on their feet. Atlanta fans were quiet, and hurt. Apostle Sheppard felt so bad for her son.

Keith gave Neal the ball.

Boom! Boom!

He got hit, the sap second he touched the ball. Billy and Truck crushed him.

They actually lost a yard. Portland moved slow as a turtle's grandmother. The clock was ticking like a bomb. The Russian was smiling like the Joker.

"Well, we live. Destiny said laughing

. Ebony wasn't so sure. She didn't speak. The baby laughed.

"Time out! I know you saw me!" Coach Brown yelled at the side judge.

It was only 5 minutes left. Atlanta was down by 7. Portland was preparing to nail the Super Bowl winning field goal that would make my family keep their lives!

"Look, I don't care what it looks like! I don't care what it smells like! Somebody, somehow, do something!" Coach Joshua Brown shouted.

Coach Brown grew up watching last second miracles. However, Coach Josh never experienced it.

"Hubby, we got to win!" Shawn yelled in Michael Lackey's ear.

He gave her a funny smile, then focused on the final five minutes.

Shawn Riley smiled at him. Then glanced at her 20 million dollar platinum, diamond engagement ring.

If Atlanta lost, like they were, Michael Lackey was firing a lot of people!

"Everybody in the dome got to go!!! Except Sexy Shawn!" Mr. Lackey roared.

Always Believe

"Man! We winning this game!" Micki shouted. Micki was a girl filled with faith.

"Red Bone, you crazy! That junk over!" A tall Atlanta gangsta name G-Nut said. In the bar, with his throw back Atlanta Falcons jersey on.

"Bet! Anybody! I still believe in Atlanta!" Micki shouted, tossing a suitcase with $120,000 on the table.

"My Gansta DJ Mac and Burke County ain't going out bad!" MacTown shouted.

"I will Bet Anybody Atlanta Lose!!!" Gino yelled.

"Hey, don't look at me. Muslims don't bet." Salaam stated.

"Bet! Let me see. 1,2,3,4,30. I'll bet everyone in here $1,000 a piece! Atlanta still win! And if I lose, yall can have this $120,000 and my car! I love Atlanta!" Micki shouted. Short in size, but Micki was big in her heart! Full of faith, and she still believed.

"Bet! Bet!" Everyone yelled.

Even Atlanta fans gambled against Atlanta. Atlanta was dead as the First person that ever ate a pickle! They just knew, it was impossible for Atlanta to win this Super Bowl! A horse flying to the moon with a broom was more possible, than Atlanta making a come back in the Super Bowl!

With 5 minutes left.

"Bet! My sister is a winner!" Kishana shouted. Cheering with Micki.

The entire floor was covered with money. If Atlanta won, Micki was gonna straight kill the bar! Boop! Not a bad kill though. A good, winning kill! Micki was gonna kill all of the doubts against the City of Atlanta! In sports world!

She didn't want the money and could care less about it.

Micki wanted to win! Micki wanted her brother, her family, and her City to win!

Go Hard or Go Home

Hearts beat across America had stopped, momentarily. I know mine did! So what? Would Atlanta lose again . . . However, I was losing a lot of blood with this lost. After so much losing, a person begins to feel like a loser! Now that's the crap I don't like!

I watched both teams take the field. I smiled, ooh! I picked up the ear device and stuck it in my ear. Click! I turned it on.

"Great lost my friend. Believe it or not, I'm a man of my word. Your family will live. I knew you would be clicking me in, soon. Keep the ear piece in. So I can tell you where to pick them up." The Russian said. He was very calm. Why would he be mad? He just won 400 million dollars!

Both teams waited for the 3 point field goal. Portland's holder, held the ball. The snap took two seconds to reach the holder, too long! The crowd went nuts!

The holder jumped up and grabbed the loose ball! Sergio flew pass the 9 blockers and leaped in the air like Jordan! Sergio was the highest jumper on the team! Plus he had the longest arms!

He quickly penetrated through the 9 blockers. Portland's kicker went for the kick . . .

Wham!

Sergio blocked it!

"He gone! He gone! He gone!"

Sergio blocked it, like J-Smooth from the Atlanta Hawks! Then he scooped up the ball and ran, fast! He ran real fast, with hunger and thirst in his eyes!

The crowd was shouting! Atlanta fans were cheering! The Russian was cussing! Destiny's mouth was open!

"Go! Go Sergio! Go bro!" Ebony cheered.

She was just so accustomed to cheering for her team. Ebony loved her baby. But she refused to let her enemy see her cry any more.

She had shed enough tears! Now, it was time to fight! Any kind of way she could fight, this woman was fighting! Nothing beats a fighting woman!

The only weapon she had was her cheers. So win or lose, she was cheering!

"Cheer or Die! In my Young Jeezy voice! Hah-hah!" Ebony laughed.

Destiny rolled her eyes and frowned, in total disgust.

"Touch Down! Atlanta!" April shouted dancing.

"42 to 42, what a heck of a game New York!" Tiffani said, from her New York radio station.

Tiffani was a beautiful announcer. She was from up north, but super cheering for the dirty south!

"Told you! Told You! Now I can breathe!" Sergio yelled.

He ran all the way to me with the football. Then picked me up, celebrating! I couldn't help but laugh.

4 minutes to go. Tie game. 42 to 42

Atlanta kicked off the ball.

Kah

Boo

Yah!

"Hah hah! What! What Now?! ATL baby! In yo face!" Kiana yelled, standing in Miss Franklin's cute face. She just stuck her hand out to block her.

"Whatever." Miss Franklin said and smiled.

"Boo Yah! Told yah! It ain't over till it's over baby! I'm a Candler Road Chick, I'ma take yall money!" Micki shouted to the instantly, quiet Stonecrest Bar.

This time Bohannon returned the kick. He scooped it up, running behind his blockers.

Man, I was very anxious. This game had me on the edge. Bam! I felt like I was about to jump. He zipped and skipped pass the 20 yard line. The 30, 40 . . . Boom! Taylor monkey dunk slammed him! Portland took over at the 43 yard line, near mid field with only 3 minutes and 48 seconds to play in the most exciting, nail biting, highest scoring Super Bowl of all time.

Keith took the snap. Keith rolled from left to right.

Bam!

Bonner buried Cooper! Then hopped up, pounding on his chest. He was pointing towards the Atlanta fans, behind our bench.

Bonner wasn't having that! Atlanta was keeping the momentum!

Cooper lost 5 yards on the sack. He stumbled to the line.

Atlanta defense was in a 4-3 front. Two defensive tackles, two defensive ends, and two outside line backers.

Keith took the snap! He scrambled . . . 3 minutes left to play . . . He took a shot down field to Bohannon.

Boom!

Bonner crushed him.

"Bonner Breaks Bones Boy!" Bonner told him, when he hammered him to the ground. Keith was hurt. He couldn't move.

However, Bohannon still caught the pass! Wesley and Zack were chasing him down! Too little! Too late.

"Touch down Portland!" April and Tiffani and the world shouted.

"Yes!" Ebony cheered. Destiny looked at her aunty and shook her head.

"You funny." Destiny said.

"Excellent, pitiful defense! Now, go lose!" The Russian yelled in my ear piece.

I had to listen to his crap, cause I could hear my family in the background. I even heard my baby crying! Lord, I hope it's a boy! My sisters are enough! Lol. No more girls! Boop!

Portland kicked the ball off with 2:59 left to play. 49 to 42 Portland.

Danny caught the ball, after it flipped. He shot out of the end zone! He high stepped and danced! Going for the tie! He broke free! Lyons zipped pass the 30, the 40.

Boom! Tackled at the 41 yard line.

"End it. We going for the kill. No ties. Score a touch down. Then go for the two point conversion. Win or lose. Ride or Die. But No Tie." Coach Joshua Brown told us, loud and clear.

This is the moment I lived for. Mr. 4th Quarter, I'm with it.

"Lose this game." The Russian said in my left ear piece.

"Win this game." Coach Brown said in my right ear piece.

Good and Bad. I ignored them both, some kind of way.

I saw their 4-3 front. I decided to let Jayhlen attack the bubble side where the two line backers were positioned.

Boom! Boom!

Jayhlen ran through both of them; 5, 6, 7, 8 yards. Bam! Grant brought him down.

We ran back to the line; trying to get one more play in before the two minute warning.

"Beep!"

Too late. Time out.

The reff let us know, it was 2 minutes left to play.

Automatic time out. "Ride or Die." I whispered to myself, beating on my chest.

"Ride or Die." Ebony whispered to herself at the same time. In her mind and her heart, she knew her man was thinking and saying the same thing.

"Good game going!" Tiffani said, up in N.Y.C.

"Lord, bless Atlanta to finally win one." Apostle Hannah Sheppard prayed.

Back on the field! Ride or die!

"Lose!" The Russian yelled in my ear, distracting me!

Ok, I guess I will do something stupid. I was tempted to turn the evil ear piece off.

I can't! I had to hear my wife, baby and my niece. So far, I knew they were really alive. So I knew, the big guy was keeping his word. Because I could hear my wife actually cheering for me in the background.

"Win it baby! Win it anyway!" Ebony yelled.

"Shut up!" The Russian snapped at her.

I took the snap. I skipped and danced. I ran backwards for no reason, losing yards.

Boom!

Howard bone, crush tackled me.

"Hand?" Howard asked, helping me up.

"Booooo!" Some obviously pissed off Atlanta fans screamed.

I couldn't do it. The crowd, the city, the hope, the win. I had to win.

1:30 left to play.

"Lose." The Russian demanded.

"Win, by any means necessary." Coach Brown said.

I lost 15 yards in that stupid play. I had tears in my eyes. I think, I had to lose.

"Be stupid, they will die. I promise you. If you disconnect this ear piece, they will die. I promise you. Listen to your stupid slut wife if you want to. I'll deliver her head on a platter; on your front door step. Now Lose!" The devil barked.

I took the snap and ran backward again.

"What are you doing?!!!" Coach Brown roared like thunder.

"Great, Loser." The Russian said.

I scrambled backwards for 31 seconds!

Boom!

I let Howard tackle me. He really thought he was doing something! Two back to back quarter back sacks, in the Super Bowl! Howard was sticking his tongue out now! Howard had the big head!

I got up feeling bad. I lost 20 yards on that play! It would soon be over. I just want to see my family.

It was 3rd and 45. 55 seconds left. Down by 7. 49 to 42.

I was losing again for my family.

Sorry Atlanta.

No! I'm a role model!

"Down . . . Set! Red, 55! Hut!" I yelled.

Then I looked left to right. No one was open. Franklin, Grant and Howard were right in my face!

Boom!

I pushed Howard down, then I slung the ball in the air!

A missile!

The defenders stopped. The offense stopped. The crowd stopped. No one moved but Bailey and Sergio . . . As they both ran looking for the ball! That I really just tossed in the air. Who would win? I didn't think anyone would!

Ebony was cheering like crazy! Had Ebony lost her mind? Did she give up and want to die?

"Catch it Sergio!" Kiki shouted.

"Yes!!!" Micki yelled, jumping up and down.

Bam!

Sergio caught it! He wasn't missing that ball, for nothing in the world! Sergio caught that ball like Julio Jones! Sergio ran like his life was depending on it!

It was! Just not his life!

"Touch down! Tigers!" April screamed.

"Atlanta! Atlanta!" Tiffani shouted, singing like a real super star and looking like Halle Berry! Tiffani had the entire New York dancing!

"49 to 48 Portland, 10 seconds left. Time out Portland."

Portland's head coach was nervous as a roach under a fast flying foot!

"Look, no field goal. Ride or Die. Crunch time. Atlanta will either win their first Super Bowl now, or lose again. But there will NOT, I repeat, there will NOT, be a tie.

Cimeon, go prove that you are the 100 million dollar man! Offense! Go prove that yall want it! Go win it for the starving, pretty City of Atlanta! Win it for all your Haters! Win it for all your family and friends!

Tigers it's now or never!" Coach Brown preached!

We went back on the field. I took, what may be my last play, the last play of my life. I lose this game. I lose my love.

"Down! Set! Hike 1. Hike 2. Hike!"

"Lose the game, or they die."

"Win the game and the city is yours!"

Win!

Lose!

Win!

Lose!

Coach was in my right ear telling me to win. Hollering it! The Russian was in my left ear, with all his power, telling me to lose.

I grabbed the ball from young Elijah. Boom!

Dog Man gave me a thundering, Atlanta Super winning block.

Bam!

Jackson stone cold laid out two defenders at the same dang time!

Jackson was a blocking football beast!

I had Franklin, Evans and Grant diving at me in 3 different directions.

The clock was ticking: 9, 8, 7, 6, 5, 4, 3,

Lose!

Win!

Dive!

Fall!

By my natural instincts, I dodged the 3 tackles.

Bang!

All three of them hit each other. I ran across the 5 yard line.

4, 3, 2 . . .

"Nooooo!" Destiny screamed when she saw Cimeon one yard away from the game winning touch down. He was about to cross the goal line.

Destiny's eyes got huge as a castle on top of Stone Mountain!

The Russian seem to be 8 feet tall, yelling.

"Win it baby! I love you!" Ebony screamed, in tears.

"Go bro!" Kiki yelled.

"Yes!" Michael Lackey shouted.

I was one inch away; the crowd was on their feet. Boom!!!

I couldn't do it . . . I fell down, one inch short of the touch down.

"Thanks." The Russian said.

"No!" Coach Brown yelled.

Hold up! The ball came lose with one second on the clock! Jayhlen picked the ball up!

"Touch Down Tigers!"

"Tigers win! Tigers win!" Tiffani and the whole world announced. "Atlanta wins the Super Bowl! Atlanta wins the Super Bowl!"

"Yeah! Yeah! Yeah!" Sergio yelled.

"I told you to lose. Now, they die." The Russian said, in a calm, serious voice.

Then I heard three gun shots, Pow! Pow! Pow!

The ear piece went dead. I just laid there, one yard short of the touch down. Everybody jumped and screamed. Everybody ran and celebrated.

Splash!

"Whooh! Baby! It feels so sweet!" Coach Brown said laughing, when Bonner and Jayhlen dumped the Gatarade on him.

Splash!

"Wooh! Yeah!" Coach Mackey jumped. Saniya, Lexi and 4 more cheer leaders dumped water on him.

"Hey! Get up boy! Atlanta finally won the Super Bowl!" Ced, our outside line backer, shouted in my ear.

I didn't move. I couldn't move. I blocked out the celebration. I won big. I lost bigger. I was paralyzed in pain.

"Cim! Get up!" Sergio shouted, laughing and hitting on my shoulder.

"Naw. Leave him alone. He is just too happy." Coach Brown said, then they walked away.

Everybody was smiling and partying. Interviews were everywhere.

Flash! Flash!

Miss Pettis was interviewing the Atlanta Organization.

"Atlanta, last year we took a very hard lost. I had to change up the team and keep some people. This Super Bowl, we really looked down and out. BUT, we kept fighting, and we came out on top! Atlanta, I promised I would bring you a Super Bowl trophy. And now we did it!" Michael Lackey shouted, laughing and rubbing on Atlanta's first trophy.

The entire Tigers organization stood on stage, taking turns speaking and touching the trophy.

"So Coach Mackey, you are the only coach in history to win as a head coach last year and as an offensive coordinator for another team the next year. What made you decide to step down with New England after winning a ring; to come to Atlanta, their opponent?" Ms. Pettis asked.

"Well, I saw that Atlanta had the talent. They have always had the talent. All they needed was a little extra desire, and that's why I came. And of course, I admire the sacrifices that Michael Lackey has done with this team. Plus this is my hometown! I love Atlanta!" Coach Mackey shouted in the microphone as he held the Super Bowl Trophy, two years in a row!

However, I laid on that field in the same spot for 2 hours; I couldn't move.

. "Cim, wake up. You have to get up." Lexi told me, sitting down Indian style.

Lexi sounded like a cheer leading angel. I just looked up in her pretty, caring eyes. Lexi really had love for me. However, my love was gone. There was no reason for me to fight any more. Football wasn't even a part of me, at the moment. Life is bigger than a game. So even in victory, I lost.

"And you! Our Super Bowl M.V.P., the first NFL game you ever played in, and you performed with excellence! The youngest M.V.P. in Super Bowl history, Danny Lyons! AKA Bald Head!" Angel, the sexy pretty, chocolate commentator said holding the microphone with her all red Atlanta shirt and hat.

"Wooh! I love it! I don't know what to say. I didn't even expect to play. But I thank God for this day! I love you Mom! I love you Atlanta! Wooh!" Danny shouted, holding his M.V.P. trophy in one hand and the Championship trophy in the other one.

Splash!

Angel splashed Danny with a cold cup of Gatorade!

"Hah-hah. Wooh!" Danny shouted again.

I could hear all the cheers for hours. Until . . . Finally . . .

There Is A God

I stood up, tears of a man, are tears of pain. Tears of my deceased wife and child raced down my brown face. Tears of my beautiful niece raced down my face. I had never experienced such a great lost, in my young life.

Lexi held my hand as we walked out of the dome. Lexi was like a daughter to me, at 18. She stayed by my side.

"Get in." Lexi said, as she opened the door to my money green Lamborghini.

I quickly agreed. I was so discombobulated, I didn't even remember how I got there. Visions of my wife flashed in front of me.

"Cim! One day, you will win the Super Bowl for your city. You will be in the history books as a champion, and be remembered forever. And I will be your wife. I will be right there by your side to share that moment with you. I love you Cimeon." Ebony told me in Columbia High School's swimming pool. Then we kissed, Ebony was right. She predicted the future, 5 years ago.

However, there would be no sharing the Super Bowl victory with my wife. There would be no smiles or tears of joy. There would be no TV interviews. I was done with Love and Football.

"You good?" Lexi asked, interrupting my pity party.

"Umm. Yeah." I said looking up, noticing I was at my mom's house in Decatur.

"You sure? You look like you just lost your best friend." Lexie said, looking at me strange. I just nodded, and told the pretty cheer leader "Thanks."

"Cim! Cim! Baby! We won son! You did it! Atlanta finally won the Super Bowl. Thank God! And my son was a part of it!" My mom shouted, running to Lexie's car, hugging me.

"Hey! Momma Sheppard!" Lexi shouted, then she hugged my mom.

"Hey baby. You are just so beautiful; looking like yo momma girl."

"Hah, hah. No I don't." Lexie said, laughing.

I left the two queens and went into my mom's huge house.

"Man!" I was hit dead in the face! The lights snapped off! I couldn't see anything!

I reached and raced for the living room wall. I stumbled into the piano, striking the keys. "Ouch!"

Bam!

I tripped over a small object and hit the floor hard! It was already dark, at midnight. Oh no, not at my mom's house! I felt his huge feet. The Russian had come for revenge. He was about to finish me off for winning the game, and losing his money. He was about to pay me back for killing his son.

Whif!

I swung for the gun!

Click!

The lights came on!

That's when I saw the biggest surprise in my life!

"Surprise!" Ebony, Bre'Shauna, Sharonda, Deon, Kiki, Erica, Levi, Destiny, Lexie, Mom, and Micki shouted. Ebony ran and jumped into my arms.

We didn't speak for seconds, then minutes. I just held her so tight; so close. I was never letting her leave my side again.

Her tears felt so good on my face. I felt like I was in heaven. Football meant nothing. Love meant EVERYTHING!!!

"I love you baby! I miss you so much!" I fought through the Real Victory of winning my wife back! She just continued to cry.

"I, I love you too. I missed you I kept my faith though. I still wanted you to win. I knew that nothing was too Hard for God." Ebony said, in tears.

"Look at my nephew!" Micki shouted, holding my adorable baby in her arms.

I gently broke my 5 minutes hug from my wife. I softly grabbed my son from my sister's hands.

"Muah. Daddy love you, little man. What's his name?" I asked.

"Nothing . . . He don't have a name." Destiny answered, with a weird, cute look on her face. Destiny is so funny. She giggled.

"Oh well, Daddy gonna name you Victory Courage Brown! Because through all of this, God brought us the Victory!" I shouted.

"Yeah!" Everyone shouted, then clapped.

"Amen." Momma added.

"I missed you sis. My nephew is beautiful!" Sharonda sexy, pretty cherry said; tickling little Victory's toes and making my baby laugh. Awwe.

"Awee. He loves Aunty Cherry Berry." Ebony said, laughing.

Sharonda smiled and gave her sister a big hug.

"We are going to celebrate our victory, and reunite. Love yall." I said holding my baby in one arm and my beautiful wife's hand, with my other.

I continued to hold my wife's hand, as if the world was about to end. My son was doing his baby giggles in my ear. If you ever want to know how it feels to be a Real Man: Try being faithful to your wife and child. Try being faithful to your family Against All odds.

ZZZZOOOOM. He stopped the ride! Then he stepped out in a purple suede suit. His purple snake skin boots, had prison knives sticking out the toe of the boots.

Tim Bushwick Jackson was funky fresh. Even though his hair was nappy as a rug in the projects! My limo driver opened the door to my candy apple red limousine.

Then I allowed my Gorgeous, Determined, Loyal Wife: to get in the car. Muah. I kissed my baby then handed him to his mother.

Then I got in feeling like a king. Immediately we went right to work on each other's body. Like a therapeutic body massage inside a Hot Bubbly Jacuzzi. We kissed with Thirst and Hunger. Feeling, touching, squeezing, pulling, rubbing and bitting all over each other. Like a hot virgin and a hard prisoner. We were two long lost lovers.

"Hold on! I heard 3 shots. The Russian said he killed yall. How did yall escape?" I asked, breaking away from our hypnotizing kiss.

Her eyes were still closed. Lips still in kissing motion; she let out a deep, disturbing breath.

"Ok. Actually, I was thinking we might die regardless. So I just wanted you to win. Seeing you win the Super Bowl for Atlanta would be a great way to die. At least I woulda died seeing my husband fulfill his childhood dreams."

"So how did you get away?" I asked again. Really wanting to know, cause the Russian seemed very precise and intelligent.

"Well, when you fumbled the football at the one yard line, and Jayhlen picked it up and scored. The Russian spoke in the ear piece that he was killing us! Pow! Pow! Pow! I closed my eyes.

I thought we were dead; then, I heard a familiar female voice. 'Come on Ebony, let's go! The bomb is about to go off!'

I opened my eyes and Micki was standing in front of me. She had an urgent look in her eyes. Micki had on all red, with two red .45 magnums in each hand.

'Come on. Hurry up Deon. Untie her' Micki yelled with desperation. Worry was written all over her face. I was never so glad to see your sister in my life! She was sweating and rushing to unchain me.

I was so shocked to see Micki and Deon. Then to see Coach Pettis who quit coaching for no apparent reason. His reappearing shocked the Noodle Soup out of me.

'I've been watching the whole time. Coach Pettis called me and told me that he think he saw you. And that you seem to be kidnapped. I told Deon when he got hurt.

I had to have as much help as possible. But less help as possible to go unnoticed by the Russian mob.' Micki explained.

Deon and Coach Pettis quickly untied Destiny; then, they unchained me. When Micki accidently found the key, I grabbed our baby as we all ran out of the huge haunted mansion.

Kah Boom!

I fell with my baby, scraping my knees on the hard pavement. Micki and Deon picked me up. Mr. Pettis pulled me into the Hummer truck and Micki sped off. The mansion was completely blown to pieces. We escaped just in time." Ebony explained, breathing hard; reliving the deadly testimony and life threatening story.

I just squeezed her hand and caressed her shoulders, as she explained through tears.

"I missed you baby." I said.

"I missed you too, my king." Ebony said, stuttering through tears.

"Hold up! The bullets, who shot who?" I asked, anxiously wanting to solve the entire puzzle.

"Who else? Your sister of course." Ebony answered.

"Micki? Hah, hah. What did she do?" I asked.

"Micki aka Red Bone Shawty saved the day! Kicking the door down in her red steel toe boots! Then the Russian let off two quick shots. But Micki hit him right where it counted: smack in the eyes with one shot!"

"Wow, Lil Sister. What she shot em with? I asked.

"Hah! I guess one of her Red .45 magnums! She tapped him on the shoulder. He turned around, and Boom! She blew his face off! It looked like one of those Scar Face guns!" Ebony said, laughing.

"Hah—hah, Lil Sis been looking at too many gangsta movies. However, she didn't do nothing wrong; protecting her family. Even the Bible says: It's a time to kill, and a time to heal. Ecclesiastes3:3

That was the time to kill. This is our time to heal." I told my gorgeous wife. As we sat on the smooth, red leather seat.

The only woman I ever loved: Cimeon and Ebony for life. Our baby, Victory, laughed and kicked his tiny feet as his momma and daddy held each other tight as an airplane door; flying in the air.

Even a baby knows when it's loved. The smooth melody of my favorite Whitney song pumped from the ten speakers inside the Limo. "Dont make me close one more door. I dont wanna hurt anymore. Stay in my arms if you dare. Or must I imagine you there . . ." Bushwick gave us a thumbs up; the coolest, wackiest Limo driver on earth.

The next day, we were in Disney World with the entire Atlanta Football team throwing a massive Super Bowl Parade. Me and Ebony were riding on our own white horse and carriage. Confetti rain down on the cheering crowd!

"Congratulation to the Atlanta Tigers. Cimeon Riley, we give you the key to the city!" Mayor Earl Brown said on the stage; standing next to his beautiful wife, Kiana.

Everyone clapped as I stepped off the horse carriage and accepted the key to the city. From the cool, smooth, Mayor of Atlanta.

I never saw a red tiger. However, today in Orlando, Florida, I saw nothing but hundreds of Red Tiger jerseys. Atlanta was representing.

"Cimeon, the city of Atlanta, and the state of Georgia have been waiting two life times for this Super Bowl victory. I like to congratulate you and also give you the key to Georgia." Governor Lawrence Rutherford told me, handing me another key.

Now I had two platinum keys: A key to the city and a key to the state.

Me and my wife hugged with pure, holy joy! No fakeness, we had real love. Anyone in any race could tell our love was real.

We had never known anyone else, sexually. My mom popped up on the stage, out of nowhere!

"To top it off, we have a Super Bowl Parade slash Super Bowl Wedding!" Momma, Apostle Hannah Sheppard announced in her long beautiful, ruby red, silk dress. It was adorned with real green emerald trimmed in real platinum! A 50 million dollar dress! Made for a Queen! My mom deserved it!

"Awee . . . Ohh . . . Wow . . ."

The entire Disney World, shocked crowd said. My mom shocked the crowd and rocked the crowd at the same dang time!

"Wooh!" I shouted. Mom even took me by surprise.

"Come on Disney World! Give it up for my home boy and home girl! Wooh!" Mickey Mouse shouted.

Minnie Mouse may have gotten a little jealous. Lol. Jealous cause my sister and Mickey Mouse were holding hands. Yes, Micki was chilling with Mickey.

Mom went straight in with the surprising, televised Super Bowl winning wedding!

Mom looked deep into my eyes. This is a woman filled with honesty, holiness and faith. I NEVER heard Hannah Sheppard tell a lie; not even a little white lie! Boop!

"Cimeon, do you solemnly agree before God and the million witnesses watching on TV and present here at Disney World: To take Ebony, this beautiful wonderful woman to be your lawful wedded wife; to love and respect her, honor and cherish her, in health and in sickness, in prosperity and in adversity; and, leaving all others, to keep yourself only unto her, so long as you both shall live?"

I looked at my mom, then searched the depths of my wife's eyes and heart.

Forget the crowd, forget any other female. Forget pleasing people. Forget temptation. Forget any fine, pretty female. This is all about the one woman I have loved my entire life.

This is only about her. I can only, truly have one woman at a time, no sharing!

This is the woman that had my back when I was down.This is the woman that cheered for me to win. Even if it caused her to lose her own life! This is the only woman that loved me when I was poor and unknown; so, this is the woman I will marry and be loyal to, forever.

"I do." I replied.

Mom, Hannah Sheppard, turned her attention to Ebony.

"Do you, Ebony in like manner solemnly agree to receive this MAN as your lawful, wedded husband; to love and respect him; and to live with him in all faith and tenderness, in health and in sickness, in prosperity and in adversity; and leaving all others alone, to keep yourself pure and loyal to this awesome man, so long as you both shall live, remaining faithful to only him, to death do you part?"

Apostle Hannah Sheppard said, in her always honesty voice, so beautiful with age and wise. She was straight to the point. Her long black and grey natural hair was dancing down her back.

Ebony stared into her husband's eyes. She melted with passion and love. No other man mattered to her; no matter how fine they were. No matter how much money another man had; no matter how much swag or how good another man talked. No other man could ever have her sexually or any other way, except her husband.

The way God created Adam and Eve, and Eve just for Adam; God created Ebony just for Cimeon. Not Cimeon for Keisha, Pam, and Angel. Not Ebony for Thad, Jeremy or Kawaski. God created Ebony only for Cimeon.

As she stared in her King's eyes, she remembered when she wasn't sure that they would ever see each other again. Now, she was thankful that God allowed them to join as one, and with their first baby.

This was life. This was love. Ebony knew Cimeon was the only man for her.

"I do." Ebony said, with tears of joy.

We kissed to the million hand claps. When I opened my eyes, I was so happy and proud. I was a real man. I didn't need 1,000 girls to prove I was macho or cool. I only needed my wife; that's all.

I was smiling. Everyone was so excited. I looked at Lexie, Nu Nu, Donte, Vetta, Coach Joshua Brown, Sergio, Alyssa, Deon, Angel, Destiny, Shawn, Michael Lackey, Levi, Erica, Mom, Kiki, Micki, Governor Rutherford, Mayor E. Brown, Shylin, Mickey Mouse, April, and Sandra.

Wait! Standing next to April clapping was the Russian! Did he have a twin? Did Micki shoot the wrong man? Would the Russian strike again?!

Naw . . . It was all in my head. I saw all of my teammates and fans. His image disappeared, or did it?!

Oh well, Love will Never Fail!

ATLANTA
FALCONS

2

YOU
CAN'
BLOC
MY SHIN